THE LOTUS AND THE DRAGON

ALSO BY BRENT TOWNS

Retribution

Deadly Intent

Termination Order

Blood Rush

Kill Count

Relentless

Lethal Tender

Empty Quiver

Barracuda!

African White

Kill Theory

Danger Close

Collateral Damage

The Death Bringers

Hunting Ghosts

London's Burning

The Cold Hand of Death

Global War

Companions of Death

Hammer Down

THE LOTUS AND THE DRAGON

BRENT TOWNS

The Lotus and the Dragon
Paperback Edition

Wolfpack Publishing
1707 E. Diana Street
Tampa, FL 33610

www.wolfpackpublishing.com

Paperback ISBN 979-8-89567-527-4
Ebook ISBN 979-8-89567-526-7

THE LOTUS AND THE DRAGON

Dragon: A mythical and deadly monster. Symbolises chaos or evil.

Lotus: Grows in murky waters, one of the most beautiful flowers on earth.

1

PILLIGA SCRUB, 1875

FROM THE WEST came the ominous, low rumble of thunder making its continuous trek across the leaden sky, headed for the eastern horizon. The big bay horse beneath me tossed its head in protest, skittish at the ongoing noise, picking its way slowly through the thick wattle scrub.

Close behind my horse's tail came Billy and George, a pair of Aboriginal trackers, their skin the colour of ebony, the white of their teeth a stark contrast when they cracked a smile. The duo rode along in silence, neither man saying much unless spoken to or when they had something necessary to say.

Jack Crowe is the name my parents gave me twenty-five years ago. I guess you might say that I'm a hunter of sorts. Where most hunters track animals, my quarry is man.

"Hey, boss. Up there."

I turned my thickset frame in the saddle to see Billy.

The tracker was pointing his long, brown hand at something ahead and to our right.

Easing my horse to a stop, I turned to face forward, looking in the direction that Billy was indicating, and saw a thin wisp of smoke rising above the eucalypts near a wall of ochre sandstone.

With a nod of my head, I said, "I see it."

"They think they're safe," George said.

"Yeah."

"That Monte Burns always was careless," Billy observed.

Monte Burns was a bushranger and scoundrel. Running with him were two others: Hollister and Grey. Though not quite as bad as Burns, by all reports, they were still wanted, dead or alive.

The trio had robbed a Cobb & Co. coach just south of Narrabri. The lousy mongrels had killed the driver and gotten away with almost five hundred pounds from the strongbox. Well, that action was enough for the New South Wales Government to put a high price on their heads, calling for the services of a professional manhunter. That's where yours truly comes in—Jack Crowe at your service.

Thunder cracked loudly overhead, and this time all three horses shifted nervously. I said, "Billy, go have a look."

The tracker climbed from his horse, handing the reins to George, and quickly disappeared into the scrub. This wasn't the first time the three of us had worked together. But it would be the last. I had decided that four years of hunting men for the police was enough. It was high time to settle down before I got too old, or worse, killed.

When I was twenty-one, I'd been travelling on a stage

that had been held up in northern Victoria, just south of Albury, by a wanted felon named Flash Bob Roberts. The bushranger had fleeced me of my valuables, down to the last shilling I had in my pockets. That incident was a turning point in my life. From that day on, I'd become a hunter of men.

If the pilferer had known then that I'd prove so problematic to him, tracking him to the ends of his days just to get my money back, he may just have left me be. But he didn't, and it wasn't long before I'd caught up with him in the Warby Ranges.

The citizens of Wangaratta stopped and stared at the gruesome sight I presented when I rode along their streets, trailing a horse with an already putrifying, fly-ridden corpse tied over its back.

The senior constable on duty at the time had questioned me thoroughly and then organised payment of a two-hundred-pound reward—which was the paper the dead Roberts had on his head. Once done, the policeman asked whether I was interested in another job. When he told me that all I had to do was ride over to Greta to pick up a young man named Edward Kelly and return him to Wangaratta, it sounded pretty straightforward to me. He was only wanted for common assault.

I hesitated for a moment before answering, but then the senior constable, a man named O'Hanlon, a short middle-aged Irishman, told me there was twenty quid in it. Gee, I didn't want to seem too keen, but I was out that door pretty quick smart.

I saddled up my horse, grabbed a bite to eat, then headed over to Greta after that rapscallion. Honestly, the hard part wasn't finding him—he was at a dance. When I entered the hall and announced that I was there for young Kelly, most everyone laughed at me.

When Kelly stepped forward, I found that the young man was rather big for his age. Huge, in fact. When asked to come along quietly, the bloke gave me a choice —fight or leave.

Well, after having been laughed at already, I wasn't about to turn tail and leave, so we fought.

Many years later, even after Ned had been hanged for his crimes, it was still talked about—the knockdown drag-out fight that saw Ned Kelly bested for the first and only time at fisticuffs, by a man called Crowe.

When I showed up later in Wangaratta, battered and bruised, definitely a little worse for wear with Kelly in tow, the jaw on O'Hanlon dropped. On the safe delivery of the young man to the cells, the senior constable paid me and then offered to shout me a beer at the pub.

I accepted readily, and the two of us talked for quite a while about different things. Then, O'Hanlon happened to mention a newspaper he'd once read, and how in America, they had men who hunted down the lawless for the money on their heads.

The thought interested me, as I wasn't really doing much else, and not long after, I began bringing in felons from Victoria and New South Wales. For the last year or so, authorities sought me out for the work I performed. They began referring to me as *The Hunter*.

The majority don't condone what I do, in fact, many think it's abhorrent, but mostly I offer a service that many can't do without.

Now, with my dark hair tucked under a brand new leather hat, I was on my last manhunt. I had decided that once we took Burns and his bunch, I was done. The toll the job was taking wasn't just a physical one, but a mental one.

Once it was all over, I intended to head west to the

Darling River country and start a freight business. With so many properties along the river region and scattered throughout the nearby areas, there was bound to be plenty of work which would set me up to grow the business real good.

But before I get ahead of myself, first, we had to bring Burns in.

LARGE RAINDROPS STARTED to fall when Billy came back. Both George and me were seated on a couple of basalt rocks as we waited for his return.

"What did you find?" I asked, standing up as a kookaburra protested another deep rumble.

"They are there, boss," Billy said. "I saw them with my eyes. They have no idea we are here."

Nodding, I said, "We'll go in on foot. Use the storm for cover."

"This is the last time, yes?" George commented.

"Yes. The last time."

I walked over to my horse and took a Martini-Henry rifle from the saddle. I checked its loads as well as those of the revolver I had tucked into my belt. Billy and George took their own rifles and followed me into the scrub.

The heavy shower of rain continued, with large drops whacking onto our hats and long coats. The red soil was soon sticky and mushy and began building up on the soles of our boots. We came to a dry creek bed, which we crossed quickly. If the rain continued to fall like this, the narrow waterway would soon roil with runoff.

Before the rain, I'd noticed a pair of black cockatoos, their wing feathers glossy in flight. And once the rain stopped, a chorus of frogs would come out and sing their melodic tunes around the scattered waterholes. But right now, all the wildlife was taking shelter for the duration of the storm.

We continued to walk, none too stealthily, toward where the bushrangers were camped. Billy had said they were set up on a small billabong with plenty of fresh water. The rain would do their fire no favours, and without proper shelter, life for the small group would probably be quite miserable.

As we crept closer, the sight of them confirmed my suspicions about how the rain was making them feel. They were huddled morosely around their already extinguished campfire, their long coats over their heads in a pitiful attempt to keep some of the rain off.

I swapped the Martini-Henry over to my left hand and used my right to draw the revolver from my belt. Then I proceeded forward.

The waterhole was on our left, its once glassy surface now dancing wildly as though under attack from the torrent of water coming at it from the grey clouds above. The sound it was making provided cover for our squelching approach.

About fifty yards from where the bushrangers were crouched, we separated, our method slow and deliberate. I eased back the hammer on my revolver.

One of the bushrangers moved, repositioning himself awkwardly under his inadequate cover, and all three of us stopped dead. My eyes narrowed. The right corner of my thin mouth twitched, and I set my square jaw firm as I readied myself to shoot should the need arise.

But then the bushranger settled again, and we moved on.

We managed to get within thirty feet of them before

the group became alerted to our presence. It was one of the horses that sounded the alarm. A sharp, shrill whicker that brought the men rushing to their feet, grappling with firearms.

Pistols came up hastily and pointed at targets. The three bushrangers cursed out loud, more at themselves for their complacency rather than at my trackers and me.

Burns had his gun pointed straight at me, and in return, I had my own revolver sighted at the killer's forehead.

Water poured from the brim of the bushranger's hat, and his unshaven face below it was grimy. He glared at me and snarled, "Who the hell are you?"

"Crowe."

Burns glanced at the two trackers. "You that Crowe? The one who works with the darkies to track men like us?"

"What do you think?"

The bushranger spat in the mud at his feet. "Shit."

"Are you going to come quietly?"

"What? So they can hang me? Fuck off."

A drawn-out silence ensued, and all that could be heard was the incessant rain striking any number of surfaces: water, ground, leaves, clothing, hats.

"What do you propose we do, then?" I asked.

"I don't give two dingos' dicks what *you* do, but I'm leaving. One way or the other. Whether you're alive to see it or not, is up to you."

"You seem to think you have the upper hand."

"I think that maybe I have, cobber."

A crash of thunder sounded overhead.

"Billy!" I snapped.

Two rifle shots rang out across the bush, and the pair

of bushrangers with Burns dropped into the mud where they'd been standing. Turning his head to look at both crumpled bodies, his face an incredulous mask, Burns realised what had happened, and I stepped briskly inside the revolver before he could fire it, driving the butt of my own gun into his face.

The bushranger dropped at my feet, blood pouring from his shattered nose to mix with water and mud that was pooling beneath his head.

I looked at Billy and George. "Get the horses."

NARRABRI

People stopped and gawked at our small procession making way along the main street of Narrabri. I was out front, followed by Billy, George, Burns, and the two horses draped with the bodies of the dead bushrangers.

We were met outside the police station by the now-superintendent Michael O'Hanlon, his grey hair cut short, revealing a lined and weathered face.

"I see you caught the bastards, boyo. It's a shame you didn't shoot all three of them."

Dismounting, I said, "Might as well have the magistrate and the hangman earn their pay."

"Where'd you catch them?"

"Down in the Pilliga Scrub. They thought they were free and clear."

O'Hanlon nodded. "A message came for you while you were gone, from down Bathurst way. Feller named Harrison is raising hell down there. Tried to rob a gold shipment and killed the driver on the stage. Cobb & Co.

They will pay you five hundred pounds to go find the bastard."

I thought about it for a while, but then remembered the commitment I'd made to myself. Shaking my head, I said, "I'm done. I'm headed over to Darling."

"What on earth are you going to do over there?"

"I'm going into the freight business. There are a lot of stations over that way. They need someone to carry their wool bales to the river for the boats."

O'Hanlon shook his head, his voice filled with sarcasm. "The bastard scoundrels and rogues will breathe a sigh of relief knowing that you're off humping some stockman's wife."

I smiled at him. "It would make a nice change."

O'Hanlon shook his head. "How about I meet you over at the pub after dark, and we'll have a beer before you leave?"

"Sure. I'll see you there."

WHEN I MET up with O'Hanlon two hours later, things didn't go quite as expected. He entered the pub, flanked by three constables. They walked across to the table where I was seated, and straight away, I knew that something was dreadfully wrong.

The superintendent gave me a stern look and said, "Sorry, son, but I'm going to have to arrest you."

"Is this some kind of joke?" I asked him.

He shook his head. "No, I'm sad to say it isn't."

"What am I being arrested for?"

O'Hanlon hesitated.

"Well?"

"The unlawful killing of two men. Namely, the two rapscallions who were with that blackheart Burns."

"Bullshit!" I blurted.

"He complained to the magistrate that you had them killed in cold blood by the darkies who rode with you. At this point, I have other men trying to find them."

"For fuck's sake, O'Hanlon, they were wanted dead or alive. They were all armed."

"That may be, but the magistrate is new, and he doesn't agree with some of the methods necessary to apprehend these bastards."

"So, I'm to go on trial at the word of a murderer?"

"I'm afraid so."

I couldn't believe it. Slowly, I stood up, hands out to the side away from my revolver.

A constable stepped forward with handcuffs and was about to place them on me when O'Hanlon snapped and said, "Leave that be. The man will come quietly. Of that, I am sure."

He shifted his gaze and said, "I'll ask this once, boyo, did your men kill them or not?"

What could I say?

ONE WEEK LATER

"JACK CROWE, you have been found guilty by a jury of your peers and are to be incarcerated for a period of no less than ten years."

I stared at Magistrate Brian Hanscomb and couldn't speak. Surely I'd heard him wrong. He continued, "You will be transported to Dubbo, where you will serve out your sentence. Be thankful that it wasn't an upstanding member of the community that was killed, Mr. Crowe, or it would be a hangman's rope for you."

The magistrate's words stung, and even though I tried to bite my tongue, I couldn't hold it in, and said, "Thankful, you overbloated horse's arse? Thankful? What the buggery have I to be thankful about?"

"Crowe!" O'Hanlon snapped from beside me. "Respect."

"Frig him," I almost shouted. "He's not the one being locked up."

The magistrate banged his gavel. "Order! Order, I say."

I took half a step forward but was stayed by the hand of the superintendent. "Stop, son. There is no changing it."

Hanscomb glared at me, and I prepared myself for something worse. Instead, he shifted his gaze to O'Hanlon. "Superintendent, have the prisoner taken away to await transportation."

O'Hanlon and another constable by the name of Brown escorted me out of the courthouse, and when I was locked away in my cell, the superintendent remained on the other side of the bars and said, "I'm sorry, Jack. I don't agree with what has happened."

"That's a real big help to me now. I feel so much better that you don't agree." There could be no mistaking the sarcasm in my voice.

He looked as though he had something more to say, but after a brief hesitation, he turned away and left me there to contemplate a future that I wasn't to have.

WHEN THE TIME ARRIVED, two days later for me to be transported, O'Hanlon came to me with some news. He stood outside my cell door, rubbing his ruddy face before speaking. "I have an offer for you, Jack. Think long and hard about it before you refuse outright or accept."

I remained silent.

"There is a sheep station out west. It's called Bindurra Station, and sometimes they are supplied with labour from the penal system. I have talked to the magistrate about your case, and he is open to you being transported there instead of the Dubbo Gaol."

I was still angry and had to rein in a savage retort before I opened my mouth. "What is the alternative? Rot in a prison?" I asked.

"Yes."

"For ten years?"

"Yes."

"I don't see I have much choice then, do I?"

O'Hanlon grew angry and snapped, "Damn it, boyo! There is always a choice. Would you rather be locked up for the full ten years, or have some semblance of freedom? Just remember this, if you run from there, you'll be hunted down and then hanged."

"All right, I'll go to this place. Considering the alternative, I guess it'll be better than Dubbo."

"You'll leave tomorrow."

Looking O'Hanlon in the eyes, I said, "Thanks, Michael."

"Don't thank me, Jack. If I had my way, you'd not be here at all."

2

BINDURRA STATION, 1879

THE COOL EVENING, coupled with the orange and red of the sunset, brought the promise of something sinister. A flock of sulphur-crested cockatoos squawked loudly in the large river gums to the west of the homestead, and I saw a male kangaroo bounding across the paddock beyond them.

Behind me, I heard a raucous cheer erupt from within the corrugated iron shearers' quarters. There was a no-alcohol rule on Bindurra Station at shearing time, but it seemed that someone had smuggled it in, and now the shearers were well and truly drunk. Being a Sunday, the boss had let them quit early. They would get back at it again the following day.

But it was only a matter of time before Greg Hearne came out of the homestead and demanded they stop, which would be a mistake. Trying to talk to drunken shearers was almost impossible, hence the no-grog policy.

A crow cawed persistently from over at the timber-railed holding yards where there were still three thousand sheep waiting their turn for the ten shearers to clip.

Another loud roar made me shake my head. For almost four years, I'd been here on Bindurra, and in that time, this was the first year that grog had made it onto the station during shearing season.

They hadn't been bad years, in fact, quite the opposite. Hearne and his wife, Mary, two kids, Bethany and Reggie, were quite pleasant, even to a convicted criminal like me.

I'd arrived with two other prisoners—Charlie Wren and Eddie Brent. Both were small-time thieves, and after their sentences of two years had been served, they had stayed on and taken a full wage for their labour.

I heard the screen door on the homestead bang open as it was thrust back in anger. Then the loud clumps of heeled boots sounded across the veranda and down the steps. When I turned around to look, the chains at my ankles rattled. They were something I was required to wear at night or when I wasn't working.

I watched Hearne as he strode purposefully toward the shearers' quarters. He was making a mistake, and I called out to him, "Boss?"

He ignored me.

"Boss?"

He drew closer.

"Mr. Hearne, wait."

On cue, another raucous roar split the evening, and Hearne was spurred on.

"Shit," I muttered and tried to hurry after him as fast as my bonds allowed.

He wasn't a big man, maybe five-ten, and thin built.

He treated men fairly and expected those who worked for him to respect his rules.

Hearne disappeared inside when I was still some thirty yards away. Already, I could hear the raised voices emanating from within. I cursed out loud and tried to break into a run. Instead, I fell flat on my face in the dusty yard when I overstepped.

Spitting dirt and wiping my lips, I scrambled to my feet and shuffled as fast as possible. The shouts had grown louder, and as I shoved my way inside, I came to a halt.

Silence descended over the room, and when I looked about, I could see that nearly every man there had a shocked expression on his face. Except for one—a big shearer named Hennessy, whose face was flushed red with anger. In front of him stood my boss. Hearne's posture seemed to be unusually stiff for some reason, and then he took a staggering step back.

Frowning, I took another step further into the room, taking in the unkempt steel-framed bunks around the quarters, and the rough men who spun around to look at me. Hearne began to turn toward me, too, and that was when I saw it—a knife. Buried to its hilt in his chest.

"Oh, shit," I swore. Hurrying forward, I caught him before he fell to the floor. I laid him down and cradled his head in my lap. "It's all right, boss. It's okay, I got you."

He looked up at me through glassy eyes and whispered, "Mary."

Without looking up, I called out, "Charlie, get the missus, now!"

The sound of his boots on the timber floor receded as he left. I said to Hearne, "It's okay, boss, Charlie's gone to get Mrs. Hearne."

With every breath he took, a gurgle escaped his throat from deep down. His lungs were filling with blood. He was dying in my arms, and there was nothing I could do.

My gaze lifted to Hennessy. Rage boiled within me, and I eased myself out from under Hearne and came to my feet. With slow, deliberate steps, I walked towards him, chains rattling.

"You're done, damn you," I cursed him. "You'll hang for sure, but first, I get my piece of your hide."

My fist hit him flush in the jaw with the first blow. Hard work over the past four years had put extra muscle on my frame, and from the jarring force that travelled up my arm and into my shoulder, I wasn't surprised to see him go down from the impact.

I moved forward to follow the blow with another, but someone hit me from behind. I found out later that the man was Williams, Hennessy's friend. For the moment, however, I fell to my knees, my head ringing from the blow.

I was hit again from behind, and this time, there was nothing I could do to prevent my body from being slammed forward onto the floor. I rolled slowly, painfully, onto my back and tried to focus my vision, but everything above me was heaving as though I was swimming in a turbulent sea.

Then everything went black.

A SIMPLE BURIAL service was held for Greg Hearne the following morning, at a small plot of graves, down under a large gum.

Already in residence in the tiny graveyard was his

brother, who had been interred in the adjacent grave six years earlier after he'd fallen from his horse and broken his neck. Also buried in the Bindurra plot were three others—the youngest Hearne child who'd died at birth, and two station hands. One had died from tuberculosis, and the other had been killed by Aboriginals who'd stolen a sheep for food. The hand had stumbled across them killing the ewe and then been speared through the chest for his trouble.

My head ached like a bastard, but I stood there listening to the service read by Porter, the station foreman. Out of all of us, he'd been there the longest. As he read from the Bible, there was a deafening silence. Even the birds failed to make a sound as though they understood the solemnity of the occasion.

Beside Porter stood Mary Hearne, a slim, not unattractive woman in her mid-thirties. Her long brown hair was tied back in a severe bun, and her hands were clasped in front of her.

On either side of her stood the two Hearne children, certainly old enough to understand the grim reality of death.

Behind them were the shearers, bar two. Hennessy and Williams had high-tailed it out of there, disappearing during the night. Obviously hoping to get a head start on the troopers. Which, by my calculations, were almost a week away. That meant Hennessy had time to make it almost anywhere by then.

I waited until the service was over before I approached Porter.

"Can I have a word?"

He stared at me for a moment and then nodded. "All right, make it quick."

"I want to go after Hennessy and Williams," I said.

Porter looked at me as if I was crazy. "You think I'm going to let you go after them? You're a damned convict. That means you go nowhere. The troopers will get them."

"That's bullshit and you know it," I snapped. "By the time they get here the trail will be cold. I can get them and bring them back."

"Damn it, Crowe, I said no."

I glanced up and saw Mary Hearne staring at us. She hesitated and then approached. "What is the problem, Mr. Porter?"

"Nothing, missus. Nothing at all."

"That's not true," I said.

"Crowe," he growled.

"Let him speak."

"Missus, I can get Hennessy and Williams back. If you have to wait for the troopers to arrive, they'll be long gone, and there will be no justice for your husband."

"But you are a prisoner here, are you not?" Mary pointed out.

"Yes, ma'am."

"So how do you propose to go after them?"

"I'd need a horse and a rifle, missus. Believe me when I say I can do this. Did Mr. Hearne tell you about me? What I used to do?"

She nodded, and tears came to her eyes at the mention of her husband. "Yes, he did."

"I ask that you let me go after them, Mrs. Hearne, and I'll bring them back to face a trial."

"But how do I know you will come back, Jack. You could just ride away."

"I'd give you my word."

"Don't trust him, Mrs. Hearne," Porter cautioned.

I continued, "Mrs. Hearne, when I was offered the

opportunity to come here instead of Dubbo, I took it. I could have escaped from Bindurra many times over. But I'm under threat of hanging if I do just that. I've seen a man hanged and it's a ghastly sight. I'd not want that for me. Therefore, I give you my word under threat of death. Please, you and your husband treated me well even when you didn't have to. Let me do this for you."

She hesitated, then said, "Let me think about it."

I nodded and walked away.

Porter followed me, and once we were out of earshot, he said, "I know what you're up to, Crowe."

Stopping, I turned to face him. "Tell me then, Porter."

"As soon as you're out of sight, you'll be gone and not come back. You're using the death of a good man to help yourself escape."

Never more than at that moment did I want to punch that bastard in the face. It would have felt damned good to do it. Instead, anger laced my voice when I said, "It's for that good man I offered to do it. Now back off."

He did. I don't know if it was the fire burning in my eyes or what, but he backed right away. He turned, and then I watched him walk back to Mary Hearne. They spoke briefly, then Porter motioned to me.

I walked over to join them, and Mary Hearne looked me in the eye. She said, "Mr. Porter said I should let you go."

I flicked my gaze to him, and he nodded.

Mary went on, "I have agreed to do so, but there is a condition."

"I already gave you my word, missus."

"It's not that. I want you to kill the men responsible for my husband's death. Don't bring them back, just kill them and leave their bodies for the dingoes."

I didn't know what to say. "Missus, I…"

Her face contorted with the pain of her loss. "Promise me."

I glanced at Porter, and once again he nodded.

"Promise me, damn it!"

Shit, damn it! I thought, and then said, "All right. I promise."

"Thank you. Come by the house after the noon meal, and I'll have everything you need."

She turned abruptly and walked away, leaving Porter and me standing there, watching her leave. I looked at him and said, "What happened? How come you changed your mind?"

"I saw the look in your eyes, Crowe," he explained. "And I knew right then that you'd come back."

"And now she wants me to kill them."

"We all want them dead."

"You seem to forget that it was only Hennessy who did the killing."

"You can't kill one without the other, now, can you?"

I saw what he meant. For me to kill Hennessy and not Williams would allow an avenue for the story to get back. I either had to kill both of them, or none at all.

"Shit."

IN FOUR YEARS, I'd never been inside the homestead. It was well tended and clean, and the rooms were spacious with high ceilings. There were lots of windows throughout the house, which picked up every breeze, providing cross ventilation during the long, hot summers.

After removing my boots and brushing the dust from my clothes, I was shown through to the kitchen where

Mrs. Hearne was waiting for me. She had prepared a sack of food, as well as providing a couple of water canteens.

"There should be enough food for four or five days, Jack, longer if you eat it sparingly," she told me.

From another room, Porter appeared, carrying a couple of weapons that I'd never seen before. He placed them on the table along with boxes of ammunition.

"What are these?" I asked.

It was Mrs. Hearne who spoke. "These came last month with the supplies. My husband was fond of the stories that came out of America. The rifle is a Winchester. An eighteen seventy-three model, I think. The handgun is a Colt."

I picked the rifle up first. It was lighter than the Martini-Henry I'd used, and the action to load it worked as smooth as any I'd encountered. The revolver was well-balanced, and when I spun the cylinder, it turned free and smooth. "They are nice weapons," I said.

Mrs. Hearne nodded. "Take them. Use them to help you get the men you seek."

"You seem to forget, missus, I'm a convict. If I get caught with guns, I'm liable to be hanged."

It was something she understood and had come prepared for. She held out a sheet of paper with delicate script upon it. I took it and frowned, looking down at it. "What's this?"

"A letter telling how you came to have the weapons and what you are doing."

"I'm sorry, missus, but I don't think the traps will worry too much about a letter from a woman. No offence."

"I may be a woman, Jack, but out here where there is

virtually no water, no grass, and no law, my word is still good for whomever you come across."

My look was sceptical as I stuffed the letter into my pocket, but I nodded and said, "Okay, then. Thank you."

"Mr. Porter has a horse picked out for you. I'm sure it will be more than adequate, as he has a good eye for horseflesh. Be careful, Jack, I fear that there is more than one danger out there awaiting you."

I knew what she meant. The Aboriginals had been active of late stealing sheep once again and would have no fear of a lone rider travelling through the vast expanse of the deserted outback. "I'll be fine, missus. I think they'll go north towards Brewarrina. Maybe they'll try to catch a coach or maybe a riverboat. Head downriver to Bourke or maybe Wilcannia. But don't worry, I'll find them."

MY ASSUMPTION WAS RIGHT. Williams and Hennessy had headed north towards Brewarrina. I'd been on their trail for two days when I saw the large eagle soaring menacingly, perhaps a mile ahead of me. The bird was doing lazy circles in the sky, each pass bringing it lower and closer to the ground.

Reaching down, I took out the Winchester from the saddle sheath. There was a loud CLACK-CLACK as my hand worked the lever and a bullet rammed into the breech. Off to the west, the rumble of thunder sounded across the plains. A row of tall river gums was up ahead of me, and I figured they marked the course of a creek, because by my reckoning I was at least another three days' hard ride from Brewarrina.

My eyes went back to the large bird as I took another

loop in the reins. In my right hand, I held the rifle, my thumb on the hammer, and my forefinger resting on the side plate. Somewhere in a large silver-barked gum to the right of the trail, a crow cawed, following up with a low sound not unlike the growl of a dog.

I rocked back and forth with the rhythm of the horse as he picked his way along. A light breeze had sprung up, whipping a small cloud of dust past me. With it came the odour—a sickly-sweet smell, regarded as the scent of death.

Drawing back on the reins, I brought the horse to a halt. Looking around, I dismounted and tied the reins to a tree, then moved forward cautiously on foot. The further I walked, the stronger the smell, until it was stiflingly thick in the air. It was Williams's body. It lay at an angle to that of another. Bloated skin, the colour of burnished copper, threatened to burst with unescaped gases. I walked forward and studied both corpses. An Aboriginal had been stabbed with a knife. That was easy enough to tell. Just like the spear that pinned the white man's body to the baked earth told the tale of his death.

A screech from above drew my attention to the eagle. It was perched on a thick, gnarled branch of one of the river gums, waiting patiently for me to move on so it could begin its repast. Looking back at the grisly scene before me, I turned toward my horse. I felt a spot of rain hit the brim of my hat, then another. Soon the storm was upon me, and the rain fell in sheets.

I left the corpses where they lay, mounting the horse and heading it in the direction of Brewarrina. There was only one thing worse than riding in the rain and that was sitting around in it. Besides, I needed to get across the creek in case it rose suddenly, leaving me stranded on the wrong side. If that happened, it would more than likely cost a hundred-mile ride out of my way, or two or three days waiting for it to recede. Either way, the loss of time was unacceptable, and the trail was getting colder.

The horse pushed its way through the water course, the brown water swirling in eddies around its knees. He climbed the steep bank on the far side and crested the top with ease. I heeled him forward, and as we continued, I had a sudden sense that I wasn't alone. My gaze was drawn into the trees to my right, and I saw him. An Aboriginal man holding two spears, his hair wet and layered, his beard dripping with constant droplets of water. Apart from a loincloth, he was completely lacking clothes, his body wiry, cords of muscle obvious.

Thunder crashed, and the bay horse I was on lurched to the side, causing me to saw on the reins trying to bring it under control. I looked back up, but the aborigine was gone.

THE HORSE HAD BEEN dead for only a few hours. A combination of hard riding and the spear wound to its chest. Hennessy had gotten everything out of the poor animal and then some. And the horse, hearty though he had been, flanks caked with mud, could finally give no more.

With a grim face, I stared at the boot prints left in the softened earth. They were deep and indicated that the man was hurrying, putting distance between himself and whatever it was that was scaring him. My guess was the Aboriginals who had killed his friend back at the creek.

Well, now that he was afoot, it made the job of capturing him that much easier. Or so I thought.

My horse snorted and turned his head to the right,

ears pricked forward. I followed his gaze and saw the line of riders as well as more on foot. They were moving slowly across the broken ground from my right towards the trail I was on. After a few minutes, I could make out the dark uniforms of the mounted riders. My heart quickened. They were traps, police, four of them. Behind them walked a trio of Aboriginal men, ropes around each man's neck that strung them together. The lead rider, a sergeant with thick muttonchop sideburns and bushy moustache, raised his hand to stop the small column.

He eyed me with suspicion for a time before he asked, "Who are you?"

For a fleeting instant, I thought about lying and then knew what would happen if I was caught out in the lie. "My name is Jack Crowe."

"What are you doing out here?"

"Nothing. Passing through to Brewarrina."

The sergeant's steely gaze shifted to the dead horse. "What happened here?"

I shrugged. "I don't know. I've only just got here."

"Do I know you, Crowe?" another trap asked me. This one was taller, thinner than the sergeant.

"I don't think so."

The man scratched at his stubbled face, uncertainty showing at my answer.

"You know him, Smith?" the sergeant asked.

"Not sure, Sergeant Kennedy. Maybe."

The man named Kennedy narrowed his eyes as he stared at me again. "You wanted by the law, Crowe. A bushranger, maybe?"

"No, not wanted by any law," I answered, which was the truth. Then I deflected any more questions with one of my own. "What did your prisoners do?"

"The darkies? They stole some sheep from a squatter up on the Barwon. We're taking them back to Brewarrina to hang."

"For stealing a few sheep?"

"That's right."

"All three of them?"

"There was five, but we left two back where we found them as an example of what happens when the bastards take what doesn't belong to them."

I saw the half smile on his face and felt my guts churn inside. Sure, I'd killed men before, but I'd certainly not taken any pleasure from it.

The trap called Smith climbed down from his horse to examine the dead one. After a minute, he looked up at Kennedy and said, "This horse was rid to death, Sergeant. But only after it was stabbed in the chest with something. My guess would be a darkie spear."

"Has to be Jarrah," Kennedy hissed.

"Who's Jarrah?"

"He's from the Murrawarri tribe around Brewarrina. There was a little trouble a while back when one of the local squatters caught one of Jarrah's tribe butchering a cow. He hung him from the nearest gum, which should have been the end of it all. The thing was, the darkie was Jarrah's brother. Now, he's been knocking off whites whenever he gets the chance to. He's a slippery bastard, I'll give him that."

I remembered the Aboriginal I'd seen earlier and wondered if he was the one they referred to as Jarrah.

"The bloke who was riding this horse is now on foot," Smith told Kennedy. "He can't be too far ahead."

"Then we best catch up to him before Jarrah does," Kennedy suggested. He turned his gaze to me. "You coming with us, Crowe?"

Slowly shaking my head, I said, "No. My horse needs a rest. I might walk him for a while before keeping on."

"If you catch up to us, you're more than welcome to share our fire tonight. Then we can ride into Brewarrina tomorrow."

"I'll keep that in mind."

I watched them continue, the three Aboriginal men at the rear of the column. Of course, walking my horse was just an excuse because I had no intention of riding along with them, especially if they caught up with Hennessy. I would bide my time and wait for the right opportunity to finish what I had started.

IT WASN'T a dingo's howl that disturbed me in my blankets. It was a scream. A blood-curdling cry that caused me to throw my blanket back and roll to my feet in a cautionary squat, taking the Winchester as I went.

It sounded again. High-pitched, carried easily on the clear outback air. Above me, a million stars winked and sparkled, a sight to behold if I'd been looking up. Instead, my gaze was focused on the small orange glow in the distance to the north.

I had no doubt that it was a campfire. And I was reasonably sure I knew whose fire it was. What I didn't know was what the hell was happening.

Sudden gunshots reached out across the dark landscape like tendrils of a vine, followed by more cries. I hurried across to my horse and threw my leg over without a saddle. Turning it toward the glow in the distance, I urged the animal forward. By the time I reached the camp, the shooting had stopped, but the sound of raised voices had replaced it.

"I can't believe we got the prick," I heard Kennedy snarl. "God damned Jarrah himself."

Hoofbeats on the damp ground drew their attention in my direction. Weapons came up, and for a moment, I thought they might fire, but it wasn't forthcoming. "I heard the sh—"

I didn't finish for I was distracted by the figure hanging at the end of the rope attached to a thick branch of a solid gum. I'd not seen it when I had ridden up, but I sure as shit did now. It was one of the Aborigines—the bastards had hanged him. I glanced quickly around the camp and saw another lying on the ground, unmoving. Beside him was one of the traps, just as dead as the man he lay next to. The third prisoner sat on his own, his eyes impossibly wide with fear of whatever he'd just witnessed.

And then there was the other one who sat in the firelight, hands tied behind his back. He stared at me, and I realized it was the same man I'd seen earlier in the day by the creek. My eyes narrowed as my hot gaze turned back to Kennedy. "What have you done?"

"We, my dear Crowe, have captured the savage known as Jarrah. I can feel a promotion coming on already. We didn't find the rider from the dead horse, by the way. His tracks just seemed to vanish."

"Why did you hang the Aborigine?"

Kennedy shrugged. "Here, Brewarrina, Dubbo, doesn't matter much where. He got what was coming to him. That darkie over there didn't like it much, though. The bastard got loose somehow and killed Bennett. But we got him for it."

"What are you going to do with the other two?" I asked, not really knowing if I wanted to hear the answer.

A cold smile split the sergeant's lips. "We're going to hang them too."

I felt a shiver run down my spine. The Colt that Mrs. Hearne had given to me was tucked into my pants, and I also had the Winchester. But a man really needs to think twice before he goes and shoots a policeman, even out here in the middle of nowhere.

"A man has the right for a trial," I pointed out. "Even if he has different coloured skin."

"Are you a darkie lover, Crowe?" Smith sneered.

I could feel my anger starting to rise at the stupidity of the men before me. They may be policemen, but right at that point in time, I felt nothing more than the urge to kill them. Instead, I said in a low voice, "You blokes hanging them without a trial just makes you all as bad as the killers you bring in."

They stared at me for a moment, and the silence was punctuated by the howl of a dingo out on the plain somewhere. Then Kennedy said in a low, threatening voice, "If I was you, Crowe, I'd turn around and leave about now. If you don't, you might just find yourself hanging beside these *Aborigines* you seem so set on protecting."

"This is wrong, Kennedy," I growled.

The sound of a hammer being cocked drew my attention to the third trap, the one who'd remained silent throughout my arrival and the ensuing conversation. But about then, he had something to say, "You heard the sergeant, Crowe. Get out of here, or the rope won't even get put around your neck."

The sight of the gun in the firelight pointed in my direction left me with only one option. I was about to take it when a howling scream erupted from the darkness to the north, and Hennessy came roaring into camp, knife raised and making for the Aboriginal known as Jarrah.

Now, I had two options. I could let him kill the man and then take my chances on telling Kennedy who the killer actually was, but then the sergeant would find out who I was, and the odds of getting out of it alive were less than ideal. On the other hand, I could shoot Hennessy then and there and take my chances on the outcome. Either way, I was hip-deep in shit, and it wasn't good.

Decision made, the Winchester came up and fired. The sound of the shot echoed throughout the darkness, and the bullet hammered into Hennessy from the side. The force of the blow flung him sideways into a sprawled heap on the damp ground. I worked the lever on the rifle, and in a heartbeat, it was ready to fire again. However, it wasn't Hennessy I should have been concerned about, for the revolver Kennedy had drawn fired, and I felt the bullet burn deep into my side.

My body stiffened as I fell from the bay and then thudded onto the ground at its feet. Things went black, and I had no idea how long I lay there before a rowdy chorus of shouts and yahoos brought me back to the land of the living.

Pain ripped through my side as I made the mistake of trying to move. A low moan escaped my parched lips. My eyes cracked open, taking in the dark as my vision swam into focus. I could see my horse standing under the branch where the traps had hanged the first Aborigine. Only now he wasn't alone. Beside him hung another, and Kennedy was preparing to hang Jarrah from the branch next to them.

I opened my mouth to say something, but all that came forth was another moan. This one, however, garnered attention, and I saw the three of them turn to look at me. It was Kennedy who came across to stare down at me. For a moment he said nothing, then, "Aren't you dead yet?"

Then he kicked me in the head, and this time, darkness settled in for a long time.

I WASN'T sure how long I lay there, but it was daylight when I came to, and the sun was high in the sky, beating down harshly. The traps were gone, and they'd left me for dead. The clothes I wore were crusted with blood, and my head hurt like a bitch. Reaching up, I gently touched the area where Kennedy had kicked me. The feel of more crusted blood told me all I needed to know.

Holding my hand up as a shield against the bright glare, I looked around at the abandoned campsite. There were three Aboriginals hanging from the gum, and the fourth still lay where he had fallen. The absence of the dead policeman indicated that Kennedy had taken his corpse with them. Not so Hennessy. He was still where I'd shot him. Obviously, not important enough to take with them or bury, just like me, which I was thankful for.

Pain tore at my nerve endings as I climbed to my feet, teeth grinding together to prevent me from crying out. I looked about for my horse but found it gone, then I realised that my weapons were missing too. The Winchester and the Colt, which disappointed me greatly because of where they'd come from. To get them back, I would have to continue to Brewarrina, and I was in no fit state to be going there. Besides, once Kennedy found out I was alive, he'd make sure I hanged by the neck.

With only one option left, I turned and started on foot back toward Bindurra Station.

3

OUTBACK NEW SOUTH WALES, 1884

THE KENNEDY GANG STRIKES AGAIN!

THE HEADLINES on the front page of the Kent's Landing Star drew my attention immediately. Since being shot and left for dead, things had changed some. The trap sergeant named John Kennedy had been declared an outlaw, and I had been released from my incarceration. I had now set up the original freight outfit that I had intended all those years before.

It turned out that Kennedy shot the wrong prisoner in '81 and was prosecuted in the Brewarrina court for his misdeed. Sentenced to hang, he was to be transported to Dubbo, where the sentence would be carried out. But alas, during the journey, the prison transport wagon was held up at gunpoint and the escort killed. Kennedy was liberated from his cell on wheels and remained that way as I read the headlines once more.

As for myself, I'd been lucky. After the traps hunting, Hennessy had arrived at Bindurra Station, and they'd not waited around but immediately followed the trail with a tracker they'd brought with them. They found me two days after I'd been shot. Their leader was my old friend, Superintendent Michael O'Hanlon.

The next few years I spent working on the station until my release came up. The decision to stay on working for Mrs. Hearne was an easy one, and I did that until the opportunity arose to start my own freight outfit. It was the missus who actually helped me out. I was outside one evening watching the sunset when she appeared at my side. "What do you want to do with what is left of your life, Jack?" she asked me.

For a moment I was startled by the question, but once I gathered myself, I said, "I had an idea that I would like to haul freight, missus."

She smiled warmly at me and placed a hand on my arm. "Call me Mary, Jack, please. I think we've known each other long enough by now."

I nodded. "Okay, Mary."

"Why haven't you gone off and done it?" she asked me. "Instead of staying here."

"Before I was sentenced, Mary, I had the money to do it. Now, I've lost all I had, and it'll take me a while to ever get the money I need to get set up."

"Oh," she said softly, and fixed her gaze on the ground.

"Oh no, it's not like you think," I added hurriedly, hoping that I hadn't offended her. "I appreciate what you pay me and all, missus, but a team and a dray will cost a small fortune."

"I see," she said to me before turning away. "Good evening, Jack."

"Good evening, Mary."

A month later, we had the sheep in ready to shear when word reached Bindurra that the usual freighter who transported the clip to the river wouldn't be coming. There was no reason given. Mary Hearne was a little more than put out by the news, and I can honestly say that I'd never heard a woman swear like she did upon receipt of the news. The clip was put on hold, and the shearers threatened to walk off the station and move on to the next mob.

In the end, Mrs. Hearne told them to shear the sheep. It would mean that she would be out of pocket a lot of money with no way of getting the clip to Kent's Landing and the riverboats.

"I have an idea," I told her.

Porter was with her when I approached. He glared at me and snapped, "Go away, Crowe. The missus needs a solution, not more complications from the likes of you."

"I'll hear what he has to say," she said, and I noticed the scowl on Porter's face, but he held his tongue.

"The flatbed dray over behind the shed—"

"Has a broken axle," Porter pointed out.

"Has a broken axle, but it can be fixed. I can fix it and then we can use it to freight the clip to Kent's Landing."

"We don't have bullocks that can haul the dray," Mary said.

"We have horses, though," Porter added. "We can hitch a team of them up, and it should be enough."

After a moment of deep thought, Mary said to me, "All right, Jack, it looks like you have a freight outfit. If you get it through, I'll pay you on your return."

I shook my head. "Missus, if I get through, I don't want your money. I'd rather the dray if you are agreeable?"

To which, Mary Hearne replied, "You get my clip to the boat on time, Jack, and you can have the dray and the team to go with it."

So, I fixed that dray while the sheep were being clipped. And when I was finished, I repaired other things on it that needed some care. Then I picked out a team of horses to haul it. However, I needed extra because Bindurra didn't have the big, strong cart horses best suited for the trip.

By the time I was ready to head for Kent's Landing, the dray was piled three high with wool bales, with four across the deck.

It took me over a week, closer to two, to get the load to Kent's Landing. Once there, I found the riverboat waiting for the bales. It was called the *Canarvon,* and it already had one wool barge half loaded.

The captain's name was Henry, a stocky man with grey hair, who'd been sailing all his life. He welcomed my load with a gruff, "You're two days late. I was about to sail without it."

"We got late notice of the freighter not coming to Bindurra," I told him by way of an excuse.

He grumbled something and then said, "Hugh Cross got himself all busted up after one of his drays rolled over him. The doctor says he'll never work again. Be lucky to see out the year, in fact. So, there's plenty of freight out on the stations and on the riverbank with no one to move it."

"How did these bales get here then?" I asked curiously, pointing at the ones on the barge.

"They were already there. I picked them up in Brewarrina."

A million thoughts ran through my mind as I suddenly became aware of the freight sitting on the bank of the river. "Is there anything there that is headed out Bindurra way?"

The sound of a steam whistle echoed along the river, drawing our attention. A paddle steamer pulled away from the bank, a barge in tow. I could see the cords of wood on the deck behind the cabin. All along the river were stockpiles of the stuff cut by various contractors.

Captain Henry said, "That's the *Tibooburra*. Fred Hayes's boat."

I nodded, watching as it started to make headway through the lazy brown waters of the river. Hayes could be clearly seen in the wheelhouse of his boat, and I saw him reach up to pull the thin rope attached to the whistle. Another piercing shriek shattered the riverside hubbub, and this time, a flock of sulphur-crested cockatoos took flight with screeching protests from a large rivergum across the other side of the Darling.

"What were you saying, Jack?" Henry asked me.

"I wanted to know if there was any freight headed back out Bindurra way?"

"I don't know. You'll have to check with the Irishman. It'll take a while for your clip to be loaded, so you've plenty of time."

"Thanks, Captain."

"The name's Charlie."

"Thanks, Charlie."

I left the riverbank and walked up into the main street of Kent's Landing, more of a dirt trail compared to some that I'd seen. The town itself was erected on a raised piece of country some distance from the river. The first settlers had learned the hard way that the Darling River may look majestic and slow, but come the rains, it could turn into a wild beast. It took the washing away of the newly erected town and the deaths of seven people to work it out, though. Now, after three years, the rebuild was going strong.

There were a few framed buildings along the thoroughfare. The hotel, one of the two pubs, plus a couple of stores, and the bank. However, there were more in various stages of construction as the small river town grew.

When I finally reached my destination, I stopped to look at the freshly painted sign: ***Dunlavin River Freight.***

I walked inside, and straight away the scent of fresh-cut timber invaded my nostrils. The man I sought was seated behind a small desk, writing in a ledger.

Michael Dunlavin was a large Irishman from County Cork. He'd emigrated to Australia some ten years earlier and made his mark on the land with one dray and a team of bullocks. It had taken the redhead a while, but now he owned one of the larger river freight outfits on the Darling.

He looked up from his work, and I saw the expression that flitted across his face. He was well aware of my past, even though we'd only met once. "What can I do for you, Crowe?" he growled in his heavy accent.

"I just brought the Bindurra clip in, and I'm looking for a load to go back," I said, not letting his harsh words get to me.

He stopped what he was doing and stared at me for a moment. Then he said, "You brought the clip in?"

"Yes."

"On your own?"

"Yes."

"And now you're looking for another load? You trying to start your own freight company, Boyo?"

"Something like that."

He gave an abrupt nod, and his expression changed

Mary came out of her mourning, and one day she found me over at the yards, breaking a stock horse.

"Do you have a moment, Jack?" she said to me.

I turned around to see her standing at the rails, her hair tied back in a braid, a light cotton shirt tucked into a pair of men's pants. I let the pony go and walked over to her. I smiled and said, "It's good to see you, Mary. How are you going?"

Up until now, we'd been getting our orders from Beth. Whether they had been coming from Mary or not, we didn't know, nor did we question them. If it had been Beth, then she knew a lot for her age. Perhaps because it had been thrust upon her.

Mary said, "I'm fine. I've been wallowing in my grief for far too long. It's time I took my life back."

"Beth has been doing a grand job while you've been resting. She's shown she can run this place and then some."

Mary nodded. "She's almost sixteen and could run this place possibly better than I can. She is all I have left."

"What is it you wanted, Mary?" I asked softly.

"I'm surprised that you are still here," she said.

"I was needed here."

She smiled at me. "You're a good man, Jack. Even if—"

"Even if I'm a convict?"

She dropped her gaze. "It's not what I meant."

A kookaburra's laugh was answered by a galah. I said, "I know."

"So then, it's time for you to leave."

"I'll go eventually."

"No." Her voice was firm. "We had a deal. You take the clip to Kent's Landing, and I will set you up with your freight outfit."

"Yes, missus," I said, feeling like a stock hand again.

"Don't you, *yes missus,* me, Jack Crowe. You will leave tomorrow with your dray and horses. But mind me when I say this. I'll expect you back here every year for the clip. Understand?"

"I understand, Mary."

So, on that very next morning, I left with a dray, horses, food, and an old Colt Navy for protection. Three people saw me off. Mary, Beth, and Porter.

I READ the headlines for a third time. Back in the old days, I would have been out there after Kennedy. A pursuit which would have ended in a fury of gunfire and one of us dead. Of that, I was sure. But now I had different work, freight work, and I would leave tomorrow to keep the promise I had made to Mary Hearne to collect her clip.

"I was told I'd find you here," a familiar voice said, and I looked up from the newspaper to see Senior Constable Albert Prior standing before me.

Prior was a middle-aged man who'd been sent to Kent's Landing after it started having trouble with hoodlums from the riverboats. Every time something had happened, an officer had to be dispatched from Brewarrina on the two-day jaunt to get there. But that was also after the two-day ride made by someone to get there to make the complaint. Or if not, then word would be sent upriver on the next riverboat. By then, everything had blown over, or the drongo who'd started the issue in the first place was long gone.

"What can I do for you, Senior Constable?" I asked suspiciously.

The tall man with a salt and pepper beard hesitated for a moment. "What makes you think I want something?"

His light-blue eyes gave his intent away as he directed them toward the dusty street upon which he stood. I stared over his shoulder at a black tracker who sat atop a bay horse. Beside him was another man I'd never seen before. "Going somewhere, Albert?" I inquired.

The senior constable lifted his gaze. "I received word that the Kennedy gang were out east of here. I could use your help."

"I don't do that anymore," I replied with a shake of my head. "Besides, I have a wool clip I have to pick up at Bindurra."

"Superintendent O'Hanlon sent word to ask you," he said, wielding the words like a weapon. "He's coming with more men from Dubbo, but he wants you along."

I stared at the man sitting on the horse beside the tracker. "Who's he?"

"Morrison. Came upriver on the *Tibooburra*. He's the only one who wants the ten pounds that the job is paying."

"Dangerous way to earn ten pounds."

"Are you coming or not?"

I studied him for a moment before shaking my head. "You want to go out there and get your nice blue uniform all dirty, go right ahead. I made a promise I aim to keep."

Prior nodded. "I thought it would be a stretch to get you to help. I don't blame you, I guess. I thought that maybe—"

"That maybe I'd come and help after what Kennedy did to me those years ago?"

"Something like that."

"Maybe one day, if we ever cross paths, then there might be a reckoning. But until that time, I've got a freight business to run. My days of hunting men are over."

"I'll be seeing you then, Jack."

"Be careful, Prior. He's a very dangerous man."

After their departure that morning, I wouldn't see them for three more days. When I did, I wished I hadn't.

4

The offside lead bullock gave out a deep moan of protest as his hooves kicked up dust from the dry trail. The creek about two miles ahead was where I intended to unhitch the team, water them, and bed down for the night. Turning around, I looked back at the other team and dray I owned, plodding along behind me. It was smaller than the one I drove and was piled high with freight. This one was guided by my hired help, Jim Craig. He would help me load the clip at Bindurra, and then once he was unloaded, would move on to Craiglea.

The crack of his whip echoed across the plains, and I heard Ralph bellow in protest. I chuckled. Jim always named his lead pair of bullocks—Big Boy and Ralph, the latter being the one he talked to the most.

Two large gums guarded the road ahead where it snaked between them and then pitched down a shallow slope before climbing the other side. The grass on either side of the road was short and brown—a fair indication of the distinct lack of rain over the past few months. A line of trees on the other side of the distant rise hugged the creek bank where I would bed the teams down. Jim and I had named it Broken Axle Creek, which should be reasonably self-explanatory. We'd hit a large, submerged rock with the lead dray some time back. The axle had snapped like a branch, and it had taken us the better part of a day to get it fixed.

A crow flying low overhead cawed loudly, and I looked up. It flew away from me, following the road in a fashion. I watched him for a few heartbeats, his blackness standing out against the azure sky. One moment it was alone, the next, another had joined him, and within five seconds, they were numerous. Frowning, I looked ahead in the direction of their flight and saw more circling above the next ridgeline.

A few sharp commands brought the bullock team to a halt. Behind me, I heard Jim issue the same commands, then he joined me beside the first team. He was a tall, stringy man with dark hair and a happy disposition. But he was also tough. You had to be to get by out here beyond civilisation. "What's up?"

"See those crows?" I asked him.

He grunted. "Something dead."

Nodding, I said, "That's what I was thinking."

"Question is, what kind of dead thing draws birds like that?"

I walked over to the dray and scooped up my Martini-Henry rifle. I thought about the revolver, an 1861 Remington, .44 calibre, and grabbed it as well. "You want me to come with you?" Jim asked me.

Shaking my head, I said, "No. Go get the other Martini-Henry and wait with the teams until I return."

He sighed, unsure. "You're the boss."

I set off on foot because I didn't own a horse. Not much point when you walk for miles beside a team of bullocks day after day. The worn road was deeply rutted toward the bottom of the slope, which revealed several large rocks jutting through the now sun-baked earth. They were something to watch when we brought the wagons through.

Once I started up the slope, I became cautiously aware of my surroundings. Old sensations kicked in, and I began to feel on edge. I climbed slowly toward the crest, my eyes darting all around, scanning all the terrain before me. In the sky, the crows continued to circle before one dropped toward the ground. It was a good sign, indicating that there was nobody in the immediate vicinity. If there had been, then the bird would never have landed.

Atop the crest, I stopped. Before me was the line of gums along the Broken Axle Creek. Down below me, I could see what appeared to be a small canvas tent. It had been set up just inside the tree line, not far from the creek, and to the side of the wagon road.

There was no sign of any horses, but that didn't mean anything. The birds were feeding on something. A knot bunched in the pit of my stomach as I thought of what I might find upon my arrival at the creek. A tent meant humans. The crows told of death. Whatever I was about to find, it wasn't going to be good.

THE CROW'S wings beat wildly at the air in its haste to escape my presence. With a chorus of alarmed squawks echoing through the trees, the black bird was quickly joined by more of its kind. I froze and stared at the sight before me. It was a body, the mottled white of its naked flesh in stark contrast to the surrounding ground and leaf litter.

I knew immediately who it was without even having to stare at the ruined facial features. Prior had been dead for more than a day, hence the gathering of wildlife. He'd been shot twice in the chest. Off to his left lay the new man, Morrison. Beyond him, the tracker. Every one of them had been stripped bare.

Looking around the campsite, I figured they'd been jumped by the murderers sometime the day before. It had to have happened not long after dawn—Morrison and the tracker both shot through the head.

Judging by what I found, it appeared that the tracker had died first. Perhaps he'd heard something due to being the furthest away. Then Morrison maybe, or Prior. The horses had been taken as well as their clothes. Weapons, too, and ammunition. I walked around the campsite in slow circles picking out tracks. There were five sets, and they told all I needed to know. Bushrangers had killed Prior and the others. Not just any bushrangers, it was Kennedy and the mongrels who rode with him. How did I know? I just did.

Walking back to the drays, I found Jim waiting for me with curious anticipation. His stare was all the question I needed. "Senior Constable Prior and the others with him," I told him. "They're dead. Murdered."

"How?"

I told him that someone had come upon them just after dawn the day before. Most likely Kennedy and his ruffians. They'd shot the tracker first—he probably heard them or had been going for a piss. The new bloke was shot just after him. Prior had been shot through the chest but not before whoever it was had their fun with him. On closer inspection of the body, I found that he'd been shot through both feet, and that three of his fingers had been removed with a knife.

"Sounds like that sadistic bastard that rides with Kennedy," Jim said, referring to Mad Dog Billy Wilson.

Wilson was a young man from Victoria. He'd come north after the trap almost ran him to ground outside of Ballarat, where he'd killed a couple of prospectors at the diggings there for their gold. One of them had refused to tell the young ruffian where his was hidden, so Billy had taken to him with his knife. After the loss of his first two fingers, the man had told him where it was, but Wilson hadn't been satisfied with that. He'd continued his gruesome job, carving and slicing until there wasn't much left to cut off.

There were three other members to the bushranging mob. An Englishman named Monte Burns, Mike Gardner who hailed from up Queensland way, and George, the Aboriginal tracker who used to work with me back when I was chasing men for money.

I wasn't sure what had happened to George during my incarceration. Some said that he'd returned to his own people, once on the run from the law. Billy, the other tracker, had been found somewhere around Narrabri on the banks of the Namoi River. The traps had shot him down cold. After it all came out, they'd claimed that he'd been reaching for his rifle. But I knew better. In those days, blacks were considered about as worthless as mud on a man's boots, and it wasn't worth the trouble to bring them in for trial.

But I digress. Mike Gardner had robbed a couple of mail coaches up around Warwick on the Southern Downs. He'd then moved south, killing a stockman near Tenterfield for his horse. Somewhere after that, he'd met up with Kennedy.

Monte Burns, however, had been inside the same prison wagon with the man himself and had escaped when Kennedy did. At that stage, Burns's only crime was stealing a cow to sell for money. Now he was wanted for a lot more, and with the introduction of the Felons Apprehension Act years before, it meant that all the bushrangers could be shot on sight by anyone with the will to take them on.

"Find the shovel, Jim," I told him. "We'll bury them."

We spent the next couple of hours digging the graves and interring the bodies away from the creek. We did this for two reasons. Firstly, raging floodwaters tend to uncover most things in their path. Secondly, fluids produced over time by decomposing bodies leach into the sand and maybe into the waters of the creek, and a man didn't want to be making *billy tea* with contaminated water.

Once we'd finished with the burying and seen to the bullock teams, it was dark, and we were tired. We ate in contemplative silence by the campfire until the food was gone before Jim gave voice to something that had concerned me since discovering the bodies. "You figure Kennedy and his ruffians have been hitting the landowners around here?"

"By around here, do you mean Bindurra?" I asked.

"Maybe."

"I don't know. I guess we'll find out when we arrive."

"We're still over a week away from the homestead," Jim pointed out to me. "It would be better if we go back to Kent's Landing and inform them there about what happened here."

He was right, of course. That would have been the logical thing to do. But like a sheep, I'm not so good with logic when I get it in my mind I want to go somewhere.

And at that point, I wanted to go to Bindurra Station to check on everyone there. "No. We keep going. There's a job to do, and we'll do it."

The flames from the fire cast orange shadows across his face, unable to disguise his knowing expression. "If it was anyone else," I told Jim, "I would turn back. But they aren't. Mary Hearne gave me my start. I owe it to them to make sure they're all right."

He nodded. "Fine. If that's what you want, Jack, then that's what we'll do."

THAT NIGHT, as I lay on the rough ground under my blanket and looked up at the stars through the branches and the leaves of the large gum overhead, I thought about past times with the Hearne family. Of how kind they'd been to me, a convict, of Mary Hearne and her two tragic losses, and of young Beth, although not a kid anymore. She was twenty, a young woman who had blossomed and grown as the rugged country around her.

I don't know why my thoughts lingered on her. I was almost fifteen years older than she was, and I was classed as a ruffian to boot. What could she ever see in someone like me?

Each year since leaving Bindurra, we had spent more time talking than the previous. Every time I saw her, she had changed. Her hair was darker, her eyes a little bluer, and her skin almost flawless despite the harshness of the outback sun.

Then, the previous year, Beth had confided in me something her mother had said, "She told me to stay away from you, you know?"

I had frowned at the comment, my brow furrowed with deep lines. "Your mother said that?"

She had nodded. "Yes, she believes you to be a kind and honourable man, but you are a convict in the eyes of the law and not for someone like me."

"Why would she say that?" I asked, and then I saw the look in Beth's eyes as she reached out and touched my hand.

I withdrew it as though burnt by a wicked blue flame and saw the hurt in her eyes. "I...I'm sorry," I stammered. "You should listen to your mother."

With tears in her eyes, she turned away and ran back to the homestead from the yards where we'd been watching the sunset. I left the following morning without seeing her again. But I knew from the way her mother stared at me that she'd known what had happened.

TWO NIGHTS LATER, Jim and I were awakened by the distant sound of gunfire that swept across the plains and into our camp. Upon hearing it, I rolled out of my blanket and picked up the Martini-Henry. I stood at the edge of the camp facing the north, listening to the crackle, which kept coming. Beside me, Jim said, "That's a lot of gunfire, Jack."

"It is," I said with a short nod.

We stood listening for another fifteen minutes before it finally died away. It was times like these I missed having a horse. "What do you suppose it was?" Jim asked.

With a shake of my head, I told him I had no idea, but it would probably be best if we took turns at standing watch for the rest of the night. So, I took first watch, rousing Jim to take over when his time arrived. Nothing more was heard for the balance of the night, which was a huge relief in a way, but the question still remained: Who was doing all the shooting to the north?

WE FOUND out the following morning while we were hitching up the bullock teams. The sun had given birth to another warm, clear, fly-ridden day, and Jim and I had to fight the damned things for each scrap of bacon we consumed. I think somewhere amongst the battle, I managed to swallow one or two.

"You want to camp here for another day, Jack?" Jim asked me. "Maybe head north to see what all the shooting was last night?"

I considered his suggestion. To do so would mean walking until we came upon the site of the drama. Out on the plains, the sound could have travelled for miles. Plus, it would mean leaving the wagons, and I wasn't about to leave them unattended.

"No, we'll keep driving to Bindurra Station."

Jim was about to say something when I saw movement on the horizon through an already shimmering heat haze. "Look," I said to him, and he turned to stare where I was pointing. He frowned, trying to get his eyes to adjust to the glare.

"It's a rider on a horse," I said as they became more distinguishable. He was coming in from the north, and I suddenly had a very bad feeling. As the pair drew closer, I could see that the rider was swaying in the saddle.

I scooped up the Martini-Henry rifle and started to walk out to meet the rider. Jim did the same and followed me on my left shoulder. When the rider was close enough to see, we worked out not only that the rider was a man, but that he was also wounded.

The horse stopped just short of us as we hurried forward, the rider slumping lower in the saddle. I heard Jim say, "It's Wilf Barlow."

Wilf Barlow was the foreman of the Bonneville Station. I helped Jim get him down from the horse, and I could see that beneath the blood that matted his face, it was indeed Barlow. A deep bullet furrow along the top of his forehead was the source of the blood, and it had flowed down across his face and dried a dark brown. There was still a narrow trickle of fresh blood leaking from the ugly wound, which the flies were furiously trying to get to. His injuries weren't limited to the head. The saddle leather and the horse's flanks, along with the man's pants, were also coated with fresher blood, and the wound in his stomach unable to crust over with the rocking motion of the horse.

After assessing his wounds, we moved him across the road into the shade of a large gum, lying him on the ground while Jim went to get a grey blanket from one of the drays.

When he returned, I looked up at him and shook my head. The wound in his guts was a bad one, and he'd not see out the day. Climbing to my feet, I said to Jim, "Keep him comfortable. I'll be back."

"Where are you going?" he asked with a look of confusion.

"I'll head north and see if I can find out what happened. I'll take his horse."

"Be careful, Jack," he cautioned me. "That was a lot of shooting we heard."

I nodded. "It was."

I took the Martini-Henry and a pocketful of bullets.

Then I climbed atop the horse Barlow had ridden in on and headed away from our camp.

I RODE FOR FOUR LONG, hot, dusty miles before reaching the object of my search. At first, a handful of crows was the early indicator, then a large wedge-tailed eagle began circling gracefully above a small stand of gums. It was in that shade I found four bodies. All had been shot dead, the explanation for the gunfire Jim and I had heard during the night. A couple had been shot three and four times. Flies buzzed greedily around the wounds, and the crows had already begun their feast.

Of the four, I knew only one by name. Sure, I'd seen the others at Bonneville Station before, but I hadn't been on speaking terms with them. His name was Brown. The hands had called him Snake, named after the bastard brown thing, responsible for more than one death throughout the west.

I looked around the camp. Five men had snuck up in the dark and opened fire. They'd killed everyone except for Wilf. Then they'd riffled the camp for all it was worth before leaving. I was puzzled as to why they'd left Wilf alive and why they didn't take the horse he'd managed to ride away on.

Maybe Kennedy figured he'd live long enough to find help and tell what had happened. It wouldn't surprise me, for the killer was a sadistic bastard.

I left them where they lay, having nothing with me to dig holes to bury them. Even though the massacre site was at least a day and a half from the homestead, it was still part of Bonneville Station land. Someone would find them. Besides, I had more important things on my mind.

So, I rode away, leaving them there for the flies and the crows and the lone wedge-tailed eagle.

UPON MY RETURN, I found out that Wilf had died. Jim said he'd woken up thrashing and yelling like a creature from hell was chasing him across the open plains. When he'd stopped, he'd given out a rattle from deep in his chest and died.

Jim had taken the time to bury him under one of the gums. "Seems like all we're doing is burying people this trip, Jack," he said to me in a sorrowful voice.

"It feels that way," I agreed with him.

"What did you find?"

I told him, and he shook his head in dismay. "Someone needs to kill that mongrel bastard," he growled. "If you were still hunting men, you could do it."

"I don't, though," I reminded him. But he was right. If it had been back in my manhunting days, I would have gone after Kennedy and his gang.

We still had half the day left, so we made the most of it, driving the teams hard until the sun was about gone before we stopped and made camp again. That still left us around four days from Bindurra Station. We'd just sat down by the fire to eat when Jim asked, "Do you miss it?"

My spoonful of food stopped halfway to my mouth. "Miss what?"

"Chasing down bushrangers."

"No."

"It was good money, wasn't it? Better than freighting."

"Why all the interest?" I asked him. "You've never worried about it before."

"I guess it's this whole Kennedy thing. I just wish

someone would get him. Not take him in to hang, mind. Just shoot the bastard down and leave the crows to pick his bones clean."

"And you figure that I might be that someone?"

He nodded. "I'm sorry, Jack, but the traps aren't doing anything, and you're the only one I can think of. From all the stories—"

"Are just that," I snapped. "They're stories."

He put his head down and started to eat while I simmered opposite him. I don't know why it upset me so because what he said was true. Maybe that was the reason.

We ate in silence, and once finished, I cleaned my plate with sand, then picked up the Martini-Henry and stalked out into the darkness, still angry but not understanding why.

FOR THE NEXT FOUR DAYS, the bullocks lumbered along the rocky and rutted trail towards Bindurra Station. It took us a day and a half to reach the homestead from the front gate. But it was that last half a day that had me on edge. It was then that two things happened. The first was the trail left by a bunch of riders, and the second was the scene that lay before us when we topped a low ridge and saw the homestead. Or what remained of it.

The house and station hands' quarters were burned black, with nothing left except a twisted pile of corrugated iron and rubble. The yards were empty and—

"They've been here," Jim said, interrupting my thoughts.

I nodded as the cold hand of fear gripped my insides.

Or was that anxiety because of what I knew I was about to find? I felt my heart race and my hands start to tremble. Reaching down, I retrieved the Martini-Henry, making sure that it was loaded, and then tucked the Remington pistol in my waistband. Jim grabbed his rifle, and we left the bullocks where they were.

Making our way slowly down the slope, our eyes darted left and right as we looked for anything out of the ordinary that might speak of danger. I felt the blood coursing through my veins, a feeling I hadn't felt since my last manhunt.

Gravel crunched beneath our boots with every step, almost loud enough to drown out the beating of my heart. Almost.

Unspeakable things had been done to these people whom I'd worked with and cared for. The hands had been shot down, all multiple times. Porter had been tied to a wagon wheel and set on fire, leaving nothing of him but charred remains. The only identifying item being his twisted and blackened belt buckle that had somehow survived the fire.

I found Mary Hearne and Bethany together. Both had been violated beyond imagination, and as tears welled in my eyes and ran through the dust and hair on my cheeks, I swore on both of their lives that Kennedy and the scum he rode with would pay for their heinous actions.

But herein laid my quandary. As much as I wanted to go after the men responsible for the atrocities that lay before us, I still had to bury the dead and get my drays back to Kent's Landing, as Jim couldn't do it on his own.

It took us the rest of the day to inter the dead. I took care of both Mary and Beth and as I looked down at the latter's grave, I couldn't help but think of the last time I'd seen her, and how much I'd hurt her.

"Now are you going after them?" Jim asked from where he stood behind me.

I didn't answer at first, instead, I listened to the mocking caw of a crow in a nearby tree.

"Well?" he asked again, trying to elicit a response.

"We'll stay here tonight and then tomorrow—" I stopped.

"What?"

I didn't know, so I just walked off and left him standing there, mouth agape.

THAT NIGHT IT RAINED. Not a sprinkle or a shower, but steady soaking rain which turned the earth to a waterlogged mess and made it difficult for wagons to traverse the terrain leading back the way we'd come. I rose the following morning to a grey dawn and a landscape covered in a sheet of water. I knew that all the creek crossings between Bindurra Station and our destination would be up, and if it kept raining the way it was, then they would be impassable.

There was also another, more bitter downside to the rain. It washed away any tracks that Kennedy and his men had left behind, so there was nothing left to do but head back to Kent's Landing when the downpour let up.

5

KENT'S LANDING

IT TOOK us the better part of five weeks to get back to Kent's Landing as the rain continued for four more days without cease and flooded the parched land with a torrent of water. All the creeks had burst their banks, and the Barwon/Darling had risen high enough to do the same.

The sudden flood caught some of the riverboat captains off guard and cost them dearly. The muddy tumult of the swollen river carried much debris, holing three boats and sending them to the depths of the murky brown river. Barges broke adrift and were carried miles downstream to be hung up on trees or holed and sunk. When the river receded, one was found a mile from the river itself in a large floodplain.

It became known as the Great Flood of 1884. One which claimed lives the length of the river from Brewarrina in the north, down through Louth until it finally reached the Murray in the south.

We'd been back in Kent's Landing for two weeks, preparing to leave the following day with two drays of freight out to the stations, when Michael O'Hanlon showed up with six men in tow, looking for me.

It was early evening, and Jim and I were in the Kent's Landing pub having a quiet drink. The interior was dim and filled with a cloud of tobacco smoke. A couple of tavern wenches were making their way around the tables, fishing. That's what I called it anyway. You see, both of these lovely ladies looked like the back end of a daggy-arsed sheep, and the only way they could get a customer was to wait until a suitable stage of inebriation was reached and then go to the table and see if they could get a bite. Hence the name, *Fishing*.

I rolled myself a cigarette and then put my tobacco away. Lighting up, I drew in a deep breath, expelling it slowly, savouring the taste while Jim poured me another drink. Over in the far corner, a table was tipped over as two men came to their feet and shaped up, waving their fists around. After a few curses and misdirected swings, they picked the table up and sat down to have another drink.

"Have you heard anything?" Jim asked me, with regard to Kennedy and his gang.

I shook my head. "I thought Dunlavin might have heard something, but all he could tell me was that some troopers were headed this way."

"What for? That bastard isn't here."

"I don't know. Let's finish this drink and turn in. We'll get away after first light."

Jim nodded his agreement. "Sure."

This trip was to take supplies to some of the stations and then see us travelling south to a small place called Byrock to deliver more wool bales. The arrival of the train line there meant that many station owners no longer needed to transport their wool all the way to the river, instead shipping it the shorter distance to Byrock to go by rail.

About to stand up from our table and head off to bed, I happened to look over at the doorway and saw Michael O'Hanlon standing there looking around the room. I cursed under my breath because I knew without doubt that he was looking for me. For a moment, I hoped that he would miss me in the dim light. I put my head down and muttered under my breath, "Fuck off."

When I next looked up, however, he was walking towards our table. "Shit."

"Hello, Jack."

He sounded happy. Too happy. I looked up at him and asked, "What do you want, Michael?"

"Is that any way to greet an old friend?" he said, sitting down and reaching for the bottle in the middle of the rough surface. "Don't mind if I do."

His face was covered in grime from many days on the road, and I figured his throat, too, was thick with the stuff the way he swallowed the first drink then another two after it. Before he could reach for the bottle again, I moved it aside and repeated my question, "What do you want, Michael?"

"I want you, Jack," he replied. "Or rather, your manhunting skills."

"No."

"Come on, Jack," he said to me. "I've been asked to put a stop to that bastard Kennedy, and you're the only man I figure who can get me close enough to get him."

"I'm done with that. I ship freight now."

"What about—"

"Don't say it," I snapped, for I knew where he was going with it.

"What about the Hearnes?" he continued.

I felt the anger grow within me as I glared at him. For more than a fleeting moment, I felt like putting my hard fist into his mouth and driving the words back down his throat. Even though weeks had passed, the wound was still raw and painful.

"Damn it, Michael."

"You're the best manhunter I know, Jack," he said to me. "I'll pay you two hundred pounds for your time, whether we catch them or not."

"What about my freight?"

"Put someone else on for a while to help out."

"You don't even know where they are," I pointed out, "do you?"

"They were seen over near Louth a week ago," O'Hanlon told me. "There's been money shipped up and down the river of late, and it's only a matter of time before they try for one. I want to find them before that happens."

I looked over at Jim, who'd remained silent throughout the discourse. "Are you okay with this?"

He nodded. "I can take care of it."

"When do we leave?" I asked the superintendent.

"First light."

"Do you have any trackers?" I enquired whether he had any darkies.

He nodded. "I have six men, including myself."

"Not what I asked."

"Yes, I have a tracker," he growled.

"Who?"

"His name is Jimmy. Tracker from over Dubbo. I've used him many times."

"Fine, I'll be ready to leave in the morning."

"I'll meet you down at the river."

I raised my eyebrows. "River?"

"Yes, we're taking a riverboat down to Louth. It'll take us too long to get there otherwise, and Kennedy could be miles away by the time we get there."

"Then, I guess we're taking the boat."

O'Hanlon climbed to his feet and held out his hand. I took it, and he returned my firm grip with one of his own. "Thanks, Jack. Don't forget your guns."

I watched him go and then turned my gaze on Jim. "All right, let's talk about what to do while I'm away."

CAPTAIN HENRY WELCOMED us aboard his boat the following morning. A low mist hung over the river, and a chilly wind cut through our clothing. Magpies welcomed us to the river with their early morning warbles. The captain saw me coming up the gangplank and stopped what he was doing. "It is you I be seeing early this morning, Jack Crowe. I've no freight for you this—" He stopped when he saw the Martini-Henry in my grasp.

"I'm meeting Michael O'Hanlon here this morning, Charlie. And since there are no other boats in port at this time, I assume that you're taking us down to Louth."

The captain nodded. "That would be me. Do you have a horse?"

I nodded.

"Put it on the barge. The others should be here soon."

By the time I got my horse aboard, the troopers had arrived. Apart from O'Hanlon and his tracker, Jimmy, there was also a solid-looking sergeant named John

Croft who'd come bush from Melbourne ten years earlier. Also, a fair-haired trooper named Pete Sellers and two others, named Able Trent and Nate James, both with dark hair.

Once all the horses were aboard, Croft ordered Jimmy to stay with them for the duration. I looked at the Aboriginal tracker and noted the hostility in his eyes towards the sergeant. One thing I'd never gotten used to was bearing witness to the treatment that the whites gave the indigenous people of our country. Not all whites treated them that way, but there were a fair few who did.

I bit my tongue and said nothing. Right up to the point where the sergeant said to me, "You join him, too, convict."

"Did you say something to me, Sergeant?" I asked him. "I must have missed it because I don't think you were saying something like that to me."

"I said you stay on the barge with the darkie. Did you understand me that time?"

"How about you take your tunic off, you son of a Dubbo whore, and we'll sort it out like men instead of you hiding behind that trap uniform."

"Is there a problem, Sergeant?" O'Hanlon snapped from behind Croft.

The sergeant ground his teeth together before saying, "No, sir. No problem here."

"Good. Jack, a word."

Croft walked off and left me standing on the riverbank with the superintendent. "What seems to be the problem, Jack?"

"Nothing I can't handle."

"Don't give me that horseshit. Tell me."

"Your sergeant wanted to remind me of my place. I was about to show him the error of his ways."

"Don't go fighting with Croft, you hear me?" O'Hanlon said grimly. "If you strike him, then I'll have to arrest you. And you know what that means."

I did. It would mean me going back to jail, and this time it would mean Dubbo for years of hard labour. But my pride wasn't about to let it go so easily. "You tell him to stay out of my way, and I'll stay out of his."

O'Hanlon nodded. "I'll tell him."

And that was it. We boarded the riverboat and headed downriver toward Louth. It was a beautiful morning as we pulled away and headed into the middle of the swirling brown water. I remembered it well in later years. The mist had burned off, the sun was higher in the sky, transforming the rivergums which stood guard over the waterway, giant silver-barked sentinels casting long shadows.

The reason I remembered it so well was because it was the day I stepped back in time and became the manhunter I had once been.

DARLING RIVER

I sat up at the bow watching the gums slide by on both sides of the river. The banks were steep, and the river flowed well as the extra water from upstream still washed down. We passed through Bourke without stopping and were now still half a day from Louth. I was deep in my thoughts of past experiences when O'Hanlon came up beside me. "It's a beautiful place, isn't it, Jack?"

With a nod, I said, "Harsh, too."

"They were good people, Jack."

"The Hearnes?"

"Yes."

"They were more than that," I replied. "You sending me there was one of the best times of my life, even if I didn't deserve it."

O'Hanlon dug into his pocket for his pipe and tobacco. He stuffed the bowl and lit it, blowing out a blue iron cloud of tobacco smoke which was whipped away by the passage of the river boat.

"Michael," I said. "If I do this, I want enough money to buy another dray and team of oxen."

He thought for a moment before answering. "I'll agree to that, Jack."

"Thank you," I said. "There is one more thing, Michael. When we catch up to Kennedy himself, I am going to kill him. No one better get in my way."

He looked at me with a steady gaze and must've been able to read my steely resolve. He thought about denying me this wish but then said, "Okay, Jack. I'll grant you that."

He walked back down the deck and left me alone with my thoughts. A couple of cockatoos flew low over the river before climbing up over the trees. I closed my eyes and returned to the past.

LOUTH, DARLING RIVER

We arrived at Louth late in the afternoon. The river and wharf were busy, and we waited for a while before a berth became available at the dock to unload the horses. I guess that with the river running as high as it was, many boats were able to traverse it more easily, whereas in times of drought it sometimes became impassable. I stepped off the deck and stood on the dock, watching the hive of activity a moment before moving to help unload my horse.

"It's busy right enough," O'Hanlon observed as he walked up to me.

I grunted, not really listening to what he'd just said.

"The men will take care of everything. Leave your horse. Come with me."

I followed him into the town, which was bustling with people, mostly men, as they moved to and fro along the main street. I stopped and caught sight of something on a hill just outside of the town. It was a giant pedestal with a cross on top of it. O'Hanlon saw me staring at it and said, "It was put up by Matthews when his wife died in sixty-six."

I nodded and followed him further along the street until we arrived at a small frame-built place with bars on its windows. When we entered, we found the local constable inside on his own. He jumped to his feet when he saw O'Hanlon and said hurriedly, "Welcome to Louth, Superintendent."

"Where is Sergeant Prendergast?" O'Hanlon asked, looking around the dusty room.

"We had a report that the Cobb and Co. was attacked yesterday, sir," the constable replied. "He rode out to have a look."

"Where?" I asked the nervous-looking man.

"Dawson's plains."

"That's the best part of a day from here, isn't it?"

His head bobbed up and down. "Yes."

"And you're the only one left in town?" O'Hanlon asked curiously.

"Yes, sir."

"What is your name?"

"Bartlett, sir."

"When are you expecting him back?"

"I'm not sure, sir."

"Is there much money in town?"

"I'm not sure. You'd have to see Banker Meldrum."

I looked at O'Hanlon. "This makes the hair on the back of my neck stand up."

"You figure it could be a ploy to draw the police out of town to try for the bank?"

"Kennedy may be a killer, Michael, but he's smart too. I wouldn't put it past him."

He agreed with me, for I could see it in his eyes. "It would seem we have a bit of a predicament."

"We could stay here and wait," I counselled, "but if they don't come, then we lose time, and they get away. If we go, and they come to rob the bank, Constable Bartlett here doesn't stand a chance."

"Damn that man for a fool," O'Hanlon exploded. "Why on earth would he—how many constables did he take with him?"

"Two, sir."

"Anyone else?"

"A tracker and a couple of locals."

"Are you able to find some men to help you out?" O'Hanlon asked him.

"Maybe," Bartlett said, in an unconvincing voice.

"I will leave one of my men with you when we ride in the morning. Once the sergeant returns, he can catch up to us."

"Yes, sir. Thank you, sir."

"Where might my men and I find some accommodations for the night?" the superintendent asked.

"There is a boarding house or four pubs to choose from. Take your pick."

"Thank you, Constable."

We left the police station and went back outside. "Are you going to stay where we find lodgings or—"

"I'll find my own way, Michael."

He nodded. "Meet us back here in the morning at daybreak."

"I'll be here."

I FOUND a place at the pub. The room was small, the bed stiff, the mattress lumpy. All the makings of a good night's sleep. It made me think I might have been better off on the ground under a gum with roots poking out of the hard-packed earth. With my fixings left there and my weapons poked under the mattress, I went back downstairs into the bar.

The room was filled with thick wood smoke from the fire in the far corner. The chimney was overdue for a clean, however, the smell of the burning wood helped cover the stench of unwashed bodies of the men filling the place.

I walked up to the bar and placed a shilling atop its rough surface. A man walked over to me, a stained shirt tucked in beneath suspenders holding up pants under his large gut. "What'll it be?"

"Beer."

He found a glass and poured the beer, placing it in front of me. I stared at the head on it. "I hope you only take half of what you're owed, publican, because by the looks of that, I only got half of what I ordered."

He glared at me and said, "There are other pubs you

can drink at if you don't care for this one, friend. Maybe you should try them."

I shook my head. "No, I just don't like not getting what I'm paying for."

His eyes narrowed. "What are you saying?"

"I'm saying that you are treating your customers like fools. You give them half the beer while still charging them full price."

Now, I was tired and more than a little irritable, which was probably why I reacted the way I did when he ducked down for the club he kept under the bar. For when he came back up with the crude weapon in his hand, I was already reaching across the short distance between us.

I grasped a good handful of hair and pulled his head down with a brutal force driven by pent-up anger. His face smacked into the bar top, and his bulbous nose flattened against the wood. Blood spurted as he reeled back, then his legs gave way, and he slumped to the floor out of sight.

"What you go and do that for?" a man asked beside me.

I turned, ready for any attack on my person. The man gave me a confused look through booze-blurred eyes. "Say," he said, blinking to clear his vision. "I know you. You're—"

My right fist drove forward, taking him in the midriff. Air whooshed from his lungs as he doubled over. I caught him before he fell to the floor and propped him against the bar. I leaned forward and whispered in his ear, "You've never seen me before in your life, understood?"

He nodded, still gasping for air.

"What's going on here, Convict?"

I froze and shook my head. Croft. Of all the people I didn't want to see at that moment, he was at the top of the list. My feet moved slowly as I turned to meet his stare. "Just having a beer," I told him.

"Looks to me like you're causing trouble."

"I'll say he is," the publican gasped, having managed to find his feet. "I want you to arrest him for striking me."

A wicked smile split the trap's lips. "I guess we know where you're going, right, Convict?"

"Call me that again, and I'll give you a real reason to lock me up."

"What are you waiting for?" Croft sneered.

I glanced at his coat.

"Oh, I see. How about I take it off, and you can have a free run at me?"

"That's enough," O'Hanlon snapped.

We both turned to stare at him. His face was red as his anger boiled to the surface. "Croft, get out of my damned sight before I take those damned chevrons from you and give them to someone more deserving."

"Yes, sir," he said through gritted teeth.

Then the superintendent focused his gaze upon me. "What did I tell you?"

Suddenly, I felt like a scolded child. My face flushed, and I had a compulsion to look away. Instead, I held his stare and remained silent.

"Lock him up, Superintendent," the publican growled. "Look at what he did to me."

O'Hanlon's gaze shifted as he looked at the bloody face of the barman. However, instead of taking pity on the man, he said, "Shut up."

"Now, Jack, what do you have to say for yourself?"

"The publican tried to impose his opinion on me with a club he had behind the bar."

"He called me a thief," the publican retorted.

"He'd be right," an observer stated, eliciting laughter from the crowd.

"Go and find somewhere else to drink, Jack," O'Hanlon said to me.

"I have a room here."

"Just do it," he snapped.

I nodded and left, but not before I drank the beer I'd bought. My act of defiance.

MAGPIES AND CROWS. The resonances of both greeted me the following morning as I stepped outside. One a nagging, grating sound, the other more, a musical warble. The air was chilled and smoke from woodfires hung low, the scent welcoming. I held my belongings over my shoulder while the Martini-Henry, I carried in my right hand. The Remington pistol was tucked into my waistband.

I started along the street towards the police station and noticed the amount of activity there, even though it was early. When I arrived, I noted the absence of one horse, then remembered how O'Hanlon had offered to leave one man behind.

I was not disappointed to find that the man would be Croft. A kind of punishment for his indiscretion the night before, no doubt.

I placed the Martini-Henry in the saddle scabbard and walked around behind my horse where the tracker, Jimmy, stood. "Have you eaten?" I asked him.

He looked at me as though I was asking him something strange. It was a simple question, so I asked it again. "Have you eaten?"

He nodded. "Yes."

"Do you have a sidearm?"

He shook his head. I dug into my things and took out a second Remington, which I had. I passed it to Jimmy, who hesitated. "Go on, take it," I urged him.

He reached out and took the weapon in his calloused palm, seeming to weigh it before he tucked it into his waistband.

"Hey!" Croft cried out. "What are you doing giving that darkie a pistol?"

I glared at the sergeant, my patience wearing thin with him and his bombast. "If we catch up to Kennedy and his men, he'll be needing it. Besides, it's not against the law."

"Quiet," O'Hanlon said, attempting to stop something before it started. "Shall we go?"

We climbed onto our horses under the hot stare of Sergeant Croft. I could tell by the set of his jaw that he was grinding his teeth in anger. I almost rode off without saying something, but alas, it wasn't in me to let it go, and I couldn't help myself. "Have fun minding the station, Sergeant."

The expletive-laden sentence that followed was much too heated to repeat, but let us say that if he were on a ship, even a sailor would turn scarlet. I gave him an impertinent salute and rode off, trailing the others out of town.

WE FOLLOWED the road east for the better part of the day without finding anything. No stage nor any traps.

The flood plain around the river turned to ridges and hills with jagged outcrops of rock exposed by the harsh Australian clime. Dirt, a deep red colour was punctuated by large tufts of grass. An escarpment rose to our north as we traversed the inhospitable but beautiful country. Gums that had fought their way into majestic trees dotted the landscape, along with flocks of emus. Every so often, a kangaroo would bound away, startled by our passage.

It wasn't until late in the afternoon that Jimmy stopped and dismounted. He studied the red gravel of the road and pointed to the right of the trail. He spoke clearly. "There."

It was one word, but I immediately knew the meaning of it. I turned my horse and started towards the south. As I rode, I drew the Martini-Henry from the saddle scabbard.

"Where are you going?" O'Hanlon called behind me.

"To find the dead."

He called out more words, but I chose to ignore them, my eyes concentrating on the ground before my horse. At first, it was hard to locate, but then the terrain changed, and soft, sandy patches appeared, spread sparsely before me. But I found what I was looking for. The deep marks of iron-rimmed wheels cut into the surface of the bitter landscape. I halted the animal beneath me and followed the direction the stage appeared to have taken. About a mile distant, I could just make out a scar on the landscape where a deep ravine, washed out by scouring waters over many millennia, had carved a path. Looking to the sky above it, I could make out the faint circling black dots of the crows. Beside me, Jimmy brought his horse to a stop. "You see them, boss?" he asked me.

"Yeah," I grunted.

"We find them White fellas there?"

I shook my head. "No. What we'll find there will be much worse."

We edged our horses forward, leading the traps behind us to the ravine. At the edge, we both stopped and looked down at the soft sandy bottom. The Cobb & Co. stage lay on its side, wheels and axles busted from the impact of hitting the base. Beside it lay the bodies. Stripped bare and thrown down so that some lay on top of the others. I shook my head in disgust.

"Oh, sweet Lord," I heard Michael O'Hanlon gasp from where he stood beside me. "What fucking animals commit murder so foul like this?"

"We both know who it was," I reminded him grimly.

"Aye, we do."

I dismounted my horse and walked towards the edge of the ravine.

"Where are you going, Jack?" Michael asked.

He already knew the answer, but I think it made him feel better asking the question anyway. So, I gave him the answer he wished for. "I'll have a look. The rest of you stay here."

As I started down the almost vertical face, I heard movement behind me. I turned and saw Jimmy following me. "What are you doing?"

"I come with you, boss. We look together."

I sighed. "Okay."

It took us the better part of thirty minutes to get to the bottom, and the closer we came to it, the stronger the smell became. When our boots touched the soft sand, a buzzing grew in intensity as swarms of flies attacked the corpses with vigour.

It wasn't just the people from the stage but the traps

who'd gone searching, too. All of them had been shot many times. I circled the macabre mass of bodies until I reached the stage. It was shattered, the journey down from the rim above having done it no favors. I also noticed the bullet holes in the different wood panels and bloodstains near the seat. My guess—from the driver or the guard.

"Hey, boss, look here," Jimmy called to me.

I looked up, and he threw an item of clothing at me. Catching it, I let it unfurl, and to my horror, saw that it was a dress. My eyes darted back to the mass of flyblown corpses as I searched for what I knew in my heart I would not find. I stuffed the dress into my shirt and started back up the face of the ravine to give O'Hanlon the news.

"GOOD LORD, I should have been told!" the superintendent exploded, after I broke the news to him. He looked at the dress and scrunched it up. "We have to find her."

"She will be dead. Kennedy will have killed her once they finished getting from her what they wanted."

"If we follow their trail, then we might catch up to them—" O'Hanlon started.

"Stop, Michael. We won't catch them. They've been dead since yesterday. My guess is that Kennedy and his gang circled around to avoid the road. By the time we get back to Louth, they'll have already done what they wanted to."

"God damn it!" he exploded.

"Hey, boss," Jimmy called out.

"What?" O'Hanlon and I both said it at the same time.

"The woman, she not with them bad fellas. She walk off that way." He pointed to the northeast.

"How do you know?" O'Hanlon asked the tracker.

"I look around. She hid over there," he said, indicating a clump of wattle. "She watch, and when bad men leave, she go walkabout."

"Maybe she escaped?" O'Hanlon said hopefully.

I shrugged. "It doesn't change the fact that you need to get back to Louth."

I didn't like the decision as much as he did, but if the superintendent wanted to catch Kennedy and his gang of scoundrels, then it was the right thing to do. However, I saw another way.

"Michael, take the others back, and I'll take Jimmy with me. We'll find the woman if we can and catch up. Not sure how she got up those steep walls. The same way we did, I guess."

"Make sure you find her, Jack," O'Hanlon growled. "Find her and bring her back to civilization."

"I'll do what I can."

"Do you want some of our supplies?"

"No, we'll get by."

"I'll see you in Louth."

"Watch yourself," I warned him.

They mounted their horses and rode back towards the road. The receding sound of their animals' hoofbeats faded further until they could no longer be heard. I looked at the sun in the sky, which was almost to the western horizon. I turned to Jimmy and said, "We will camp here for the night and start fresh tomorrow."

6

We followed the woman's trail across the hostile terrain, through small stands of stunted trees and scrub, and traversed red dirt plains and clumps of grass. We found the spot where she'd spent the night and then left that morning. At one point, her path intersected a dry creek bed lined with box and redgum. She paused there for a while in the shade before continuing. Jimmy said to me, "She not far ahead now, boss."

I nodded. "An hour, maybe."

He pointed at the ground. "She tired, see?"

I did see. Where her footprints had been clear earlier, they were now long, distended where she'd begun dragging her feet from exhaustion.

We climbed back onto our horses and continued, aware that we were running low on water. I said to the tracker, "Do you know where we can find some water?"

"Yes, boss."

"I'm not your boss," I told him patiently. "My name is Jack."

"Yes, Boss Jack."

I opened my mouth to rebuke him, but instead said, "Find water for us, Jimmy. The horses need it, and so will the woman when we locate her."

"Yes, boss."

We moved off, and Jimmy led us further to north, away from the trail we had been following. Three miles from where we deviated, we crested a rise in the red landscape, and there before us was another creek bed. This one, however, had a billabong in it surrounded by gums and other trees and backed onto a small escarpment. Out on the plain to the east, I saw a flock of emus as they slowly browsed through the grass tufts, looking for food. "There, boss," Jimmy said. "Down there. Place never dry."

As we rode closer, I could hear the abundance of birdlife in the trees. Cockatoos, galahs, and even smaller parrots screeched greetings to us as we approached.

"Black fella come here all the time," Jimmy told me. "Special place."

I'd learned about the Aboriginal special places from my previous trackers. I said, "Maybe we shouldn't go down there."

"It fine," Jimmy said, and urged his horse forward.

The billabong was a hive of activity. Wildlife abounded. Even in the pool of clear water, we could see the fish swimming. I watered the horses and filled our canteens while Jimmy walked around the pool to a tall tree. He looked underneath it until he found a reasonably straight branch. I watched him as he used a knife to carve a point at one end. Then he slid quietly into the billabong, careful not to spook the fish we had seen.

He seemed to glide through the water, creating but a small ripple on the surface. Beneath it, the fish swam lazily, unconcerned with the intrusion into their habitat.

Then Jimmy stopped, and the spear in his right hand lifted slowly before plunging down through the surface of the water.

With an exultant yelp, he lifted it into the air with a fat fish impaled on the end, tail flapping in its death throes. He pulled it from the spear and threw it to me on the bank. He repeated this twice more, and I realized what he was doing. The fish would be our dinner that evening.

Horses watered and canteens filled, we rode back to pick up the woman's trail. Once rediscovering it, we kept moving. Then, two hours later, she appeared on the plain before us. We urged our horses to go faster, and they broke into a ground-eating lope. Up ahead, I saw the woman turn and then start to run away from us.

Maybe she thought us to be the ones from the stage holdup: part of Kennedy's gang. I saw her stumble and fall. She never rose again. It was as though she just gave up then and there, resigned to the fate about to befall her, no matter how brutal it was.

We reined in our horses at a distance to show we posed no threat to her. I could hear her sobbing, her shoulders shuddering with each one. "Miss?" I called to her.

She didn't look up, dared not. I tried again. "Miss, my name is Jack Crowe. I'm with the traps—the police."

I heard her sobs stifle, and she looked up at me.

"We will not come closer unless you say it is all right. But I assure you that you are safe with Jimmy and me."

"How—how do I know if you tell the truth?" she managed to ask.

"Do you see the clothes that Jimmy wears. That should tell you enough. We found the stage yesterday with Superintendent Michael O'Hanlon. They have gone back to Louth in the hope of capturing the scoundrel who did the murderous deed."

"It was horrible," she gasped. "Murder most foul."

"Aye," I said, and nodded in agreement. "I've seen it before."

"You are a policeman?"

"No," I replied truthfully. "I was asked to help capture the man responsible."

"And you are called Jack Crowe?"

"I am. Please, have some water." I leaned down to hand her one of the full water canteens.

She rose to her feet, wobbled from fatigue, took a hesitant step forward, and held out her hand. She looked nervous, and I wasn't surprised—she'd been through a lot. "What is your name?" I asked her as she took the canteen in both hands.

"Clara Watson."

"Where were you headed, Miss Watson?"

"Kent's Landing," she replied, uncapping the lid and taking a couple of tentative sips.

Thoughts roamed my mind. The stage would have ended at Louth from there. "Were you taking a boat from Louth?"

"Yes, one of my father's."

"Is he Thomas Watson?"

"Yes, do you know him?"

I nodded. "Yes, I know him. I have taken freight from his barges on more than one occasion."

She stopped short of the horses. Under the grime on her face, she was quite pretty. Her hair, though messed, was dark, almost black, her features fine, and one would guess an age in her late twenties. "Can you ride?"

She nodded. "I think so?"

I leaned down in the saddle and helped Clara up

behind me, taking the canteen from her right hand. I felt her arms wrap around my waist as she pressed herself against my body. The pressure of her firm breasts on my back made me want to squirm, for I felt a little uncomfortable at their touch. But I brushed it off, and Jimmy and I turned the horses, pointing them towards Louth.

THE SNAP of a small twig in the fire sent a stream of sparks into the darkness on the eddies of rising heat. Each of us was bathed in the orange glow of the flames and the jumble of shadows being cast. We dined on the fish Jimmy had caught at the billabong, and now, stomachs full, we talked. I, for one, was eager to find out what had happened to the stage.

From what Clara had told us, they'd been stopped on the road. As soon as the stage ceased movement, she'd heard voices, and then the gunfire erupted. "The men inside the coach rushed to get out. In the crush, I was forced out too."

"How did you get away?" I asked her.

"I don't think they saw me. I ran into the scrub while they were still shooting, and I hid there."

"When did the policemen arrive?"

"That same day?"

I was confused. "Are you sure. You didn't get a knock to your head or anything like that?"

"I know what I saw, Mr. Crowe," Clara snapped. "I will remember it for the rest of my living days. They shot the wounded who were lying on the ground. I'll never forget that."

"But Louth is the best part of a day from the site where the coach was robbed—"

"They never robbed the coach," she said, cutting me off.

I felt my eyes narrow, and my mind was filled with thoughts of the possibilities. There was never going to be a robbery, it was all about getting the police out of Louth.

"What happened when the traps arrived?" I asked.

"The bushrangers were hidden at the side of the road. The police rode right into their—" she went quiet then. "All except one. A man who rode at the rear of their group. He wasn't shot because he was one of them. Once the shooting had stopped, he dismounted, and they all slapped him on the back like he was some kind of hero."

So, they sent for the traps before they even held up the stage. Kennedy had planned it well, and now there were only two policemen standing between the killers and the money they coveted within the bank. I just hoped that O'Hanlon would make it back in time.

I DON'T KNOW what time it was, but during the dark hours of the early morning, I vaguely remembered Clara joining me where I slept, pressing herself into my back. I guessed at the time that it was a case of her feeling safe. When I woke up the next morning to the warble of magpies, she had moved away again. Jimmy had already started a fire to warm ourselves before starting out towards Louth.

"Did you sleep well?" I asked Clara, who turned scarlet at the question.

"I'm sorry, but I needed you—to feel safe, I mean," she stammered.

"It's okay. I figured something like that. I can't offer

you breakfast for we have nothing. We should reach Louth today, though."

"That's okay. I can wait."

Clara climbed up behind me again for the journey. At around midmorning, with the sun once more nestled in a clear blue sky, she surprised me by asking, "Are you married, Mr. Crowe?"

"Call me Jack, ma'am."

"Then you must call me Clara," she stated.

"I guess that's fair, Clara."

"*Well?*" she said after I failed to respond to her question. "Do you have a wife?"

"That's kind of a personal question to be asking a man who is a stranger to you, isn't it?" I asked, trying to avoid answering.

"My father always told me when I was a young girl, if you want to know something, ask. It's the only way to learn."

"No, ma'am, I'm not married."

"Is there a—"

"No," I replied abruptly.

She went quiet, and I was afraid that the tone of my voice might have upset her. "Are you okay, Clara?"

"I'm fine." Her voice was clipped, and I knew that I'd offended her.

We rode in silence for the next couple of hours until the town came into view. Straight away, we could tell something was terribly wrong. A thin brown smudge of smoke rising into the sky above it told me all I needed to know. The Kennedy gang had been here.

THEY HAD RIDDEN into Louth under the cover of darkness. Five killers led by John Kennedy. Their first port of call had been the home of William Burnett, the Louth manager of the Northwest Bank branch. They had casually knocked on the door, and when his wife had opened it, forced their way in. The killers gathered the family in their sitting room, Burnett, his wife, and son and daughter, both young adults.

"What do you want?" Burnett had asked them.

"We want to get into your bank," Kennedy had replied calmly.

When the manager hesitated, Billy Wilson walked over to the man's daughter. "Mr. Manager, I'd do what the man asks, or—" He ran a grime-covered hand down the young woman's shoulder. She cringed, repelled by his touch. With his free hand, he grabbed a handful of hair while the other travelled down to the swell of her breasts.

"Don't," the manager whimpered.

"Then you'll do as we ask," Kennedy told him. "My boy Billy here will take good care of your family while we're gone."

That was when they had left for the bank. After the robbery, someone had gone to check on the family, and they had found them all dead. All three had their throats slashed wide, the daughter's only after she'd suffered at the hands of the crazed killer kid.

As we rode along the street, we saw the bank, burned to a pile of rubble and ash. So too, the few buildings around it. When Burnett couldn't be found, it was assumed that he was still somewhere inside.

O'Hanlon was at the station when we arrived there. Even before we dismounted, he was out to greet us. "Thank God you're back. We need to get moving again.

The black-hearted bastard—" he stopped when his gaze settled on the woman. "I beg your pardon, Missy, I'm emotional at this present time."

Clara nodded. "That is quite fine, Superintendent, and totally understandable."

"Are you the woman from the coach?"

"I am."

"Good thing you found her, Jack," he said to me. "Now get ready to ride again. I'm sorry, Missy, but we need to get after these…"

His voice trailed away as he looked for words to fit.

"Black-hearted bastards?" she supplied.

O'Hanlon gave a forceful nod. "That's them."

I shook my head. "We're going nowhere on these mounts, Michael," I told him.

"What?" he blurted out.

"They're spent. They need food and rest."

"Get some fresh ones," he demanded.

"Michael, it'll be dark soon—"

"They killed two policemen, I'll not let them get away."

I said nothing.

"That's right," he continued, "the constable and Sergeant Croft. Both dead."

"I'm sorry, Michael, but it still doesn't change the fact it'll be dark soon. Even Billy can't track in the dark."

He knew I was right, but his emotional state had him letting out a string of epithets that had him apologising once more to Clara. "All right, Jack, get yourselves some food and rest. But I want you ready to go before sunup tomorrow. Understood?"

"I'll be there."

"Now, Missy," he said to Clara, "let's find you somewhere to stay."

Clara turned to face me and said, "Thank you for all you've done, Mr. Crowe. I'll be sure to let my father know what you did for me. He will be grateful without doubt."

Her gaze lingered on mine for a long time before she turned and started off with O'Hanlon. Jimmy said from beside me, "That woman like you, boss. I can tell."

"Shut up, Jimmy."

THE MOOD that evening in the Ironsides Pub was bleak. Everyone was still in shock about what had happened. The butcher's bill in all, I was told, had been nine dead. Nine good souls—eight good souls gone to meet their God, and one bastard sergeant gone the other way, no doubt. I sipped my beer and finished my dish of mutton stew. While not overly hot, it tasted good and was filling. I'd bought Jimmy one too, but as per pub rules, he had to sit outside and eat his. I didn't agree with it, but I was in no mood to argue the point with a second publican in town.

I sensed her at first. I don't know what it was that made me look up, but I did and saw her coming straight towards me. An attractive woman, who had obviously not long bathed, for her long black hair was still damp. My first impression of her was confident, as the way she walked told me that she was no wilting wallflower. When she stopped and stood before me, she gave a wide smile, revealing straight white teeth. In an accented voice, she said, "Would I be considered too forward if I asked to join you?"

I shook my head and said, "If there's two things I've learned over the course of my life, miss, it's not to care about what other people think about me, and never turn a pretty lady away."

She laughed and sat down. "You sound just like my brother."

"I hope I don't look like him," I replied. "Would you like a drink?"

She nodded. "I'd kill for a beer."

Now it was my turn to laugh. "Coming right up."

We sat and talked well into the evening. Her name was Alice, and she came from a place called Georgia in the United States. Apparently, she'd come to Australia with her brother Charles, who owned a couple of river boats and was in the process of negotiating a business venture with another owner. But all the while, I could sense she was holding something back. Then she surprised me by saying, "I asked around about you, Jack."

I stared at her brown eyes, looking for some kind of sign as to what was coming next, but she gave nothing away. She would have made a good card player. Maybe she would surprise me there, too. "Aye," I said.

"I was told you were a man to be careful around," Alice said gently, as though her words might wound me.

"I've heard that said of me before."

"And that you were a killer of men."

I nodded. "I've killed men, that's true."

Still, she didn't seem too moved by my admission. "I find that intriguing."

"Nothing intriguing about killing a man," I replied.

"My brother is looking for someone like you to oversee his business ventures," she told me.

"A killer?" I asked.

She smiled, and her eyes sparkled in the lantern light. "No, a man who can get the job done."

"I've got a job at the moment," I told her.

She pouted at me and asked, curling a finger in one of her long tresses, "Is there anything I can do to change your mind?"

NOW, I'm not one to take advantage of a lady and talking about it, but that woman was like a she-devil in bed. I'm still unsure who made the iron-framed bedhead bang against the plank wall harder, her or me, but she sure could sing up a storm. Thin walls and all that, I wouldn't have been surprised if Superintendent O'Hanlon had knocked on the door to see who was murdering who. Now, in the early light of morning, as I stared at myself in the mirror, I could see the scratches and bitemarks she'd left there in her throes of passion. I turned and stared at her as she rested against the battered bedhead, sheet halfway down her torso, exposing her voluptuous, pale breasts.

"Rolling with you is like trying to hug a damned possum," I explained to her.

"Is that a bad thing?" Alice asked innocently.

"Depends, if you're the one doing the hugging."

"You can't tell me it was that bad."

"Never said it was bad," I replied.

"Have you reconsidered my brother's offer?"

"I can't," I told her truthfully. "I already told you I have a job."

Her eyes flashed before she could get control. Hoping I wouldn't notice her brief fit of anger, she said, "Take some more time to consider. We're travelling up to Kent's Landing today to finalise the agreement with the Watson fellow we're dealing with."

I nodded. "I'll do that, but I won't change my mind."

"WHERE THE DEVIL HAVE YOU BEEN?" O'Hanlon demanded when I finally showed. "We've been waiting here for God knows how long."

"I'm here now," I told him.

The other troopers smiled knowingly at me. "What are you lot gaping at?"

"Yes," O'Hanlon said. "What indeed?"

We rode out of Louth and headed southwest, following the meandering path of the river towards the port of Hawesville. The port itself was new. Another to serve the ever-expanding wool trade. The tracks were plain to see, and after we'd covered ten miles, the trail turned away to the southeast in the general direction of Cobar, the new copper mining settlement some eighty or so miles from where we were.

Jimmy dropped back beside me and said, "Them fellas not worried about being followed, boss."

"I'm not your boss, Jimmy."

Suddenly, he stopped, reining his horse to a stop. I heard him take a deep breath before he climbed down and started to walk around in a circle. "What's wrong?"

"That black fella with them is a smart one."

He was talking about George. "What's wrong?"

"They split up." He straightened and pointed in different directions. "They go that way, that way, that way, that way, and that way."

Hoofbeats sounded from behind us as O'Hanlon and the others approached. "What's up, Jack?"

"They've split up, Mike. I guess they figured that we wouldn't be able to follow all of them at once."

"Damned inconvenient. Which one should we follow?"

I looked at Jimmy. He shrugged his shoulders. "Don't know, boss. You pick."

O'Hanlon muttered a curse under his breath. "We'll split up. Take two of the trails and see where they take up."

A pained expression came to my face, and the superintendent obviously saw it. "What is it, Jack?"

"I don't like that idea. I say we follow one trail and stick with it. Eventually they'll come back together."

O'Hanlon shook his head. "You and Jimmy follow one together. I'll take the others and follow another. Between us, I'm sure we can manage that."

"They'll either head towards a nearby station or back to one of the river settlements," I told him.

"Why do you say that?"

"Look around you. We've had some rain, so water won't be an issue for a while. But they'll need food. A man gets enough of eating kangaroo after a while."

"That means Yuraba Station, or they'll circle back and head for Hawkesville."

I nodded. "Take your pick."

"You take Yuraba. If they're not there, we'll meet you in Hawkesville."

"All right."

O'Hanlon looked grim. "You realise if we're wrong, then we'll have lost them."

I pointed at the sky. "We'll get a storm this afternoon. We'll lose their trail anyway."

"Fucking weather," the superintendent swore bitterly.

7

I'D BEEN RIGHT about the rain. In the early afternoon, there was a gradual build-up off to the west, and a couple of hours later, the sky overhead became darkened with steel-grey clouds that boiled angrily. The dense curtain of rain could be seen coming across the rugged landscape towards us, and before it wrapped the pair of us in its shroud, we took our oilskin coats from our bedrolls and put them on.

Jagged streaks of lightning were followed by the booming crash of thunder. Large drops of rain fell sporadically at first before it became a torrent. The outback terrain seemed as though a thick fog had settled like a mantle on the tops of the gums. The rain out here transformed the landscape, giving it life where there seemed to be none. And after twenty minutes of solid precipitation, it was gone.

We continued to ride until it was time to make camp by a creek, which I theorised would have been slack earlier in the day, but with the sudden cloudburst, it was now flowing well.

We ate from our rations before turning in, to the sound of the creek burbling along beside us.

The galahs roused us early the following morning, and Jimmy had the fire going by the time I crawled out from under my blanket. The wood was damp, and the campfire smoked and struggled to burn with any authority, but eventually the coffee was ready. Once finished, we were back in the saddle and headed towards Yuraba.

AFTER CROSSING ONTO STATION LAND, we were greeted by three men. Still a couple of miles from the main house, but the three men who stopped us on the trail were working a mob of sheep.

They spotted our approach after Jimmy and I crested a low rise where the trail veered around a clump of copper-coloured rocks. They moved away from the sheep and positioned themselves across the trail.

Jimmy and I eased our horses to a stop. I nodded to the man in the centre. "How do?"

The man's lip curled in the corner as a sneer touched his thin lips. His eyes were fixed on Jimmy. "What's he doing here?"

"He's with me."

"We don't want darkies on Yuraba," he growled.

"That's strange," I said evenly. "Considering the name of the station is an Aboriginal word meaning *place of spotted gums.*"

"I don't care what it means."

I studied him. His face was weathered and lined. His hair dark, and his hat stained with sweat and salt marks burned white in the sun. The men beside him were younger than the speaker, who was maybe forty years or so. "Fella, we don't want any trouble. We're here looking for news on the Kennedy gang. That's all. I just want to talk to the owner."

"You're welcome to talk to Mr. Worth," he allowed, then looked up and gave Jimmy a dismissive look. "The darkie gets off the station."

Jimmy's face remained impassive. Over the years, I guessed he'd faced this kind of bigotry wherever he went, maybe even worse. "Who are you?" I asked.

"Yates. I'm the foreman." He reached up with his right hand and lifted his hat to wipe away the sweat from his brow. His shirt sleeve dropped down his arm to reveal the darker ring of scarring around his wrist. Manacles was my guess. "Who are you?"

"Jack Crowe."

The man's eyes narrowed. "I heard of a Jack Crowe once. Used to hunt bushrangers and lawbreakers for money."

"I heard of him, too."

"Ended up on the wrong side of the law, the rapscallion did. Got off light."

I could see where this was headed from the bitterness in the man's voice. "Are you going to let us pass or not?"

"You want us to move, you'll have to make us."

I was in no mood to put up with his urge for trouble, so I reached for the revolver in my belt and took it out. I pointed it at Yates and thumbed back the hammer. "Move."

Yates stiffened, but there was still defiance in his face. "You won't shoot, Crowe. They'd hang you this time."

He was right, of course. I moved the weapon, so it was pointed into the air and fired it three times. The sound of the shots was enough to startle the sheep so that they began to run, bleating as they went. With a snarl of rage, Yates yanked on the reins of the horse he was riding and started off after them, his friends following in his wake.

I glanced at Jimmy. "That'll keep them busy for a while."

"Him bad man, boss," Jimmy stated. "You see his arms?"

I grunted. "Yeah, I saw them."

Jimmy pulled back his sleeves to reveal similar scars. "I got them too."

I heeled my horse forward. "Come on, let's get on up to the homestead."

THE OWNER of Yuraba Station wasn't what I expected. He was a young man in his early twenties and looked more like a boy, not old enough to shave. He stared at us and then said, "Who are you?"

"I'm Jack Crowe. My friend here is called Jimmy."

He ignored Jimmy and asked, "What do you want?"

"We're tracking the Kennedy gang. We are looking for news."

"They're not here," the young man said.

I was aware of more station hands moving to gather around us, and it was starting to make me nervous. Behind Jimmy and I, the sound of hoofbeats grew louder, and I guessed that Yates and his bastard mates were coming into the yard. He rode over to where the young man stood and said, "I tried to stop them, Mr. Worth, but he fired his weapon at the sheep and scattered them."

"You're a liar, Yates."

"Mills and Ryan saw it, too. We was trying to tell him

that the Aborigine wasn't welcome here. He took mad at us and shot at the mob we were shifting."

Worth studied me for a long time, and I edged my hand closer to the revolver in my belt. "Where's your father, son?" I asked him. "The last I heard, this place was run by an older man."

"Climb down, and I'll take you to him."

"All right," I agreed. After all, I felt I had nothing to worry about, for I had done nothing wrong.

I climbed down, and Worth said, "Follow me."

However, instead of taking me toward the homestead, he walked towards a large red gum outside the yard. As we grew closer, I could see where we were headed. A small family plot marked out with rocks, at its centre, rock cairns in place of headstones.

"My father is there, next to my mother," Worth said in a dry tone. "Tell him whatever you want. I'm sure he'll listen without interrupting you."

I heard a shout of alarm and turned to see Jimmy being dragged from his horse. "Hey! What are you doing?"

I was about to take a step forward when I heard a footfall behind me, and old instincts warned me I was in trouble. I started to turn, and everything went black.

CRACK!

The sound was followed by a moan. In my mind, I frowned then grimaced as pain lanced through my head.

CRACK!

I opened my eyes, and the sun's glare made me close them again. I gasped.

CRACK!

I rolled onto my side and opened my eyes again. This time, I was able to leave them open, although I had to blink to clear my vision. With that done, I could see what was happening and felt white-hot rage surge through my veins.

Jimmy was tied to the red gum near the cemetery plot. Yates was wielding a stockwhip, and the wicked lash was cutting deeply into the Aboriginal tracker's flesh, opening his back to the bone. His dark skin glistened with blood, and his head hung down as mercifully, unconsciousness claimed him.

"Stop," I croaked.

Worth turned and looked at me. He walked across to where I lay beneath the burning sun and stared down. "Did you say something?"

"I—I said stop. He's done nothing to you."

"He's a darkie. They steal our sheep and cattle. For all I know, he could be behind it."

"He's a tracker for the traps," I grated.

"So you say. A convicted criminal. For all I know, you could be working with him."

"Don't be a fool," I growled and tried to rise.

CRACK!

"I told you to stop," I tried to shout.

Worth lashed out with a boot, and it caught me just above the ear. I collapsed onto my face. I tried to rise, and blackness claimed me once more.

WHILE I WAS UNCONSCIOUS, the whipping continued. Jimmy's back was open to the bone in several places, but mercifully, though, he wasn't awake to feel it. Then they hanged him from a large redgum.

I didn't find this out until later, as Worth and Yates had thrown me over the saddle of my horse and sent me on my way. When I finally awoke, I was face down, disoriented as to where I was, my horse standing quietly under a large river gum.

I groaned, the ache in my head worse than what it had been the first time I'd come to. I slid from the saddle and slumped to the hard ground. It was gravelly, and a large chunk of rock dug into my spine. I arched my back and ground my teeth together. "Bloody hell."

Rolling to my left I stopped on my side. Then lying there, I touched my head, found it sticky with drying blood.

Jimmy! Where was he?

I tried to get to my feet, using the stirrup on the left side. At first attempt, I failed. The second time, I managed to drag both of my feet beneath me and stand. The landscape swam sickeningly as everything spun around. The sun was setting to the west, the sky tinged with orange and red. It would be dark soon.

So, I sat down, rolled back onto my side, and went to sleep.

8

WHEN I AWOKE the next morning, I felt two things—better physically, and a deep burning anger. My head was still sore, and when I first climbed to my feet, my legs were a bit wobbly. After a short time, my head cleared, and my strength returned.

Checking over my horse, I found him to be sound. In the saddle scabbard sat the Martini-Henry, and in my saddlebags was the spare Remington. Well, they'd left me with weapons. Their mistake. If they'd thought I was going to let it lie, they were sadly mistaken. I tucked the revolver into my waistband and climbed onto the horse. Then I pointed the animal back towards the Worth place and kneed it forward.

ABOUT FIVE MILES out from the homestead, I left the trail. So far, I'd seen no one, but even if I had, I wasn't prepared to have them stop me. I let the horse pick its way through a stand of trees and then down into a gully lined with tall gums and large granite rocks.

I followed the gully for an hour before turning the horse towards the bank. It climbed out, and I drew it to a halt beside a gum. Overhead, pink and grey galahs screeched at me for the intrusion. Ahead on the tree-dotted plain was a ridge which I figured would be the one I'd seen to the north of the homestead. Before I crested it, I dismounted and approached the top, bent double.

Kneeling, I studied the scene below me. The homestead looked quiet. The hands would be out working. My gaze drifted to where I'd seen Yates whipping Jimmy, and that's when I saw him, hanging from the tree.

The anger I'd been carrying with me turned to despair. But then, hatred kicked in along with the desire for revenge. I turned away from the scene before me and sat down. I needed to think, clear my mind. There was no doubt I was going down there, that was a given. They were going to pay for what they'd done, but if I went riding down there all hot and bothered, it was a sure way to get killed.

Then, there was the other issue—the one that would see me hanged for murder should I kill any of them out of revenge. Common sense told me to ride away and find O'Hanlon, tell him what had happened, and then let him deal with it.

But those bastards had whipped Jimmy within an inch of his life, then they'd taken that inch and hung him with it.

I got to my feet and walked back to the horse. I took the Martini-Henry out of the scabbard and made sure there was a round under the hammer. Then I climbed aboard and rode over the rise towards the homestead. It was time to make it right.

The first person I saw when I rode into the yard was one of the hands. He saw me there atop the horse and clawed for a revolver in his pants. Obviously, Worth had told his men to go armed, worried about me returning. The Martini-Henry crashed, and the bullet punched into the man's chest, flinging him backward.

Dismounting the horse, I pulled the Colt Navy from my waistband and started towards the homestead, thumbing back the trigger as I went.

Yates appeared on the veranda, a revolver in his hand. He raised it to fire, but I beat him to it. My first shot hit him low on the left side. He grunted, staggering a little. He gathered himself and fired his first shot. It missed, digging into the dirt at my feet.

My second shot flew truer and hit him in the chest. The snarled expression on his face changed to shock, then pain. He sagged to his knees, blood from his wounds spilling onto the dry wood of the veranda.

Another shot to the chest and he spilled backward, his legs tucked under him at an odd angle.

I kept walking towards the homestead. My gaze focused on the front door. Worth never appeared.

Climbing the steps, I was aware of the sound of my heart beating in my ears. I stopped when I reached the top and waited, listening. I heard nothing.

Yates was well and truly dead. His eyes were open as they stared sightlessly at the corrugated iron roof of the veranda. A pool of blood gathered around him, some of it trickling through the cracks between the floorboards. As was the way of the outback, flies were attracted to the bloody wounds and began to feast.

I heard the creak of boards, and my head snapped up with my eyes fixed on the doorway.

I could see nobody, but it was apparent there was someone inside.

Before going any further toward the door, I turned and scanned the yard. There was no one visible.

I opened the door with my left hand while holding the Colt in my right. I stepped into the hallway, and the first thing I noted was the smell of stale woodsmoke, which filled the interior of the house.

I closed the screen door behind me, not wanting to remain outlined in the doorway for longer than necessary. My second step found a loose floorboard, and the squeak sounded like an explosion in the silence. Even the fly that buzzed past my ear sounded deafening.

I took two more tentative steps, reaching the first room on my left. My fingers touched the dry wood of the door, pushing it open gently. It was a bedroom, and I could smell the sour odour of sweat emanating from within.

The room itself was empty, and I kept going. Each footfall sounded louder than the last. Somewhere outside, I heard a sheep bleat. It was answered by a cockatoo, a screech which had startled many people unfamiliar with the white parrot.

The next room was on the right. It was the sitting room and the obvious source of the strong woodsmoke smell. As I eased myself into the dim room, the clock on the mantel chimed, causing me to start and almost blow it off its perch.

My eyes scanned the rest of the room. Worth wasn't much of a housekeeper. Dust coated every surface. A large wool rug covered the floor, and a long leather lounge grounded the space. A gilt-edged mirror hung behind the clock, and long drapes covered the window. The room was empty.

I stepped back out of the sitting room and moved to continue along the hallway.

The loose floorboard warned me that I was in trouble. I heard the squeak and whirled instantly. The sunlight from outside framed the figure standing just inside. I saw the gun and fired as well, our shots simultaneous, blending as one, the crash echoing along the hall. I felt the bullet strike my side and go deep. I staggered, a cry of pain escaping my lips.

My legs gave way, and my knees hit the floor. I remembered the shooter and tried to straighten. Pain ripped through my side, but with teeth grinding, I fought to bring the Colt up.

At the end of the hallway, the shooter was already down and no longer a threat.

I stayed there like that for a moment as the burning radiated outward from the wound. I climbed to my feet, the pain steadily growing worse. Each step was an effort, but I fought through the fire in my side and stood over the man at my feet. It was Worth. His eyes were open, and there was a hole in his chest where my bullet had taken him. Jimmy had been avenged, but now I had to get out of here and see about the bullet that was in my side. And I was days from anywhere.

I HAD no idea how I managed to get to Hawkesville. The days blurred together with pain and fever. Sometime later, when I had healed, I was told that I'd been picked up by a station owner—Jones from Mount Morgan

Station. He'd dug the bullet out and shipped me in his dray back to Hawkesville.

I was surprised to find out that Clara had been taking care of my needs. I was on her father's boat in a downstairs cabin on a cot, which felt soft and sagged in the middle. When my eyes fluttered open, and I was able to focus, I saw her face above mine. With a dry throat, I rasped, "Have I died and gone to heaven?"

She smiled at me. "Words like that will get you a long way, Jack Crowe."

"Where am I?"

"On my father's boat. The Lady Liza."

I lay there with my eyes closed for a moment and could hear the water of the river lapping at the steamer's side. "How long?"

"A few days." She went on to explain the rest.

"Does O'Hanlon know?"

Clara nodded. "Yes, he's been checking on you. He left with the others to find the Kennedy gang. They robbed a station further up the river and killed the owner."

Something dawned on me. "Have you been tied up here all this time because of me?"

Clara shook her head. "No, Father is having trouble getting freight."

I frowned. "Why? I thought there was a lot moving at the moment."

"Don't worry about it. It—"

The sound of footsteps reached my ears, and the cabin door opened, admitting the outside light into the lamplit room. "I thought I heard voices. How are you, Jack?"

"I'm mending, Thomas. Thanks to you and Clara."

"Not a problem, son. It wasn't like there was urgent freight to be delivered."

I glanced at Clara, who dropped her gaze. "I'm sorry you've been having trouble, Thomas. Once I'm mended, I'll get out of your hair."

"Take your time, Jack," the grey-haired riverboat captain replied. "Do you feel like a trip upriver?"

Clara's head whipped around. "Do you have some work?"

"I do, in fact. Have to deliver some supplies to Walgett."

Clara looked at me. "Well? It's not like you can go anywhere, and Michael won't be back for about a week."

"I'll have you back by then, Jack," Watson said to me. "You can answer all the superintendent's questions when he gets here."

With a nod, I said, "All right, it's not like I'm in any shape to be going anywhere."

"Fine. I'll have Vic and Hank get the girl ready. We'll get loaded and out of here before anyone gets wind of it."

I frowned, thinking it was an odd thing for him to say. Before I could ask, he was gone. That left Clara. "What did he mean?"

"Pardon?"

"He said before someone gets wind of it. What did he mean by that?"

"I told you he's been having trouble getting loads."

"Yes, but you didn't say why?" I reminded her.

"Someone has been trying to buy up riverboats for themselves. When they refuse, the captains find it hard to get work. Father was made an offer about a month ago. The buyer was really pushy, so Father knocked the offer back."

My mind worked for a few moments and then the

shilling dropped. "The buyer wasn't an American, was he?"

"Yes, it was."

"Name of Charles something?"

Clara nodded. "Charles Travis. How did you know?"

"I met his sister in Louth when I took you there."

"Oh."

"Tell me more," I encouraged.

"There's not much more to tell. Father refused to sell, end of story."

"You said they'd made offers to others."

"Yes. Father said he made offers to Charlie Henry and Fred Hayes for the *Carnarvon* and the *Tibooburra*. Both of them knocked him back, too."

"But some have taken up the offer. He has two boats."

"Yes. The *Atlanta* and *Virginia*."

I frowned, racking my brain trying to work out if I'd heard of those boats before. "I can't place them."

"That's because their names were changed. "One was the *Darling Rose* and the other the *Murray Flyer*."

"That's why."

"After Father wouldn't sell, he made an offer on the *Western Mist*."

"Sam Miller's boat?"

"Yes, that's the one."

"Did he sell?" I asked.

"No."

Her expression told me she wasn't telling me everything. "What happened?"

"Two days later, he was found floating beside his boat in the river," she explained. "They said he must have slipped and fallen because of the bump on his head. Got drunk and gone in."

"But?"

"Father said he was talking to Sam that evening. He was sober because he had to sail early the next morning with a load for Willow Station up past Walgett. The river gets tricky up that way, and a captain needs his faculties about him all the time. A hungover skipper invites trouble."

"What happened to the boat?"

"Charles Travis bought it from the bank two days later and renamed it *Persephone*."

The news was troubling.

"Anyway, enough of the dark talk. I'll let you get some rest."

Clara turned to leave the cabin. "Wait."

She stopped and turned back.

"Thank you," I said. "For everything."

"That's fine. It was no trouble at all." Then another thought entered her mind. "What happened to your tracker? I thought he was with you."

I could feel my face grow dark. "He was killed."

9

We left port later that day. The *Lady Liza* sailed through the darkened waters upstream. The river was up a few feet from heavy rains somewhere in Queensland, and by all reports, it was likely to go higher. In the setting sun, the giant river gums stood watch over our passage as though guarding the boat from any unseen threats. Cockatoos and galahs came in to roost, screeching in protest at our encroachment on their territory.

Just before the sun finally disappeared, Watson tied the *Lady Liza* to a stump on the eastern bank for the night. I lay in my bunk and listened to the water lap against the hull. I was bored already and decided to try my luck at getting up.

The first step was rolling onto my side. It didn't seem much at the time, but the pain that ripped through my body told a different story. I gasped for a moment and then pushed myself up into a sitting position.

More pain.

That was the easy part. Now I needed to get to my

feet. Things kind of came apart at that step, for I found myself on my knees on the cabin floor, breath heaving in and out of my chest as I tried to make the pain go away. I think I may have cried out at some point because Clara appeared in the doorway.

"Good heavens, what are you doing?" she gasped, one fluttering hand to her mouth while she began to reach out to me.

"Getting up," I growled abruptly, angered by my helplessness.

"More like crawling around pretending to be a wombat," she scolded. "Get back into bed."

"I can't," I shot back at her. "I can't move."

"Oh, dear."

She crouched beside me, her arm going around my shoulders. Suddenly, I felt uncomfortable. The reaction I was feeling from her touch was disturbing to say the least. It was like little jolts going through my body, making my skin turn to goose bumps. I knew what it was but hadn't felt it for a while, and it troubled me.

I turned my head and stared into her eyes. The orange glow of the lamp on Clara's skin made her even more attractive. Our eyes locked, and I was suddenly lost in their watery gaze. I could feel myself being pulled toward her and realized that I wasn't the only one. And just as our lips were about to touch, a voice said, "Is everything all right?"

Just like that, the spell was broken, and we turned our heads to see Vic, one of the deckhands standing in the doorway. Clara rubbed her hands on her dress and stammered, "Yes—yes, I might need some help to get Jack back in his bunk. It seems he was a little ambitious and tried to get up too early."

"That's all right, Miss Watson, I can help you."

Vic moved in beside me and effortlessly helped me to my feet. "You shouldn't be up, Jack. Takes a while to get over being shot."

"So I realise," I replied.

He put me back on the bunk, and I lay down.

"If you want to get out, Jack," Clara said, "maybe tomorrow you could be helped out on deck for a while."

I nodded. "That would be great."

"Fine. Thank you, Vic."

The deckhand nodded and bowed his head before leaving the cabin. I looked at Clara and said, "About before. I—"

"I'll go and get you some dinner and bring it back," she said curtly, cutting my words off mid-sentence. "I won't be long."

As I watched her turn and leave, mixed feelings began coursing through my body. This woman had gotten under my skin, and I had no idea what to do about it.

THE FOLLOWING MORNING DAWNED EARLY, and the birdlife let us know that we were no longer welcome. The river had risen another half a foot, and eddies were clearly noticeable in the water.

Before we sailed, Vic had helped me on deck, and I sat on a grain bag near the bow of the paddleboat so I could enjoy the view. It was also Vic who brought me breakfast, as Clara was avoiding me due to our shared moment the previous evening.

But soon we were on our way as the *Lady Liza* moved away from the bank and out into the current.

The morning was spent navigating the many twists and turns of the river, travelling many times the distance required if one was to traverse a straight line. I was enjoying the sun on my face and the landscape of steep banks and giant trees when the sound of a steam whistle drew my attention to a boat coming around the bend further up.

As it sailed into view, I could see that it was the *Maybelle,* skippered by Jock Peters, a Scottish migrant who'd come to Australia twenty years back. The boat was towing two barges, both loaded high with wool. As she sailed past, I could hear Peters and Watson calling out to each other.

Then she was gone.

"Father says we're going to stay overnight in Bourke before we keep going. He has one more load to pick up while he's there."

I turned and looked at Clara. "Sounds fine."

"Father says you can stay there if you want."

I stared at her. "What do you want?"

She stared back at me as she hesitated to speak what was on her mind. A kookaburra laughed in the trees on the western bank, and it seemed to break her resolve as she whirled around and walked off. I muttered a curse under my breath and turned to look once more across the bow.

I stayed there for most of the day, contemplating what to do. By the time Bourke came into sight, I'd decided to stay with the boat. Besides, I still wanted to talk to Clara.

THE SUN WAS on its way down when I saw a familiar figure boarding via the gangplank. O'Hanlon looked tired and drawn. He smelled of horse and sweat, and when he spoke, his voice sounded tired. "So you're still alive, Jack, I see."

I glanced at Clara, who had emerged from the lower cabin. "Been getting good care," I replied.

"I ran into Watson up in town. He said you were here. Are you able to sit a horse?"

"No!" Clara blurted out.

We turned and looked at her. "Pardon, miss?" O'Hanlon said.

"He's most certainly not able to sit a horse."

"Does she speak for you, Jack?" the superintendent asked me, his voice carrying an edge to it.

I nodded. "On this occasion, Michael. I'm still not right."

"Now that you're able, will you tell me what happened and where Jimmy is? I thought he'd be back by now."

It took a few minutes, but I told O'Hanlon everything, even the part where I exacted revenge for what had been done to Jimmy. "I'll understand if you lock me up."

The superintendent snorted. "As far as I'm concerned, you were acting under directive from me. There'll not be an enquiry."

I saw Clara disappear over O'Hanlon's shoulder and found myself wishing she had stayed. Instead, I turned my attention to the trap. "What about you, Michael?"

The Irishman's face turned into a snarl. "We lost the bastards again. I think they crossed the river, but we missed where they did it. Not having a tracker didn't damn well help. Now I'm going to have to find another one."

"You feel like a beer?" I asked him.

He sighed. "I need a bath and about twenty hours of sleep, Jack, but a beer sounds good. Do you think you can get away from your nurse?"

"If I can run fast enough."

O'Hanlon chuckled and helped me towards the gangplank. A familiar voice said, "Where do you think you're going?"

Shit!

"To get a beer," I replied.

"I don't think so, Jack. You're not strong enough."

"It might stiffen a man some, Clara," I told her. "I tell you what, why don't you come with us, and you can keep an eye on me?"

I expected her to turn the offer down, but instead she said, "Wait, I'll get my shawl. I suspect Father is there somewhere."

A few minutes later, we walked up the gangplank onto the riverbank. From there, we made slow progress into town to the pub. It was busy as usual, but we found a vacant table and sat down. O'Hanlon got the beers, and while he was away, Watson appeared, a little worse for wear. "What's going on, Thomas?" I asked, concerned.

"I'm having a drink for a friend," he replied, his words slurred.

"What friend?"

"Charlie Henry went over the side of the *Carnarvon* last evening. He never came back up, and they never found his body. Accident, they say. Accident, my backside."

"Oh, Father," Clara gasped.

"What makes you think otherwise, Thomas?"

"Because his deckhand said he'd been drinking before he went over."

"Could he have been?" I asked him.

He gave me an indignant look. "Not on your life. He never drank while he was on the water. You knew him, Jack."

I nodded. I did, and there was no way he would be drinking while he was afloat. "Where did this happen?"

"About a mile upstream. He overnighted there before coming in. Only he didn't make it."

"Who brought the *Carnarvon* in?"

"Stubbs, his deckhand."

"Why the serious faces?" O'Hanlon asked when he returned.

I looked at him. "Thomas was just telling us about Charlie Henry."

The superintendent's face grew grim. "Yes, I see."

"Did someone check it out, Michael?"

"What for? The man was drunk and fell in. Wouldn't be the first time it happened."

"That's bullshit if I ever heard it," Watson growled.

"Now, Thomas, we've been through this."

"And I told you, Charlie never drank while he was on the *Carnarvon*."

"Not what Stubbs said. Apparently, he'd been hitting the bottle of late."

"I wouldn't believe anything that liar said," Watson growled. "Tell him, Jack."

O'Hanlon turned his gaze in my direction and waited for me to speak. "He never drank on the boat, Michael. He was religious like that."

"I can only go on what I was told, Jack," the superintendent replied. He sighed. "If it will make you feel happier, I'll have someone ask around and see what others have to say. Now, how about drinking that beer?"

The incident to do with Charlie wasn't forgotten about, just set aside for the rest of the evening. By that time, Watson was well and truly drunk and asleep at the table. Clara leaned close to me and said, "I don't know how we'll get him back to the boat."

I gave a wan smile. "Michael, do you figure they've got a spare room here for the night?"

He looked at the sleeping riverboat captain and nodded. "I'll find out."

"Thank you, Superintendent," Clara said.

"I'm afraid, Miss Clara, you might be stuck in Bourke tomorrow."

She nodded. "I'm *afraid* you could be right."

As luck would have it, there was a spare room, and a couple of riverboat crew helped get the drunk skipper upstairs. O'Hanlon left Clara and I at the table while he went out the back to the outhouse. "You know, I'm starting to feel stronger already," I said to her.

Clara looked at me suspiciously. "What are you up to?"

I opened my mouth to reply when the bar was pierced by a shriek. Suddenly, the sound of gunfire erupted, and I felt myself lunging forward. I crashed into Clara, forcing her to the floor, laying my frame atop her, feeling the pain in my side. She cried out in alarm as it happened, but I heard myself say to her, "Stay down."

Shouts erupted all around us, and soon, a high-pitched cry of pain could be heard above the din. "Get under the table," I said into Clara's ear. She wormed her way beneath the wooden structure, and I struggled to my feet. Another shot was fired, and the bullet ricocheted off the table where I stood, leaving a splintered furrow in the rough top. I ducked reflexively but never went below the table line. Across the room, I could see a man staggering around, waving a pistol. "Damn strike breakers," the man howled. "Where's that bastard captain that's taking scab labour up the river? I'll shoot him in the guts, I will."

I walked forward gingerly. "Hey, what's going on, bloke?"

He turned towards me, the gun aimed directly at my guts. The last thing I wanted was a bullet there. "Who are you?" he growled, his words slurred. "Are you the bastard?"

All around me, customers were shrinking back against the wall. After taking another step forward, I saw the man on the floor on the other side of the table. He was writhing in pain but not much was passing his lips. "What bastard's that?"

"The riverboat captain who's taking shearers up past Walgett towards Mungindi. Getting them into Queensland for Bremer Station. I was told it was him, but now I'm not so sure."

"What's going on there?" I asked him, as I took another step forward.

"The shearers laid down their tools. The station owner refused to pay the asking rate. Now he's trying to get replacements in to do the work. Word is that the bastards are being picked up here by some captain they're paying a heap of money to."

"Not me, friend. I'm just a dray owner and freighter." I looked at the man on the floor. "Is he all right?"

"Who gives a damn about him?" the man spat. "He got what he deserved. Especially if it was him."

"Can I take a look at him? If he dies, you'll hang for sure."

The expression on the man's face suddenly changed as though it finally dawned upon him what he'd just done. The effect of the grog seemed to just fall away. He looked down at the weapon in his hand then back at me. "What did I do?"

"Give me the gun, cobber, and I'll help old mate out on the floor there."

The expression on the shooter's face turned from shock to horror and then he turned and ran out of the pub, dropping the pistol as he went.

I limped forward, aware of my recent injury, and struggled to crouch beside the shot man. From the flickering orange light, I could see that he'd been shot in the chest and his clothes were slick with blood. His breathing was shallow, and it didn't take a smart man to work out that he wasn't long for this world.

I looked up at the crowd that had started to gather around me. Clara had joined them, and she knelt beside me. "He doesn't look good."

"He's dying."

"How terrible."

With a slow nod, I said, "Yes, it is."

O'HANLON CAME across to the table where I was seated with Clara and pulled out a chair. "He finally died."

"Dick Turner, skipper of the *Lazy Lady*."

"Is what the killer said true?" I asked. "Was he taking shearers north?"

"Yes and no," O'Hanlon replied. "Shearers are being taken north, but he wasn't the one taking them. It's Thomas. The shooter had the wrong skipper."

I glanced at Clara. "Did you know he was doing this?"

"No, I—I didn't. He said he had to pick up a well-paying cargo, but he didn't say what."

"He's paddling in dangerous waters here, Miss Clara," O'Hanlon cautioned her. "Getting mixed up in something like this, as you can see, lassie, it can get a man killed."

"I'll talk to him tomorrow after he wakes. Hopefully, he'll see reason."

There was a moment of silence before O'Hanlon muttered something I couldn't quite hear. "What was that?"

"I said *strange*."

"What is?"

"The fact that Travis was made an offer for his boat a while back, and now he's dead."

"You have a theory, Michael?" I asked.

"No, no. I was just wondering out loud. It just seems convenient that the man who shot him was given the wrong name."

His words got me thinking. "Don't tell me, the person who offered to buy it was American, right?"

"That's the word."

"Shit, Michael, you've got it all going on."

He nodded. "Bushrangers, trap killers, some bloke trying to take over the river boats, and now, reports of damn Chinese people disappearing from the diggings."

"Wait, what?"

"You heard me. There are reports of Chinese just disappearing."

I grunted. "If it doesn't rain, it pours."

"Isn't that the truth?"

"What now, Michael?"

"I'll take some men and try to find this killer. Now that Kennedy has disappeared, I'll have to wait until he raises his head again, or I'll be wandering across the damned country chasing my tail."

"When I get back, I'll come find you."

"You do that."

BUT AT THAT TIME, Kennedy hadn't disappeared. Not totally. He'd crossed the river, ridden upstream, and then crossed back over. He and the others were camped outside the small river town of Silver Gum. That's what I was told, anyway. They were eating a meal of kangaroo and wallaby when a rider came out of the darkness and into the firelight of their camp. He was a tall man with long, muttonchop sideburns and a bushy moustache. He sat there on his horse while every man in the Kennedy gang pointed their weapons at him. "You blokes were hard to find."

"And why might you be looking for us?" Kennedy demanded.

"I have a message for you."

"A message?"

"Well, not exactly a message, more of an offer."

"Well, tell me what it is so I can shoot you in the guts and leave the rest of you for the dingoes."

The rider slowly reached into his coat, took out a leather pouch, and tossed it onto the ground near the flickering fire where the shadows danced across its dark exterior. On landing, it made a clinking sound. "One hundred sovereigns."

Apparently, that got their attention because the words that came out of Kennedy's mouth were, "What's it for?"

"My boss wants to hire you and your men."

Kennedy licked his lips greedily and stared at the pouch of coins. "Who is this boss of yours?"

"That doesn't matter. What does, is that he's willing to pay you for your services. Starting right now."

It must have been enough money because Kennedy decided then and there that he would do just that and work for the mystery man he'd never met. And my life became even more violent than what it already had been.

10

"You need to listen to her, damn it," I growled at Watson. "This is just asking for trouble." I pointed at the men on the bank. "They—they are trouble."

Watson's eyes were red from fire and alcohol. "I don't have a choice, blast you. I'm almost broke. The money I'm getting from this trip will see me clear until at least next year's clip."

"Someone wants you dead, Father," Clara pleaded with him. "Last night proved that."

A steam whistle sounded from downriver, putting a flock of cockatoos on edge. I looked downstream and saw a riverboat coming towards us, towing two fully loaded barges. I frowned. I knew the boat but not the name. Then it came to me. It was the old *Darling Rose*. In the background, I could still hear Clara and her father exchanging words as I watched the boat sail past.

Steam belched from her whistle, and a low, almost mournful moan floated across the river. "And that there," I heard Watson say, "is why I'm almost broke. All the freight on those barges is enough to keep three skippers in money for a couple of months."

He was right. When the clip was in, there was plenty of freight. But in the off-season, the riverboat captains depended on the freight coming upriver. With Travis taking the lion's share, there wouldn't be much left for the others.

I turned back to Watson. The helpless expression on his face made my mind up for me. "All right, Thomas, get them on board. But you're not getting behind the wheel."

"What?"

"Clara can work the helm, can she not?"

She shot me a worried glance, which I ignored. "Sure, she can," he replied.

"Then she is skipper for today at least. You're too hungover from last night."

"Listen, Jack, the *Lady Liza* is still my boat, which means I'm in charge—"

"No one's saying you're not, Thomas."

"Father, listen to him. I can do it. I can." She touched his arm.

"All right. Just for today. Now, get those men aboard."

TWENTY MINUTES LATER, we had enough steam and the *Lady Liza* sailed from Bourke with our cargo and shearers, Clara at the helm. I stood beside her as we left, and she handled the boat like an old hand. Her father was on the lower deck shouting orders at her, ones she chose to ignore. She saw me looking at him and asked, "Has he turned purple yet?"

I smiled. "Not yet, but he's a dark shade of red."

"I haven't done this for a long time, so he's understandably nervous, but it's like riding a horse."

Once we were in mid-stream, she seemed to relax a little more, as did her father. For the next few hours, we made slow progress along the river, passing a couple of boats coming the other way with dismal-looking loads. One of them was named the *Clementine*. Watson called up to his daughter, "Steady as she goes, Clara. Ring down for slow."

As the two boats drew abreast, the captains called across the gap between them. "You've finally given up the helm, you old reprobate?" the skipper of the *Clementine* shouted.

Clara giggled. "That's John Sutton. He's another of Father's old friends."

"Pull your head in, blast you. How's business?"

"I hope you're not looking for a backload. They're scarce at the moment. I'll be lucky if I can earn drinking money with what I'm carrying back to Bourke. Where you headed?"

"Mungindi."

I saw Clara stiffen at the words. "What is it?"

"Strewth, Thomas. Take care up there. Although there's more water coming down, I hear. Been some hard rain up in Queensland."

"Good. See you in a month."

"Yeah, you can buy me a beer."

Then the *Clementine* was gone from sight. A blast of the steam whistle, her last hurrah before she disappeared around one of the many bends in the river.

"What's wrong?" I asked her.

"He's planning on going up as far as Mungindi. It's very tricky. If there's not enough water, we may not even make it. Only the experienced captains go up that far."

"I see."

We travelled in silence for the next hour or so, when she looked at me and said, "Would you like to try?"

I was puzzled. "Try what?"

She stepped back a touch from the wheel. "Here, have a go."

"I—I don't think so."

"Really?" She grinned at me. "Are you afraid?"

"No—maybe a little."

"It's easy. Come here."

As I walked over to her, she stepped in closer to the wheel. "Wrap your arms around me and put them on—"

I stepped back.

"What's the matter?"

"I—" I could feel the blood rush to my face.

"I do declare, Mr. Crowe, you're blushing."

I was, and I knew it.

"Come on, Jack, I won't bite."

I edged my way forward and put one hand on the wheel.

"That's right," Clara said. "Now the other."

My opposite hand reached around to grasp the wheel. As I did so, I couldn't help but press my body against hers, and my discomfort became noticeable. "Is—is this all right?"

"Uh, huh, it's just fine." Her voice was soft, gentle.

Clara looked up into my face, her eyes burning into mine. For the first time, I noticed how strikingly blue they were and how they seemed to draw me in...closer... closer. Her breath felt warm on my cheek and made my heart beat faster.

I gently turned Clara to face me and leaned in closer, our eyes still locked. When I felt our lips touch, all the anxiousness fell away. We kissed for what seemed like forever before a voice roared, "Are you going to turn the flaming boat or hit the bloody bank?"

"Oh dear," Clara gasped and turned away from me to steer the boat.

I glanced down to the deck where her father stood glaring straight at me. "I don't think your father approves."

"Do you approve, Jack?" she asked without looking at me.

"More than you know."

"Then that's all that counts. You leave him up to me."

"Are you sure I'm what you want, Clara?"

"I haven't thought of anything else since we first met."

Suddenly, I felt uncomfortable and stepped away. Clara turned to look at me. "Where are you going?"

"Down to the deck so I don't distract you anymore."

When I reached the lower level, I found Thomas Watson waiting for me. I could see the anger in his eyes, and I knew he had something to get off his chest. "I like you, Crowe, so don't get me wrong when I say this. Stay away from Clara. A man like you has no right to a girl like her. Understand?"

There it was. My past rearing its ugly head. But I had pride, and I couldn't help it when I said, "Clara is a woman, Thomas. Don't you think the choice is hers?"

"The girl doesn't know what she wants, Jack. She should be back in the city instead of out here riding the river with her old man. Then the first man comes along she thinks she likes and..." He didn't finish.

"I think she does, Thomas, and that scares you. Clara is a grown woman, and that scares you, too."

His voice grew harsh. "Stay the hell away from her."

I held my hands up placatingly. "All right, Thomas. I'll do as you ask."

OVER THE COMING DAYS, we continued making our way further upriver. The water started to rise around Collarenebri, and Thomas pulled in for the night so he could get news about conditions further up. Before he disembarked, he told the shearers to stay on the boat. But they were shearers, and like a mob of dry cattle who smelled water from a mile away, it wasn't long before they all abandoned the boat, and the first wave of problems came our way.

"Jack, wake up, we've got trouble."

I opened an eye to see Clara bending over me. I'd been sound asleep when she shook me. "What are you doing? You shouldn't be here. Your father—"

"Father isn't back, and the shearers are gone."

I sighed with frustration. "That's all we need."

I got to my feet and struggled to put my boots on before grabbing the Colt revolver and hiding it beneath my coat. I turned to Clara. "Stay on the boat."

"Jack—"

"Stay here. I have a feeling that things here are going to get out of hand. These shearers are nothing but bloody trouble, and I want you out of it."

"What about Father?"

"I don't know."

Thomas should have been back a while now, which told me one of two things: He was either drinking grog again, or he was in trouble.

When the river was low, one would have walked up the gangplank onto the bank, but now that there was water flowing down from Queensland, the slope was mostly negated.

I walked into town and heard the noise before I saw

anything. I knew the town had a new police station, and from the sounds coming at me along the dusty street, I would expect that the traps would be close by.

As I entered the pub, I saw a scene of carnage before me. Men were going everywhere in a display of fisticuffs I'd not witnessed in a long time. I stepped aside as a shearer crashed past me, bleeding from a wound above his brow. My shoulder hit a man watching on, and he turned, anger on his face.

"Hold it. That was an accident," I said by way of an apology. "What's going on?"

"Scabs," the man growled. "Shearers going upriver to Queensland to break the strike."

"Where are the traps?"

"They left this morning after the murderous bastard John Kennedy."

How could that be? "I heard he was down near Bourke."

"Not by a sight he's not. Pilfered horses from Caringi Station, night before last."

"Have you seen Thomas Watson?"

"That bastard, he's getting what he deserves."

"What do you mean?"

"Like I said, what he deserves."

I grabbed the man's coat lapels. "Speak, damn you."

"They took him out back before the fight started," the man blurted out.

"To do what?"

He remained silent.

"To do *what?*"

Fear came into the man's eyes, all signs of bravado gone. "I don't hold with hanging a man without a trial. But..."

I thrust him away from me and lurched towards the

rear door of the pub. Bursting through the doorway, I glanced left and then right. Fifty yards away from where I stood, a crowd was gathered around a tall gumtree. Some of the people held lanterns, others with burning torches. From the light forming an umbrella over them, I could see a rope looped up over a thick, gnarled, low-hanging branch. The rope was taut, indicating the weight it was holding.

Trying to get up to a run, I put my hand on my side, and I pushed my way through the cheering crowd using a fist and an elbow. When I broke through, I stopped dead, a cold hand touching my heart as I stared at the scene before me. Dangling from the end of the rope like a bunch of grapes on a vine was Thomas Watson. His head was lolling to one side, his tongue protruding from his open mouth.

THOMAS WATSON'S earthly remains were buried under a large gum beside the river he loved. Just a mound with a crudely shaped cross indicated the final resting place of the riverboat captain. I stood beside Clara two days later as she said a final farewell to her father.

When she was finished, I put my hat on. She turned and looked at me. "Is everything ready?"

I nodded. *Lady Liza* was loaded with cords of wood, and the shearers were back aboard. Two of them had required medical attention after the melee, but they could rest while the trip upriver continued.

The day following Watson's death, I sent word to Bourke for O'Hanlon. Not that he could do much, for he was no doubt trying to find the tearaway Kennedy. Even now, the local traps were still out hunting the bushranger.

That same day, Clara had announced she was going to continue upriver and deliver the shearers. I tried to talk her out of it, but she was adamant. There was an iron resolve inside her, formed by the brutal death of her father. I could see the change, and I wasn't sure it suited her. She was normally a gentle, kind, and happy soul. Not cold and heartless. In the end, I told her that I would go with her.

There was no one there to see us off. The good folk of Collarenebri, I use the term loosely, were obviously feeling the guilt of the few who had committed the low act of lynching a good man known by many of them.

Before we cast off, Vic and Hank approached Clara. "Miss Clara, we would like you to reconsider what you are about to do. Your father was a good man, a great riverboat captain, but he knew the risks of what he was doing."

"And I don't? Is that what you are saying?" There was a curtness to her voice.

"That's not what we're saying, miss," Vic said. "But your father had a lot of years navigating the river's shoals and snags. Even for him, the trip to Mungindi was risky at best. With the river up, it will be possible, but you have to be able to read it as well as avoid the debris being washed down. We heard that there is more water to come down, meaning it will go higher."

"If you wish to stay behind, then do so. I will find men to come with me." Her voice was cold, and I could see the hurt in the men's faces. They had served her father faithfully for years, and to be spoken to in this manner by his daughter cut deep.

"That's not—"

"Then cast off," she snapped and made her way to the wheelhouse.

I looked at Vic and Hank. Vic's eyes were pleading. "Maybe if you had a word to her, Jack."

"I tried, Vic. This thing with her father has changed her. I don't like it either, but if she's going to make it, then she's going to need us all. Are you coming?"

"If you're going, we'll come too."

Lines were thrown, and the *Lady Liza* drifted away from the bank and out into the fast-flowing tumult of brown surge headed downstream. Her stack belched black smoke as her paddle wheel started to turn, fighting against the force pushing her back. Soon, the boat was making headway, a bow wave visible as she thrust forward.

Clara pulled on the chain near her head, and the steam whistle blew its high-pitched goodbye to the ones who had murdered her father.

For the next few hours, Clara stood tirelessly at the wheel of the *Lady Liza,* negotiating the river and the debris surging past. I went up to the wheelhouse to help watch for hidden dangers. She was like a seasoned captain who'd navigated the river for years, having learned everything her father had to teach.

As we progressed, the river eddied, and small whirlpools formed. Large logs and dead animals floated past, and watching them, I suddenly felt as though we were headed further and further into danger.

Vic came up from below. "Would you like me to take the wheel for a while, Miss Clara?"

Clara shook her head. "No, I'm fine."

The sky above us was clear and blue. Not the kind one would expect while navigating a swollen river, its trees on the bank normally clear from the torrent sprouting from the brown murk.

"This is getting worse, Clara," I said to her.

"We'll be fine as long as we stay in the main channel," she replied.

Looking around, I saw nothing but a mass of water which looked more like a lake than a river. "What main channel—look out!"

As I looked, a large log came floating towards us, the current rolling it over and twisting it around.

Clara worked the wheel, and the *Lady Liza* started a slow, painful turn. For a moment, my breath caught in my throat as it seemed that the log would collide with the boat. However, just as all seemed lost, the *Lady Liza* managed to claw her bow far enough around it to avoid the catastrophe threatening to engulf it.

"Clara, this is damn crazy," I growled at her. "We need to turn around now before it's too late."

Her head turned upon me, eyes blazing. "No! I will not. This is what my father set out to do, and I will do it for him."

"This is foolhardy."

"It is right."

Suddenly, the *Lady Liza* gave a great shudder as though struck by an invisible fist. We both lurched, fighting to stay on our feet. Then came the splintering sound from below as planks gave and the side of the *Lady Liza* opened up, allowing tons of water to rush in.

"She's holed!" Hank called from below. "There's no saving her."

I grabbed Clara by the arm. "Come on, it's time to leave."

She stared at me, a horrified expression on her face. "What have I done?"

"We don't have time."

By the time we made it to the deck, it was already awash. I grabbed up a small wooden crate and thrust it into Clara's arms. "Use this."

All around us, the shearers were jumping clear of the sinking vessel, being swept away by the strong current. I heard one cry out, "I can't swim."

An older man next to him, gave him a piece of wood. "What am I to do with this?"

"Just go, son."

I saw him leap into the water and get swept away. He travelled possibly ten yards before disappearing below the surface. The man who'd given him the wood followed. He jumped in and disappeared. I never saw him come back up.

I looked around the deck, which was now completely submerged. A small barrel floated past me, and I picked it up. Clara and I started to move toward the side when I realised something. "Wait."

"What is it?"

"Your dress is too heavy. It will drag you under."

I started ripping the garment from her body, revealing corset and pantaloons. When I was done, I helped her towards the exposed gap in the rail. I swapped the small barrel for her crate and said, "Whatever you do, don't let go, and kick towards the bank. Don't fight the current."

Clara nodded. She looked scared, the fear in her eyes piercing my heart. I took her chin in my right hand and leaned in and kissed her. "Stay alive. I will find you."

"Jack, I love you."

"Just stay alive."

Then we went into the raging torrent.

11

A MURDER of crows took flight as I approached a corpse that lay above the high-water mark of the river, now that it had receded. I knew who it was before even looking at the face. Vic, one of the hands from the *Lady Liza*. That made ten I had found, not one of them Clara. And none of them alive.

I didn't remember much about my time in the river. Once I was in, I could feel the tumultuous water tugging at me, trying to pull me below the surface as though it was a monster beginning to devour its prey. At one point, a man bumped into me. When I looked, I could see that he was already dead. It was one of the shearers.

Fighting to keep hold of the wooden crate, I kicked with my legs, trying to make the submerged bank where the current was less fierce. The harder I kicked, the further I felt I was moving away from it.

Something large loomed up at me from the side. I turned my head and saw the wheelhouse of the *Lady Liza* surging towards me. It was canted at an odd angle telling me it had most likely detached from the rest of the paddle wheeler. But that was far from my problem, for right then its track had it passing over the top of me.

My tired legs worked faster, harder, trying to propel me towards the bank. I heard a shout from behind and saw a shearer flailing about in the floodwater, trying to drag himself clear of the wheelhouse's path. When I'd last looked about, I hadn't noticed him, but somehow the many currents had converged on that position and sucked him into a deadly vortex.

I watched on in horror as he gave one last cry when the swift-moving object passed over the top of him, forcing the struggling man deep below the surface. I never saw him after that.

But my predicament was real as the unstoppable object came on. Beneath the surface, my legs flailed faster and faster until dread washed over me, and I realized I was about to suffer the same fate as the shearer I had just witnessed. And there was nothing I could do about it.

Then, like a large whale out in the ocean, the wheelhouse seemed to swallow me, and the last thing I remembered was being forced deep below the river's surface.

When I opened my eyes later, I found the top part of myself on dry land with my legs still partially in the water of the river. I had no idea how or why I was still alive, nor did I care. The fact of the matter is that I was, and that's all that counted.

I looked once more at Vic's body and left it where I found it—after all, there wasn't much I could do. Both sides of the Barwon River were lined with debris where the boat had eventually broken up. I had been looking for Clara for two days and still had no luck. My heart was sinking by the hour as I started to fear that the raging waters had claimed her.

I kept moving along the riverbank. I was hungry, not having had anything to eat for those two days. More crows seemed to be taunting me as I walked slowly between the river gums. My legs were feeling very heavy, leaden.

I sat down on a log that had been deposited between two large trees. I leaned forward and rested my head on my hands. Closing my eyes, I let the sounds of the bush seep into my mind. Crows, galahs, small parrots, a woman's panicked cries...

My head snapped up, all signs of exhaustion gone. I heard the sound again—it was coming from further along the river. I came to my feet and commenced a stumbling lope.

There were two of them—shearers—survivors from the *Lady Liza*. Both were pushing a woman around—my woman. They didn't see me coming.

"Hey! That'll do right there!" I shouted at them.

They were both surprised when they saw me. I guess they thought that nobody else had survived, but they thought wrong.

"Jack!" Clara exclaimed. "Help me. Get me away from these heathens."

They forgot about Clara for the moment and turned to face me. One of them had a knife, the other bent down to grab a piece of branch from the riverbank. "You need to stay out of this, convict," the one with the knife said.

I shook my head. "I'll not let you harm the woman I intend to marry."

Knifeman chuckled. "You can marry her, convict, but after we both take our turn with her."

There was a lack of conversation as they stared at me, sizing up their options, the sound of the Barwon rushing past, along with the breeze in the treetops filling the void.

They took a few steps towards me. "Do you really want to do this?" I asked. "Fight the man who went toe-to-toe with Ned Kelly and brought him in for trial."

One of the shearers snorted. "That was just a story. Lies told by old men around the campfire and in the gold camp bars."

"Then come at me, you pair of larrikins, and we'll see who has the better of who."

The man with the branch charged straight at me, swinging wildly with his crooked weapon. His first mistake was to swing it at my head, which made it easy for me to duck under. His second was not being quick enough.

I came up from my crouch and punched him in his stomach. The muscle there was hard, sinewy, from years of shearing, but I was strong, even recovering from my wound, and he doubled over, dropping the branch. I scooped it up with my right hand and swung hard. The blow hit him along the side of his jaw, breaking it along with the branch.

His head went back, and he staggered before falling onto his arse. From there, he rolled over and lay still at the muddy water's edge. I had no idea if I had killed him, nor did I care. I turned to face the remaining threat, the one with the knife. He smiled coldly, revealing blackened teeth. I said, "Make your choice, rapscallion. If it is the wrong one, be damned to you, for I will kill you before I am done."

"You are wrong, convict. I am the one who will kill you, and the bitch will be mine. I will listen to her calling your name as I hump her. Then I will cut her throat and watch her bleed."

He chose that moment to come at me, eager to finish me quickly. The knife slashed at my stomach, and I leaped back. He smiled again, closing the distance between us. He waved the knife around, his tongue flickering across his lips. "Come on, Crowe, fight like a man."

"You talk too much, scoundrel."

He lunged at me, knife arm extended. I stepped to the side and chopped my hand down on his wrist. His fingers sprang open, and he dropped the knife. He bent to pick it up, but my foot lashed out, and my boot caught him in the jaw, a glancing blow.

The shearer staggered back, his arms waving wildly as he tried to regain his balance. I moved in and hit him hard, first to the stomach and then to the face. He stopped cold and went down to his knees. Then I hit him again, and he fell to his side and never moved.

"Oh, Jack," Clara cried and rushed into my arms. Her face pressed against my chest, and she started to sob. "I killed them. I killed them all."

My hands cupped her face, and I lifted her head. "No. It was an accident."

Then I wrapped my arms around her, and she wept some more.

THAT NIGHT, we spent a cold camp in each other's arms as we tried to keep warm. Night birds haunted our embrace, and the breeze kept up its hissing sound through the treetops. "Where are we going, Jack?" Clara asked me.

"A little farther downstream is Piggott's Run. We will

go there. On foot, we should make it tomorrow afternoon. I will try to get some horses and some clothes for you, and we will head down to Collarenebri to see if Michael is there."

"Did you mean what you said earlier, Jack?" Clara asked me.

"About what?"

"That you were going to marry me?"

I thought about it before answering. "I did. If you would have me."

She turned in my arms and looked up at my face in the moonlight. "Yes, oh, yes, I would have you, Jack Crowe."

Then she kissed my lips, and even on that cold night, I felt warmer than I had in a long time.

PIGGOTT'S RUN was sited overlooking the Barwon River amongst some large river gums. It was a sheep station with approximately ten thousand sheep. The owner was Les Monson, a Brit who'd come out to Australia in the '60s to earn his fortune. He managed to do that and more.

When we arrived, Monson and his hands were tidying up debris deposited by the flood where the river had broken its banks. Although situated on a high point, the floodwater had encroached on their property.

Watching us walking out of the heat haze, Monson removed his hat to swipe at an annoying fly, taking in our bedraggled appearance. He called over to one of his hands, who ran to the homestead. A minute or so later, Monson's wife appeared on the veranda.

"You two look a little worse for wear," he said, stating the obvious.

"Boat sank upriver," I replied.

"Which one?"

"*Lady Liza*," I replied.

"Thomas Watson's boat?" he said, cocking his eyebrow.

"That's right."

"But he's dead, murdered, I heard in Collarenebri."

I nodded. "Right again."

"Then who was skippering it upstream?"

"I was," Clara said.

He looked at her, the doubt obvious. "Who are you, miss?"

"Clara Watson."

"And you were at the wheel?"

"I was. My father taught me how to sail and navigate the river."

"Just not how to keep the boat afloat in a flood," he shot back at her.

"Enough, Les," the man's wife said. "If you can't be nice, don't say anything at all."

"Blasted woman," he growled.

"My name is Dulcie Monson," she said, introducing herself. "Come inside, please, you look done in."

"We are, missus," I replied. "Clara is in need of some clothes, and we could both use some rest and some food before we keep going south."

"To Collarenebri?"

"Yes."

"You can't walk that far," she pointed out.

"I was hoping to ask your husband for a couple of horses which I could leave there for him to pick up at a later time."

"I don't—" Monson began to bluster before Dulcie cut him off.

"I'm sure we can come to some arrangement."

"What's your name, mister?" Monson asked me.

"My name is Jack Crowe." I held out my hand to shake, but he ignored it.

His eyes narrowed. "You the manhunter?"

"Once. I've been working with Michael O'Hanlon recently to track the scoundrel John Kennedy, before going upstream with Thomas Watson."

"You used to work with the darkies, didn't you?"

"I did."

"Then I don't want you in my house. The woman is welcome, but I won't have the likes of you in there."

"Les Monson, you take that back," his wife admonished him.

"Hush, woman. The man is a killer who used darkies to help track men down and murder them."

Dulcie looked at me. "I'm sorry, Mr. Crowe, my husband seems to have forgotten his manners."

"That's all right, missus. If you could take care of Clara, it would be appreciated."

"I will, Mr. Crowe, and I will have someone bring you out some food." She looked at her husband. "As for you, get your own."

Monson scowled and walked away. I looked at Clara. "Go, get some rest. I'll be fine."

I ate and found a place in the shearing shed to lie down. I slept most of the day and into the evening. I woke to Clara in a dress standing over me with a plate of mutton stew. "Are you hungry again?"

Nodding, I said, "I think so."

She sat beside me while I ate.

"We will leave tomorrow," I said to her. "I will see if

Monson will let us have a couple of horses in the morning."

"Don't expect too much, he is a man set in his ways."

"I can only ask."

In the distance, I could hear thunder, a storm building to the east. I frowned, storms didn't come from the east.

Then they exploded into the yard, firing guns as they came. I looked at Clara and said, "Stay here."

I stood in the doorway of the shearing shed and saw them in the moonlight. Five riders, shooting at anything that looked like a threat. Scoundrels they were, and death was their business. For a moment, I thought it was Kennedy and his black hearts, but I remembered they were elsewhere. So, who were they?

I ran down the steps and leaped the fences across the sheep pens. There were figures emerging from the station hand's quarters, shouting in alarm. I saw one fall, shot down by a murderous figure atop his horse.

Clearing the last fence, I ran at him, dragging the hooded rider from the saddle before he could shoot anyone else.

He hit the hard earth with a thud, and the air pushed from his lungs. I hit him twice in the face and left him lying, scooping up his Colt handgun.

I looked around to see the station hands' quarters on fire. The bastards had set it alight. Bad for them, good for me, for it illuminated the yard enough to give me clear targets. I sighted on a rider who was about to shoot another hand and shot him through the back.

He straightened and toppled from the saddle to join his friend in the dirt.

I heard a voice barking orders and saw a large rider in the orange firelight, waving a weapon around above his head, directing his killers. I brought the handgun around to shoot him, cocking the pistol as I did so. He was clearly silhouetted and provided a good target.

I squeezed the trigger, and the hammer fell on an empty chamber. I cocked the weapon again, and the same thing happened.

Suddenly, I heard the thunder of hoofbeats from behind me, and too late, I turned to see a large, hard-ridden beast charging down on top of me.

If the animal had hit me squarely, I would have died, ground into bloody meat below its hoofs. But as luck would have it, only a glancing blow caught me, and as I went down, I looked up at the image of a hooded rider looking like the devil from the fires of hell, grinning down at me.

I tried to regain my feet but instead rolled onto my side. I blinked my eyes, trying to refocus them and caught sight of another hand being shot down. Then the night closed in on me, even though it was illuminated by the ever-growing blaze.

Then I remember nothing.

I CAME AWAKE with the smell of woodsmoke in my nose and a dull overcast above me stained by black. I moaned lowly and tried to move. "Stay there, my love," Clara said in a soft voice. "Regain your strength before you try to stand."

My head ached, so I did as she told me to. I reached up and massaged the side of my head where the pain seemed to stem from. "Black-hearted bastards," I growled. "Tell me what happened, woman."

"The riders, do you remember them?"

I nodded. "I got two of them before I was ridden down."

"I saw," she said to me. "I watched from the shearing shed. Then watched on in horror as another rode you down. I thought I had lost you. Something I don't think I could face so soon after losing my father."

"What happened after that?" I asked.

"They managed to steal the horses from the yards and then they rode away."

"How is your man, lass?"

I opened my eyes and saw Dulcie Monson standing over me, her face blackened by soot from where she had tried to help with the fire. Clara said, "I think he is going to be fine."

I rolled over and stood erect, wobbled, but then gathered myself. "I'll be fine. How many people got hurt?"

"They killed three hands and wounded two others," Dulcie said. "It was most awful."

I looked around the yard and saw the pile of smouldering rubble that used to be a building. Then I saw Monson walking towards us, his face grim. "Frank just died. Bastards."

"Who were they?" I asked. "It wasn't John Kennedy and his scoundrels, I know that."

"Jim Pike."

I searched my memory for the name. The only Jim Pike I remembered was a miner who had a claim near what would become Broken Hill. "Miner," I said.

"Was. Now he's a thief and murderer."

"Are you going after them?" I asked him.

"Yes—"

"No," Dulcie said, cutting him off. "I cannot keep this place running if you go off and get yourself killed by that rascal. I won't have it, Les Monson."

"We need those horses, woman, blast your eyes."

"Send for Michael O'Hanlon," I told him.

"By the time O'Hanlon gets here, Pike will be long gone and so will the horses."

I remembered the mention of Caringi Station and of the horses stolen from there. I was told it had been Kennedy, but I was now thinking that Pike was the more likely culprit.

I looked at Clara and then at the devastation around us. "I will go."

"Jack, no," Clara gasped.

"If I do, Monson, then there are some things I want from you. I'll not do this lightly."

His stare hardened. "I'm listening."

"You need to see that Clara gets to Collarenebri, where she will be safe."

"I can do that."

"Jack—"

I turned my head and glared at her. This was men's business, and I didn't want her interfering. Then I said to Monson. "I want a horse and supplies. Two weapons. A rifle and handgun."

He nodded stiffly. "Done."

"And a thousand pounds."

"Just wait a damn—"

"Done," Dulcie snapped. "It is worth my man's life."

I turned to Clara. "Is that enough to get a down payment on a riverboat?"

She nodded, stunned at what I was proposing. "I—yes."

"But only if you bring the scoundrel Pike, his men, and my horses back, Crowe," Monson growled at me.

"Alive or dead?" I asked.

His eyes narrowed. "I don't really care."

"WHAT ARE YOU DOING?" Clara demanded when we were on our own. "I don't want you to go."

"That is not for you to decide," I told her.

"If I am to become your wife, Jack Crowe, I think it is."

"You need the money."

"I need you."

"These people need their horses back. Do you not think they've lost enough?"

She stared at me. "What do you mean?"

I hesitated. It wasn't my place to say, but I'd gone too far to turn back. "You have talked to the woman?"

"Dulcie? Yes."

"Has she ever mentioned children?"

Clara gave me a confused look. She shook her head. "No."

"They used to have two sons. They've not told me. I heard it from Michael O'Hanlon a long time back. The oldest boy drowned in the river trying to get some stray horses back across. The river was running higher than normal, and his horse was struck by a log. He was unseated and disappeared below the brown murk. They found him two days later."

"I didn't know." Her hand fluttered to her chest—the pale blue muslin dress she wore had come from the Monsons.

"They also had a daughter. She died of a snakebite."

Clara turned and looked at the homestead. "That poor woman."

"It is a tough land," I said to her. "You ought to know that by now. But if I can get the horses back then it will be a little less tough for them."

She knew I was right. "I will wait for you in Collarenebri. But by God, you'd better come back to me, Jack Crowe."

Then she kissed me, long and hard.

WHILE I WAS PREPARING to leave, an old foe was further south making good on a deal with his new boss. Kennedy and his scallywags were hiding in a stand of scrub waiting for the small train of immigrants walking the path to the newly opened Genadi Diggings south of Walgett. Things had quietened down after the gold rush days, but with this new strike, the Chinese seemed to be coming from across the country. The last count had been five thousand.

George, my former tracker, but now an accomplished killer for Kennedy, had appeared moments earlier and advised his boss of their approach. Kennedy readied his men, and they were lying in wait.

I could imagine the sounds of the bush: galahs, cockatoos, cicadas—the damn bush beetles that chirped so loud it sounded like they were inside your head. Even crows sensed that something was afoot and made ready for the chance of an offered meal.

They sat in silence until Billy Wilson started to get too excited and fidgety. Kennedy turned in the saddle and glared at the kid. "If you don't calm down, boy, I'll cut your damn throat with your own fucking knife."

The words elicited an almost maniacal giggle from the young killer. "Can I have one, John?"

"One what?"

"One of them Chinee girls?"

Kennedy stared at the kid and saw the look in his

eyes. It was one he got every now and then and wouldn't go until his thirst had been sated. "I'll think about it."

"You're a good man, sir." Wilson giggled again.

"They coming, boss," George said.

The group could hear them now. Voices and footsteps on the road. George had told Kennedy there were maybe twenty men and women in the party. No children. The men would be put to work, and the women sold off as prostitutes in the camps.

"Get ready," Kennedy rumbled. Then, "Now!"

The brigands erupted from the scrub, shouting for the Chinese to hold. Startled and overwhelmed by fear, the men and women started to run. Kennedy signalled to Hill and Gardner to ride around them, stopping their flight. One of the Chinese men grabbed at Hill's leg, trying to unseat him, until the bushranger shot the man dead with a bullet in the chest.

Nothing like watching someone die to change the mood of a crowd. This one was no different. Kennedy shouted, "Who here speaks English?"

A man stepped forward. He looked to be in his thirties, but it was hard to tell. His hair was in a pigtail halfway down his back. "I do."

"Tell these people they will come with us. All of you."

There was a shriek from the bushes off the road, followed by the sound of a high-pitched giggle. Then came a shout of anger, rage. A few moments later, Billy Wilson emerged, his bloody knife in his hand. Kennedy stared at him. "Are you done?"

The young killer looked at Kennedy. "Tight bitch made me shoot my load as soon as it went in."

Hill spat in the dirt. "Send a boy," he muttered.

Billy pointed the bloody knife at him. "What did you say?"

Hill straightened. "I said you're a little boy who couldn't hump a real woman. Stick to the prostitutes you normally screw."

The kid started forward. "I'll kill—"

Kennedy drove his horse between the two men. "Enough. Keep it up, and I'll kill you both."

They glared at each other, their eyes like firebrands. In hindsight, if they'd been permitted to kill each other now, it would have solved problems later, but that wasn't to happen. Instead, they backed away. Kennedy nodded. "Get them moving towards the river. We're losing daylight."

12

The horse I rode had belonged to one of the killers who'd attacked Piggott's Run. There was still blood on the saddle where I had shot its owner. Monson had provided me with a Martini-Henry rifle and twenty rounds of ammunition for it. The handgun had the same.

Pike and his remaining two men, along with the stolen horses, had gone west and then south, away from Collarenebri. That first night, I camped beside a creek under a large gum. Normally dry at this time of year, the recent rain and floods had it holding well.

I picketed the horse beside my camp and built a fire. An hour later, the sun began to drop below the horizon, leaving the sky a bright orange hue which grew redder the lower it got. Just before the blackness of the outback took over, I climbed a tall gum, careful not to fall and possibly break something. I stayed there for an hour as the plains grew darker.

Satisfied that I was on my own, I was about to climb down and stoke the fire when I saw it. Maybe a couple of miles distant. Just a flickering spot on the landscape but enough to tell me that my campfire wasn't the only one burning this night.

Returning to the ground, I dug through my packs and found some dried meat and boiled the billy for coffee. When my meagre repast was done, I rolled out my swag. Maybe I would catch up with them tomorrow, or the next day.

That night, my dreams were filled with Clara. Her face came to me out of the darkness, her smile, her bright eyes. Then it changed. Her eyes grew dark, mean, her jaw squarer, and her voice deeper. Before I knew what was happening, I was staring at John Kennedy, who was gloating at me.

I saw Clara lying on the ground, her skirts hoisted high. Mad Dog Billy Wilson was lying between her legs, a knife held to her throat. His crazed cackle brought the cockatoos to flight from the trees as he stared at me. The others stood around them as they waited their turn. Then, as he finished, the knife flashed in the sunlight, slashing Clara's throat.

I cried out and shot upright, my chest heaving from the dream. A night bird seemingly laughed at me, mocking the existence of my fear. I lay back down and tried to settle, but sleep remained elusive.

RIDING SLOWLY, I encountered the remains of their camp around midmorning. Like myself, they had taken advantage of the presence of water in a normally dry creek bed, but theirs was through necessity. The number of their horses had grown by six. Those robbed from the station, I guessed.

The trail was headed southeast, and I knew by this

time that they were riding for Carnegie Flats, a small stop on the stage route. My guess, they would try to sell the horses there or stop at the small pub attached to the stage station.

The possibilities from there were either Walgett or Narrabri. My money was on Narrabri because Walgett was too close to home.

So, I rested my horse for a few minutes longer and then pointed it towards Carnegie Flats.

I had to hand it to them: they were making good time. Even with the small herd of horses. Although herding horses was a lot easier than herding cattle or sheep. I crossed a couple more creeks before drawing rein around mid-afternoon. Ahead of me, against a backdrop of deep blue sky, dark specks, undoubtedly crows, were circling. I stared at them for a long time before picking up the Martini-Henry rifle.

With slight pressure from my knees, the horse started forward again. Its hoofs stirring small puffs of dust with each step. Flies buzzed around my face, trying to distract me from whatever I was riding into.

It wasn't long before I found out.

The crows were picking at a corpse. Gone already were the eyes, and a hole had been opened in the dead man's throat. The bullet wound in his chest had been widened by the carrion eaters who were now cawing loudly in protest at being disturbed.

I climbed down and checked his pockets, knowing the chances of finding anything were slim to none. Nothing is exactly what I found. Leaving me puzzled as to whether he was one of Jim Pike's men or a wayward traveller unlucky enough to fall foul of the murderous bastards led by the former miner.

My next quandary was whether to bury him or not.

He was already smelling of decay, and I didn't much care for it. So, I climbed back onto my horse and kept riding.

For about twenty feet.

A booming shot rolled across the western plains, and the horse shuddered under the bullet's impact. I felt it going down and kicked free of the stirrups. Grabbing at the Martini-Henry rifle, I rolled clear of the dying beast.

Another shot sounded, this time disturbing the roosting crows in the trees. A bullet hit close to me. I came to my feet and ran across the open ground to a tall gum, putting its four-foot-wide bole between myself and the shooter.

I cocked the hammer on the rifle and peered around the tree. My would-be killer fired again, and the round burned into the trunk of the gum where it would remain for hundreds of years.

However, that shot gave away the position of my ambusher. Raising the rifle, I fired at the hidden assailant. I saw the bullet strike a rock he was hidden behind and blow chips off it.

He fired again, and the gum was tattooed with another scar it would bear till the end of its days. I reloaded the Martini-Henry and fired. This time, I did not miss, and the .557 round blew half of the shooter's head away.

I walked forward and looked down at the ghastly sight before me. There was no telling who he was, but I guessed he was part of Pike's remaining trio, or duo. I would find out.

Locating the man's horse, I decided that it was only fair that it should replace the one that I had lost. But the poor beast was lame. So, I uncinched the saddle from the dead animal that I'd ridden and placed it upon my shoulder. I still had at least one more man to catch.

ARRIVING at Carnegie Flats two days later, I noticed the split rail yards containing horses that appeared to have been pushed hard. I dumped the saddle under the awning of the main hut and went inside.

There were five people inside. One, a fat prostitute with blackened teeth, appeared to be averse to bathing, or if she did, it was likely in a pig's wallow. She came over to me and smiled. "Buy me a drink, mister?"

Ignoring her, I walked up to the counter, slow and easy. Persisting, she followed and said, "I can be real nice if you do. By the look of you, you haven't had a real woman in a while. I can tell these things."

I placed a coin on the bar and said to the man behind it, "Get me a rum."

"I guess that's a no then," the woman said with a pout.

Apart from the man fetching my drink, the other three sat at a table playing cards. One called over, "Hell, Rosie, come over here, darling, and I'll show you how nice I can be."

"I already had your dick today, Clarke. I don't want it again just yet."

"Then stop bloody complaining."

The bartender gave me a rum and took my money. I threw back the drink, and it tasted like week-old watered-down piss. "I need a horse," I said to the unshaven man who'd served me.

"We ain't got none," he replied, his voice gravelly, likely from a long tobacco habit.

"What about the ones in the yard?"

"Apart from the ones owned by the company, the only others are owned by that man over there playing cards with the others."

I turned and asked, "Which one?"

"That would be me," answered a large man with a bushy beard.

He had to be Pike. He had miner written all over him. "How much for a horse, mister?"

"Twenty pounds."

"I get to pick which one I want."

"You want to do that, you pay thirty," he replied.

"You do me a bill of sale?"

He lowered his cards to the table and stared at me. "Why would you be wanting a bill of sale?"

"I had some trouble once with a rascal selling me a stolen horse. Almost got me hung."

Suddenly, I realized that there was a heavy tension in the hut, and it was all directed at me. I left the Martini-Henry down at my left side, pointing the muzzle at the floor. My right hand, however, was close to the butt of the Colt. My luck was about at the end of its string and was about to snap. Might as well give it a helping hand.

"You're Jim Pike, aren't you?"

The man's eyes narrowed. "Who wants to know?"

"Jack Crowe."

"Jack Crowe is dead."

"No, he ain't," said one of the other card players. "Last I heard, he was freighting out of Kent's Landing."

"Was. A few days ago, I was at Piggott's Run when you stole those horses outside, Jim."

He lurched to his feet as he went for his gun. Mine came out in a fluid motion and roared before his could come into line. Pike staggered back, falling over the chair he'd been sitting on. I walked forward and stared down at the killer. Seeing that he was dead, I looked at the two he was playing cards with. "You with him?"

They held their hands up at shoulder height. I could

see the fear in their eyes as they shook their heads. "No, sir. He come in on his own."

"Who are you, then?"

"We ain't no one, sir. No one you would be interested in anyway. Now, them people who are stealing them Chinee people away, thems people you might like to pay a visit to."

I frowned. "What do you mean?"

"Down near Walgett a few days past," the second man said. "Someone took some Chinee people off the road. Butchered one of the girls, they did."

This was the second time I'd heard about someone taking Chinese people, miners. "What are the traps doing about it?"

The barman came out from behind the counter. "What they normally do, stuff all. You want to give me a hand to drag Pike out of here?"

I looked at the dead bushranger on the floor. "Not particularly. I've got horses to take back to Piggott's Run."

I went outside and almost immediately saw the dust cloud in the distance. As it grew closer, I saw the riders at its base. Then I saw the dark blue uniforms. Traps.

There were five of them, accompanied by a black tracker. Their leader, a sergeant, with thick muttonchop sideburns, called a halt just as the bartender brought out the dead Pike. He stared at the corpse and asked in a gruff tone, "Who killed this man?"

"I did," I replied.

His eyes fixed on me and said, "You, sir, are under arrest. You'll be lucky if you don't hang."

THE SERGEANT'S name was Murphy. He was an Irishman. Once a Redcoat but now a trap in charge of the station at Walgett. The cells were separate from the small station. They were built from mud brick with iron bars in the windows.

I tried to explain what I was doing, what had happened, even, but the bastard Irishman wouldn't listen. So I sat in the cells for the next month waiting for a judge to hear my trial.

All the time, not knowing what had happened to my betrothed or even if she was that anymore.

Early that morning, a trap brought me two buckets. One had fresh water, the other for me to shit and piss in. He left them side by side in the corner and took the other. I said, "Can you get a message to Superintendent Michael O'Hanlon for me somehow?"

"Why would I do that?" asked the policeman.

"Because he will sort this out."

"No."

"What about Piggott's Run?"

"Too far away."

"Shit, man, it's my neck we're talking about here. It's not like I'll be fined and let go. The bastard magistrate will hang me."

"I can't help that, Crowe. You shouldn't commit murder."

"It wasn't bloody murder, you fool."

"That is for the judge to decide."

"When?"

"Tomorrow."

Not news I was wanting to hear. "Have you heard anything of Clara Watson?"

"She's a right enterprising young woman that one," the trap said. "Got herself a boat."

"A boat?"

"The *Carnarvon*. Charlie Henry's old boat."

"How did she manage to get that?" I asked.

"Word is that after Charlie died, she—"

"What do you mean, died?" I asked him. "He was fine the last I heard."

"Some freight fell on him. He died underneath it. The woman came along at the right time. Made a down payment and went to work straight away to help make repayments."

I thought for a moment. If she made a down payment, then she must have got the money from Monson. Then why didn't she come and see me?

"Can someone tell her where I am?" I asked.

"The police aren't your own messenger service."

He walked away, leaving me locked up and contemplating my future, and the trial to take place the following day.

THEY BROUGHT me an extra bucket of water the next morning so I could wash. Once I had finished, the bucket was removed. It was the cleanest I'd felt in a week of incarceration, being the first they'd permitted me to have. A man's aroma can become quite distinct in that amount of time, especially in such a confined space.

With little to do with my time, I'd spent much of it listening to scuttlebutt, learning that the magistrate's name was Dennis. Apparently, he was a tough harbinger of law and had hung his fair share of those who appeared before him. Not a man I was looking forward to meeting.

There were other things I heard whilst interned.

More whispers of Chinese immigrants destined for the gold fields disappearing. Kennedy and his rapscallions had vanished into the outback, and coaches were getting through regularly. But more riverboats had been snapped up by a mysterious buyer with lots of money to spend. And the railway was almost to Bourke. Something that was going to prove the undoing of freighters and send the river boats to the bottom.

Not that work was going to dry up like the waterholes and creeks in a drought. There would still be work for the river captains. However, they would slowly be strangled until their lifeless bodies would be found on the banks of destitution.

These thoughts brought me to Clara. How would she go on her own?

I was taken from the cell about ten in the morning. The sun beat down, and people lined my walk towards the courthouse. Ladies with their parasols erect, trying to look ladylike beside men dressed in suits, trying to appear gentlemanly. Then there were the children. Snot-nosed little bastards who thought that it was good sport to throw rocks at the prisoner.

I was taken inside the courthouse by Murphy, chained at the wrist and ankle. I was positioned in a seat beside a man in a suit. I looked at him and asked, "Are you my lawyer?"

He looked horrified at the suggestion. He took off his spectacles and said, "Good Lord, no, man. I'm a store owner. Lawyers don't come to Walgett. It was my turn to be defending counsel."

I could feel the noose tightening around my neck, the small prickling strands digging into my flesh. And I hadn't even had my trial yet.

Looking across the aisle, I saw that Murphy was to be

prosecuting me. Behind me, there was noise as the good folk of the town shuffled in for the spectacle. Suddenly, in my mind, I was transported back to Narrabri again.

"Jack, Jack Crowe," a hushed voice said from behind me. I turned to see Monson and his wife standing there. He said, "We'll get this sorted out."

"Did you get your horses?"

"Aye. Thanks to you. We have your money."

"Didn't Clara get it?"

"No, never saw her."

I nodded and turned back, facing the bench. The magistrate came in not long after. He was a short, stern-faced man with more than one furrow in his brow. He sat down and looked at me. "You are Jack Crowe?"

"Yes, Your Honour."

"You have been charged with the murder of one Jim Pike?"

"Yes, sir."

He looked at Murphy. "Call your first witness, Sergeant Murphy. A quick trial is a good trial."

"Yes, Your Honour. We would call Jeremy Hart."

I frowned. Who the hell was Jeremy Hart? I found out when he appeared. It was the bartender from Carnegie Flats.

He took a seat, and Murphy walked forward, holding out a battered leather-bound copy of the Bible. "Put your hand on this and repeat—"

He did as he was asked, and then my trial commenced.

"Do you recognise the defendant, Mr. Hart?"

He nodded. "Yes, sir, he was the man who shot Jim Pike. But it—"

"No further questions, Your Honour."

I looked at my defender to see if he was getting to his

feet. When he didn't move, I said, "Aren't you going to ask him some bloody questions?"

"Did you shoot him?" he asked.

"Yes, but—"

"No questions, Your Honour," the storekeeper said.

If I could feel the noose tightening before, then I could hardly breathe now. "I have some questions, Your Honour," I said, standing up.

"You are not a lawyer, sir," the judge said.

I pointed to the man beside me. "Neither is he."

"But he's been appointed to defend you, Mr. Crowe."

"I'm sorry, Your Honour, but if he's the best they have here, then I'd rather defend myself. After all, it's my neck."

Dennis stared at me for a long moment before he sighed. "Very well, Mr. Crowe. Ask your questions."

"Mr. Hart, could you tell everyone who Jim Pike was?"

"He was a bushranger, sir. A black heart and scoundrel."

"Did you know it was him in your establishment that day?"

"No, not until you came and said who he was."

"Did he deny the accusation?" I asked.

"No, sir."

"He arrived with a herd of horses, did he not?"

"Yes, sir. He tried to sell them to me for the coach line."

I nodded. "What happened when I told him that I knew he stole the horses?"

"He tried to shoot you."

"Then what happened?" I asked.

"You shot him," Hart replied.

"Would you say that I acted in self-defence?"

"Without doubt."

"Thank you, Mr. Hart."

He got up and moved to take a seat in the audience.

"Your next witness, Sergeant Murphy?"

"Don't have any, Your Honour. It has been established that Crowe shot and killed Pike."

"What about defence witnesses?"

My storekeeper looked at me. I shook my head. "You just sit there and say nothing. Your Honour, I would like to call on Les Monson."

"All right, Mr. Crowe, do so."

Once Monson was seated and sworn in, he waited for my first question. Instead, I said, "Mr. Monson, could you tell everyone in your own words what happened at Piggott's Run?"

"Your Honour, I don't see the point in this," Murphy said calmly.

"Your Honour, I think the background to what happened is important. It explains why I was looking for Pike."

Another sigh, and Dennis said, "So much for a quick trial and verdict. All right, let's hear it."

Monson began at the start and finished at the end, leaving nothing out. When he was done, I asked him, "Do you have any doubts that the man who led the attack on Piggott's Run was Jim Pike, bushranger, murderer, and scoundrel?"

"No doubt at all."

I sat down, and Murphy stood up. "Mr. Monson, did you not say it was dark?"

"Yes, sir."

I could see where this was going, and I had an uneasy feeling about it.

"Then, sir, how could you tell if the man was Jim Pike or someone other than him?"

"Might I remind you, Sergeant, that Pike was a murderer and thief?" Monson shot at him.

"Supposed, sir. He'd not been to trial to have any charges answered."

"Not yet."

"Would you please answer the question?"

"Because I knew it was him."

"Did you see his face?"

"No, but—"

"No more questions."

Monson stared at me helplessly. Then he was ordered to sit down.

This was going so well.

"Mr. Crowe, any more witnesses you would like to call?"

I was about to answer when there was a commotion at the doorway, and two policemen walked in, their uniforms covered in dust from a hard ride. One was a sergeant whom I'd never seen before. The other was Superintendent Michael O'Hanlon.

He walked forward and said, "Sorry to barge in on you like this, Your Honour, but I do believe you are trying an innocent man."

FOR THE FIRST time in days, I felt the constriction around my throat loosen. As we stood outside the courthouse, I took a moment to savour my freedom. O'Hanlon moved in beside me and said, "Buy me a beer, Jack."

"I would buy you two—"

"Good," he said, slapping me on the back.

"If I had any money."

"It's a good thing that I have your pay in my pocket then," he said.

Surprised by this revelation, I said, "Lead the way."

Heading for the nearest pub, I bought us some beers, and we found an empty table. Before he could speak, I asked, "Do you have any news on Clara?"

"The last I heard, she was working freight up and down the river on that boat of hers. Why?"

"I thought I might have seen her before now," I said. "We were going to be married."

"Did she know that?" O'Hanlon asked me.

"Of course."

"Well, from what I hear, she's been keeping company with some American. Man by the name of Charles Travis."

I felt my anger start to build. While I'd been locked away in jail, she had moved on, even after a month. "I need to go see her."

"After you do something for me," he said.

"I don't have time, Michael."

"Listen, I've been riding all over the blasted country looking for Kennedy. I've worn out more horses and men than I care to count. Now someone is taking bloody Chinese immigrants off the roads as well as the diggings. I want you to find out who."

"Shit, Michael."

"You owe me, Jack."

I repeated my last words.

13

GENADI DIGGINGS, NEW SOUTH WALES, 1885

Seven months. I had been working for O'Hanlon for seven months and had found nothing except lost trails that led into the outback of nowhere. In that time, while my freight business floundered with Jim Craig, I had yearned to see Clara but hadn't laid eyes upon her. When five months had passed, news came that she had married her American, and I lost all hope.

Now, I was in Genadi Diggings looking for answers and finding none. Under the blankets beside me, the lump I lay next to stirred. A head full of long, dark hair belonging to a woman ten years younger than I, rose from beneath it and then I saw the face. An Ni took one look at me and said, "Shit, it's you."

"Yeah, it's me."

"Did I have that much opium last night?" she asked in a hoarse voice.

I closed my eyes, trying to remember what had

happened. Limbs entwined, naked bodies, cries of passion. I nodded. "I think we both did."

She rolled onto her back, and the blanket fell away, revealing small, firm breasts. It wasn't the first time I'd slept with the Chinese prostitute in the past months. Each time, I swore it would be the last, but here we were again.

An Ni had come to Australia looking for gold with her family twenty years before. She had been five at the time. Now, most of her family was dead. Those who had survived were spread out everywhere. When money was tight, she'd turned to the arts of the flesh.

Sitting up, she swung her legs over the side of the bed, grabbed the dish of brown water and a rag and started scrubbing herself, paying extra attention to the thatch between her legs.

"Damn, Crowe, did you empty a frigging bucket inside me last night?"

My head ached. "I can't even really remember screwing you, Annie."

"That's good because I can't either. The last I remember was sucking on that damn opium pipe."

After she'd finished scrubbing herself, she stood up and walked to the opening of her tent. Outside, the sun was up, and voices were growing louder as the diggings came alive. I lay on my back and clenched my eyes tight as An Ni opened the flap, admitting the bright sunlight.

"Bloody shit," I growled. "Are you trying to blind a man?"

"Shut up and get out of my bed," she growled. She came back in and found a sack of tobacco and packed herself a pipe. Lighting it, she inhaled deeply, drawing the smoke into her lungs. She looked at me. "You want one?"

I shook my head. "Not now."

"Then fuck off."

She stood there looking at me, her hips thrust forward, eyes burning deep. I swung my legs across and sat on the bed as she had done before getting up. I stared back. She sucked on the tobacco-filled pipe and blew out a stream of blue-grey smoke.

I stood up, and she looked down at my crotch. I could feel what she was staring at. My cock was hard again—not by choice. She stuck the pipe into her mouth and sucked on it again. "You want me to suck that like my pipe?"

I just stared at her.

An Ni held out her pipe. "Take it."

I took it in my hand and stared at the burning coal in the bottom of the bowl. I felt An Ni's mouth envelop me, sliding back and forth. Her rhythm grew faster, and my toes curled into the dirt floor as my pleasure built.

I could feel myself heading for the precipice when the flap was thrown back, and a man with red hair appeared. "Fuck off, you bastard!" I snarled at him.

"You need to come, Jack," he said to me. Looking at the motion of An Ni's head.

I threw the pipe at him, making him duck. "Piss off, or I'll shoot you when I'm done."

He backed out, but the damage was already complete. I felt my cock soften, and no amount of coaxing was going to bring it back. "Shit."

An Ni started to giggle and rose to her feet. "Come back and see me tonight, Jack, and I'll finish it for you."

I pulled my pants and boots on and then put the rest of my clothes on as well. I spied a half-empty bottle of rum beside the bed and picked it up. Taking a drink, I pulled a face, passed it to An Ni. "Here, Annie, a present."

She took it and drank. Then, before I walked out, she kissed me, her tongue darting into my mouth. "That's just to remind you to come back."

I started towards the tent flap and stopped. "Where's my guns?"

An Ni reached under her bed and pulled them out. The Colt handgun and Martini-Henry rifle that I'd been given by Monson when I went after Pike. "Thanks."

Ducking out through the flap, I stood looking around at the diggings. The landscape had been raped of all it had to offer. What once had been covered in trees and rock with a creek was now a barren panorama of people and tents and mineshafts.

"What did you want, Hank?" I asked the redhead.

"A Chinee man was killed last night over by the cut," Hank told me.

"What is so special about that?"

"He had four friends that can't be found. Word going around that they killed him and pissed off."

"What do you think?"

"Might be true."

Hank was my source of information around the diggings. When I arrived, he was destitute. Like others, he'd come to Genadi to find his fortune. When in fact he'd found bugger all. So I paid him for information. Not much, but enough to get him by.

I stared towards the cut. It was a section of the diggings where a handful of Chinese miners had started cutting through a hill, following a small quartz vein in the hope they would find gold. They did in patches, but mostly it was a dry hole. Not enough to kill someone over and shoot through. "Show me."

I followed Hank over to the cut. We took the short route through the tent city. It stank like a damn shit ditch from all the excrement that had been discarded nearby. Next would come the disease, and people would get sick and die.

We walked past the meat tent. Out the back, a tall man was butchering a cow hung from a frame over a hole where the guts would be dropped. Another disease pot ready to unleash itself on the people of the diggings.

Not far from where he worked was a series of smaller tents that the miners called Prostitute Row. Even at this early hour of the morning, they stood outside in their corsets and pantaloons, breasts exposed as an extra incentive to reel customers in. One looked at me as I walked past and smiled. She had dark hair and a dirt-smudged face. "You want some early morning fun, Jack Crowe?" she catcalled.

I heard the woman from the tent next to hers say, "Good luck with that, don't you know he only likes to fuck Chinee girls?"

"That bitch over the other side?"

"That's the one."

"She's a lot cleaner than you two cows," I snapped as I kept going.

"I hear she does special things," the first prostitute called after me. "Does she let you stick it in that tight little arse of hers, Jack?"

I ignored her.

"If that's your thing, I'll let you do me like that, Jack."

I kept walking, a chorus of high-pitched cackles reaching out behind me. For some reason, I found that the comments about An Ni annoyed me, and my fists were clenched.

"Is that true?" Hank asked me as we kept up a brisk pace.

"Is what true?"

"That Annie lets you diddle her arse?"

I stopped suddenly, and Hank's momentum wouldn't let him stop in time. As he ran into me, I grabbed a fistful of his shirt and said, "Just shut the fuck up."

"All I wanted to know was—"

I shoved him away and kept walking. We dipped down across the muddy cesspit that had once been the creek. When the diggings had been started, someone had the common sense to make a dam further upstream so there would be some semblance of fresh water that could be used.

When we reached the cut, I stopped. "Where was the body found?" I asked.

"Up in there?" Hank said, pointing towards the rear of the cut.

I walked up into the cut where the steep walls showed the scars of picks from months of work. "How was he killed?" I asked Hank.

"They said he was hit in the head with a rock," he told me as he looked around. "That one there."

I looked where he was pointing and saw the cannon-ball-sized rock with blood on it. Looking around, I started to slowly shake my head. "No."

"What do you mean *no*, Jack?" he asked.

"Pick it up, Hank."

"What?"

"Pick up the rock."

He bent down and picked up the heavy object. "Where was he hit?"

"The Chinee man?"

"Yes."

Still holding onto the rock with one hand, he tapped the left side of his head just in front of the ear. "There."

"Did you see the body?" I asked Hank.

"Yes, sir."

"Was he hit on that side?"

His head bobbed. "Yes."

"Now hit me with the rock."

He looked at me as though he thought me crazy. "What?"

"Not literally, Hank, just stand where you think the person was who killed him and lift the rock up."

He stood behind me and brought it up. "That's the wrong side."

"Come around the front."

When he did, he said, "He would have had to hold it in his other hand."

I nodded. "How many people do you know that use their left hand for everything?"

He frowned. "Not a lot. But there are some."

Fair enough. "Put the rock back on the ground and show me where the body lay."

Hank dropped the rock, pointed at the gravelly ground and said, "There."

With a heavy sigh, I said, "Lay down and show me."

Crouching, he lowered himself to the gravel and lay face down, his head turned so that the left side touched the ground near the bloody rock. "Just like that?" I asked.

"Yes."

"He wasn't killed in the cut," I told him.

Hank looked up at me, confused. "What?"

"Get up."

Getting to his feet, he brushed some loose gravel from his hands and clothes.

I said, "He fell from the top of the cut."

"Are you sure, Jack?"

"I will be. Let's go up top and have a look."

Leaving the cut, we began climbing the slope to the

top. The terrain at the summit was dry and dusty and told me all I needed to know. There were footprints that led to the cut, mixed with those of boots. I pointed them out to Hank and said, "See that, the Chinese man was chased. It was dark, and he must have misjudged where he was. Run off the cut and hit his head on the rock."

"Well stuff me."

I walked back a way and found more boot prints. "The others were taken away."

"How do you know that?" Hank asked me, staring at the ground, not seeing what I saw.

"I learned my skills from the Aboriginals I worked with," I told him.

He nodded. "I forgot you worked with darkies."

"Ask around and see if anyone heard anything last night," I said to him.

"Sure, what are you going to do?"

"Going to see the man."

"You know what he said last time, Jack," Hank reminded me. "He said he'd cut off your balls and eat them with rice."

"I'll take an escort with me."

He was about to ask who when he realized. "No, not her, Jack. She was the reason he wanted to cut them off in the first place."

AN NI WAS DRINKING COFFEE, sitting on a log out front of her tent. She looked up at me and said, "Are you back for another go around already?"

"I need to see Chen," I said to her.

She smiled at me. "And you need me to come with you?"

"The thought had crossed my mind," I replied.

"You think that my father will not kill you if his daughter is there?"

I nodded.

"You forget one thing, Jack," she reminded me. "He disapproves of you fucking me."

"I need to see him, Annie. A miner was killed last night, and his friends have disappeared."

"Chinese?"

"Yes."

"Give me a moment to get some clothes on."

Moments later, she had changed into a drab grey dress which swept to the ground. She brushed her hair and tied it into a ponytail. I stared at her, and for a moment, forgot what she was. "Come on, Jack, let's go and see him. Though it might be appropriate if I wore black."

I muttered something, and she grabbed my hand. "Come on."

Chen's tent was one of the biggest on the gold field. He was also one of the very few who made money from not digging an ounce of gold.

Chen Hu was a trader, crook, opium dealer, gold assayer, and standover man who ran a bunch of nefarious scoundrels who held the Chinese population to account. The white miners had their own rogues, but the Chinese had Chen, and he was a dangerous man when crossed.

I was one of those he despised, but we had an understanding. I wouldn't sleep with his daughter, and he wouldn't kill me.

You can see where this is going.

An Ni pushed the flap of the tent back and walked in.

I followed, my hand on the butt of my Colt handgun. The Martini-Henry I'd left at An Ni's.

There were four men inside. The one we'd come to see sat on a large, crude chair, he made it resemble a throne and he an emperor watching over all he commanded.

His bodyguards took a step forward, and I tensed. The bastards had their swords half drawn when Chen said, "Wait."

He stared at his daughter and then at me. "What have I told you about being with my daughter, Crowe?"

"We're going to go back over that again, Chen?"

"I was told you were with her last night." His eyes narrowed. "Tell me why I should not kill you now?"

"Oh, Father," An Ni growled. "I'm an adult. If I want to fuck Crowe, I will."

For a moment, I thought the self-proclaimed ruler would fly off his throne and strike his daughter. I tensed to intercede, but he remained seated. "Sometimes I wish you were more like your mother, daughter, but I know if you were, this damn country would devour you. You have strength, but would you not speak to your father that way?"

"I'm sorry, Father." She looked down contritely.

"If you want to blame someone, then look at yourself, Chen," I said. "You and your blasted opium."

"If you cannot take it, do not smoke it. Besides, it is no excuse. I warned you about An Ni."

I drew the Colt and pointed it at Chen's heart. "I'd prefer not to shoot you, Chen, but if I do, then I don't get the answers to the questions that I have."

He looked at me thoughtfully, and for a moment I thought we had ourselves an understanding. "Ask your questions and piss off."

"Last night, a Chinese man fell to his death—"

"Was killed."

I shook my head. "He fell to his death because someone was chasing him."

He stared at me and waved a hand, gesturing for his men to sit down. One of them picked up an opium pipe and lit it. "Why do you say this? I was told that his friends killed him and took the gold."

"Come on, Chen, you know as well as I do that the cut hasn't produced shit since they were digging it. If it was, you'd be richer than you are."

He nodded slowly. "Why do you think someone was chasing the dead man?"

"I had a look around. He was chased by white men. I could tell by the boot marks."

"What do you want me to do about it?"

"Could you ask around your people to see if they know something?"

"Why would I do that?" Chen asked, steepling his fingers contemplatively.

"Maybe because your people keep disappearing into thin air. The next one could be Annie."

I blinked furiously to clear my vision. The opium smoke was starting to get to me. Chen nodded. "I will see what I can find out for you."

"Thank you."

"But it will not come cheap."

I dug into my pocket and took out five sovereigns. "Here. I'll give you another fifteen when I get something."

"You bastard," An Ni swore at me. "You told me you had no money."

I stared at her dark, glittering eyes. "You should wear that dress more often. It makes you look pretty."

Then I walked out of the tent, An Ni close behind me, fuming at my dishonesty. I stopped and turned, taking out another five sovereigns. She stood before me, hands on her hips. I tucked the money down the front of her dress and said, "Happy now?"

"You're still a bastard, Jack Crowe," she called after me as I walked away.

Without looking back, I said, "I'll be by tonight to get my rifle."

MY NEXT PORT of call was to an Irishman named O'Farrell, a big man who ruled with his fists. His domain included the Irish and Italian immigrants, as well as any other Europeans who came to the strike. I found him sitting outside his tent, shaving a five-day stubble with a straight razor. He looked at me and said, "I hear you've been asking questions about the missing Chinee mans from last night."

"Word travels fast."

He clicked his fingers, and one of the four men who were watching over him went into the canvas tent. "I don't like people asking too many questions."

"I'm here doing a job, Colin," I said, using his first name.

"I don't care what you're fucking doing. It has to stop."

The man re-emerged from the tent, shoving Hank in front of him. Hank's face was bloody where he'd been beaten. The redhead staggered and fell at my feet.

I helped him up and looked at his face. "All—all I did was ask if anyone knew anything about the Chinee man, Jack."

The diggings were a brutal place with only one kind of law. The law of the toughest, and O'Farrell lived by it. We'd had words before, but nothing like this had ever happened. "You shouldn't have done that, Colin," I said to him.

The big Irishman climbed to his feet and wiped his face on a stained rag. "You know, Jack, I always thought this day would come."

"It doesn't have to, you know. All Hank was doing was asking about the miner who was killed last night."

"He was killed by his own and then they ran away. You start making anything else of it, and the traps come nosing around. And that would be bad for business."

"So, I should forget that he was running away from white blokes, and that it's possible that the same ones took the others?"

O'Farrell nodded. "Yes."

"Not what I'm hired to do, Colin."

"Maybe it should be."

I turned to Hank. "Get out of here, mate. I'll take care of it."

Hank looked to protest but thought better of it and then disappeared. O'Farrell stared at me and said, "I heard once that you bested Ned Kelly in fisticuffs? Would that be right?"

I nodded. "That's what they say."

The big Irishman spat in his palms and flexed his fingers. "Then maybe we should see if you still have the skill it would have taken to beat the young braggart."

Shaking my head, I said, "Not today, Colin. Today I'm looking for a murderer. So, unless that happens to be you, we should wait until another time."

I turned to walk away. "Take heed of what I said, Crowe. I'll not warn you again."

I caught up with Hank. "Are you all right?"

"The bastards waled the bejaysus out of me, Jack."

"What happened?"

"I was just asking around if anyone had heard anything."

"And?"

"Well, I came across a woman—"

"What kind of woman?"

"One of the girls," he replied, looking at me with a knowing look.

I knew what he meant. "Keep going."

"She heard one of the Irishmen talking about them getting extra money."

"What for?"

"Something about slaves."

My blood ran cold. "What prostitute?"

"Big Sal."

"Fine."

14

IT SEEMED that I wasn't the only one who had heard about the *slaves* thing. Chen had too, and while I was looking around the diggings, he was making plans. He'd gathered his people and was explaining what he wanted done.

"Once it is fully dark, we'll show the Irish bastards that we won't put up with what they're doing to us."

"What will we do to O'Farrell?" a man named Fu asked.

"We kill him if we can. But the aim is to drive them from the diggings. If we have to kill them to do it, then we will."

Little did I know at the time, but what was being set up was possibly the most brutal incident between whites and Chinese since the Lambing Flat Riots. Only this time, the shoe would be on the other foot.

I never heard about what was going to happen until it was too late. All day, the diggings had a feeling about it, but I put that down to the murder the night before. I planned on talking to Big Sal, but it had to be after dark when I was less likely to be seen.

While I waited, I went back to An Ni's tent, where she was washing some clothes in a large metal tub. The water was the colour of the silt-filled creek. I looked at it and said, "Did that come from the dam?"

"Yes," she replied.

"It's dirty."

"There is a lot of fresh water running into it from rain upstream."

I nodded. There had been distant thunder the night before, so obviously there had been a good downpour. Too much and the dam would overflow, and the water would course down through the diggings.

An Ni looked at me. "What are you doing here, Jack? Don't you have anything else to do?"

"If you want me to go, I'll go," I replied.

Her gaze softened. "You're not like the others."

"How do you mean?"

"The ones that hang around only want one thing, but you don't. You're not like them."

"Until I get all twisted on opium," I pointed out.

"But the sex is wild, right?"

"I wish I could remember."

She giggled, and I saw the spark in her eyes. "You should laugh more, Annie," I said to her. "It makes you pretty."

Her expression changed from happy to one of anger. "Fuck off, Jack. Get out of here."

"What? Why? All I said was that—"

"I know what you said. Maybe I was wrong. You're just like the other bastards. They say nice things, so I'll be nice to them."

"That's not it, Annie."

"I'm a prostitute, Jack. The only thing you want from me is what is between my legs."

I shook my head and swore. Then I started into her tent.

"What are you doing, Jack?" she growled at me.

"Getting my rifle."

I found the Martini-Henry where I'd left it and came back out. An Ni was scrubbing her dress again, this time with more vigour. Her anger was driving her tempo. As I started to walk away, she said, "Jack, wait."

I looked back and saw the wetness on her cheeks. "Will you come back tonight?"

"Do you want me to?"

"Yes."

I nodded slowly. "Tell you what. It'll be dark soon. I'll go and shoot us a kangaroo. Fresh meat for the fire tonight."

An Ni smiled at me and said, "That would be nice."

I walked about two miles before I was far enough away from the diggings that I might spot a kangaroo around sundown. Maybe. The one thing the diggings didn't lack was the sparseness of fresh meat. I walked a little further and stopped. Ahead of me was a small waterhole I knew that still held water in the bottom of it. With a bit of luck, it might have some wildlife come in soon.

I sat down in the grass and contemplated my life. I enjoyed the wildness of the outback. Times like this made you feel all alone, and the sounds were magnificent. Then I thought of Clara and wondered what she was doing.

Then my thoughts came back around to An Ni. A Chinese prostitute to whom I was attracted. I don't know why I was, I just was. Maybe it was because we were alike. Lost souls drifting on the rough seas of life like sinking ships with bilge pumps working overtime.

Maybe after everything was done for O'Hanlon, she would come with me, wherever *there* was. Maybe I would ask her, and maybe she would say no. But I would ask anyway.

Movement near the waterhole brought my attention back to the present. Through the dried grasses, I saw the grey fur of a kangaroo as he approached the water. I brought up the Martini-Henry and tucked the butt into my shoulder. Then I sighted along the barrel and squeezed the trigger.

The rifle roared and kicked back into my shoulder. Through the cloud of gunpowder smoke which spewed from the barrel, I saw the kangaroo go down. Climbing to my feet, I walked over to where it lay, the dry grass beneath it now wet with blood.

I lay the rifle down beside the animal and took out my knife. For the next thirty minutes or so, I went to work butchering the animal until I had both haunches off. They would roast well over the fire.

By the time I was finished, the sun was almost down, and a red sunset crept across the landscape, turning the bare earth of the diggings a deep indigo colour.

Making the trek back, I arrived in the dark, with numerous small camp and cook fires dotting the landscape. I found An Ni sitting beside her fire waiting. She looked up at me and smiled. "I'm glad you're back, Jack."

She stood up and stepped toward me. Her hand slipped in behind my head, and she pulled it down so that our lips met. Normally, when we kissed, it was with me as the customer. But this time it was different. It felt different.

An Ni stepped back. "We need to talk, Jack."

I nodded. "I guess we do, but first I need to see someone."

"Who?"

"Big Sal about the miner who was killed."

"The food will be ready when you return."

"Sounds good," I replied with a grin.

"And tonight, when we lie with each other, there will be no opium."

"Sounds even better."

BIG SAL WAS in her tent with a customer when I called. The sounds coming from within made me think of grunting pigs followed by the squeals of the newborn. A few moments after the noises ceased, a bearded miner emerged with a starry expression on his face. He gave me an amazed look and said, "I never knewed a woman could do things like that."

He disappeared into the darkness, fixing his trousers, and a few moments later, Sal emerged. She looked at me and asked, "You come for a root or for something else?"

"Something else."

"Figures. Rumour has it you only hump that Chinee girl."

"You got a minute or so?" I asked her.

She made a show of looking around, and with an abrupt nod, said, "Don't look like they're knocking my tent down tonight to get in, so yeah, I got time. What do you want?"

"I wanted to ask you what you heard that the Irish were doing?"

"I don't know what the Irish are doing," she lied.

Her breathing had quickened, and her pale breasts

started to heave up and down. "I know you know something, Sal. About Chinese slaves."

She seemed to get angry with herself for having a big mouth. "Aw. Shit."

"Tell me what you heard, and I'll leave."

"I heard one of the Irish talking about O'Farrell and his people getting extra money from some bloke for the Chinee."

"What do you mean?" I asked her. "You must have heard more than that."

"Someone was paying ten sovereigns for each Chinee man delivered."

"Do you know where they were being sent?" I asked her.

"To the river. I don't know after that."

"Where on the river?" I asked.

"Stuart's Rest."

The riverboats sometimes tied up for the night at Stuart's Rest. "And you heard O'Farrell was behind it?"

"Yes."

"Who else have you told, Sal?"

"No one," she blurted out. Instantly, I knew that was a lie.

I grabbed her arm and stared hard at her. "Who, damn your eyes?"

"I might have told Wang."

"Holy shit," I hissed. "He would run straight back and tell Chen."

I was about to ask her who else when the first shot rang out through the night. My head snapped around, and as it did, more gunfire filled the air. It was closely followed by angry shouts and yet more gunfire. I turned back to Sal and said, "Get in that tent and don't come out."

Then I ran towards the sound of the guns. But when I got there, the situation was too far gone. The great Genadi Riots were on, and people were already dead.

SOMEWHERE IN THE MELEE, I saw a Chinese miner swing a pick with enough force for its point to smash through the Irishman's skull and into his brain. The man went down to his knees, and the Chinese miner put his foot on the Irishman's head to provide more leverage to extract his pick.

Tents were on fire, and the canvas burned and illuminated the chaotic scene across the diggings. Some three thousand Chinese had risen up and faced around fifteen hundred Irish, and even though the Irish were outnumbered, the Irish had the bulk of the firearms, whereas the Chinese were armed only with picks, shovels, handles, and knives.

I watched a Chinese miner get shot in the stomach at close range, and then when he sank to his knees, his Irish attacker shot him in the head. Miners stood toe-to-toe in hand-to-hand combat. The dry ground across the diggings was fast becoming blood-soaked and strewn with the dead, dying, and wounded.

I saw one miner drag a Chinese woman behind a tent by her hair. Her high-pitched shrieks cut abruptly short as he hit her in the face. I hurried forward and found him behind the tent, pants down, buttocks seemingly glowing in the flickering orange light.

I hit him in the back of his head with my Colt, and he collapsed onto the ground. I reached down and grabbed the woman by the arm. "Go and hide until this is over."

Her eyes widened in warning. I whirled and saw a

large man with a pick raised about to bring it down and bury the point into my head. I threw myself to the side, away from the downward blow that the snarling, crazed figure intended.

The pick came down in a crashing blow, missing me but finding an unexpected target. The Chinese woman stood rigid, her eyes rolled back, blood running down her face from the embedded iron in her skull.

With a sickened curse, I fired my Colt, the bullet hammering into the miner and killing him.

I pushed the ghastly sight from my mind and started through the camp towards An Ni's tent. If this was the chaos, she was in grave danger, and I needed to get her out.

There was a melee of bodies to my right in the old watercourse. Except there was water flowing through it from the spill from the dam. Knee deep and rising. Chinese and Irish fought in the watery battleground with knives and shovels.

Amongst the throng, I saw Chen, eyes wild, a snarl on his face covered with blood. I saw him raise a knife over a miner already on his knees in the water. It plunged down into the junction between neck and shoulder. Blood spurted as he pulled the blade clear and then he kicked the man, making him topple over.

Before long, the Chinese had the outnumbered group of Irishmen overwhelmed, and they disappeared beneath the water.

Chen must have sensed me watching as he turned and looked in my direction. The whites of his crazed eyes stood out against the backdrop of his blood-covered face, and I knew from that instant he'd lost all control.

He barked instructions, and his followers waded out of the water and ran toward the next battle to be fought.

Shaking with the thought of getting caught by a crazed mob, I kept going. I still needed to find An Ni.

Ahead of me, I saw another disturbing sight. One of the only remaining gums that stood watch over the diggings had several large branches reaching out their giant arms, a macabre fruit dangling from each one. A rope hung from each branch, and swinging in the slight breeze were three Chinese miners strung up by a separate angry mob.

The riot was fast becoming a massacre on both sides.

I reached An Ni's tent and found it flattened. The kangaroo she'd been cooking was charred black on the fire and there was a wounded Irishman lying beside it. He'd been stabbed in the chest and was obviously bleeding inside. A line of bloody spittle ran from the corner of his mouth as he struggled for breath.

"What happened to the woman?" I growled at him.

"Bitch stabbed me," he gasped.

"Where is she?"

"They took her."

"Who took her?"

He said nothing.

I grabbed his shirt and dragged him up. "Who, damn your eyes?"

"O'Farrell. He f-figured that if he couldn't get Chen, then he would take his daughter."

"Shit. Where were they going?"

"To the river."

"Why? Why the river?" I hissed.

"Why do you think?" He chuckled. "She's a damn prostitute. He can make good money for a woman like her."

"He's going to sell her?"

"Get fifty sovereigns at least."

I let him fall back and looked at the tent. I was about to move when I was suddenly hit from behind. I staggered and fell forward, lights flashing through my head. Then, after I tried once to rise, darkness engulfed me, and I was swallowed by silence.

I CAME AWAKE to the bright morning sunlight and the sound of distant crying. My head throbbed but at a level I could live with. The man I'd questioned the night before, amidst the chaos, was dead. His eyes were open, sightless, the blood now dried and blackened.

I climbed to my feet, steadied myself, and then looked around. The devastation was everywhere. In every direction I looked, people were helping the injured. Others limped along by themselves. Tents were destroyed by fire, and those not burned were just misshapen lumps of canvas on the ground. In the daylight, I could see the bodies still hanging from the tall gum.

Crows were helping themselves to a sumptuous breakfast of the dead.

I checked for my Colt and found it where it had spilled. Looking at the tent behind me, I checked for the Martini-Henry rifle, locating it under the bed.

Rubbing at the sore patch on the back of my head, I started walking towards the trail that would lead me to Flintville. From there, I would go to the river.

I never got far before Chen appeared with six of his men.

"Where are you going?" he snarled at me.

"I don't have time for this, Chen," I said to him. I could see in his eyes that his bloodlust was still up, and there was dried blood all over him.

"I have not finished with you yet," he said to me in a cold, distant voice.

"Listen, someone has taken your daughter. I'm going after them. Do not get in my way."

"You will stay away from her," he snapped.

"O'Farrell has taken her to the river. I guess he means to sell her to get at you. I can get her back." I stared at him, trying to see through the bloody façade.

"You will leave her be," he said.

"Then you get her back."

He shook his head. "It is her destiny. If she comes back to me, it will be because it was meant to be."

I stared at him incredulously. "You are going to do nothing?"

"That is right. As are you."

"Then you will have to stop me, Chen, because I'm going to find her and find out what happened to the rest of the Chinese."

With an enraged roar, he came at me with a large knife. I had two choices. I could kill him or waylay him. And as much as I wanted to kill him, I chose not to. Instead, I brought the Martini-Henry's butt up and caught him under the chin. The man stopped dead in his tracks and crashed to the ground, out like a light. His men started forward, attempting to help Chen. I pointed the rifle at the closest one and said, "Stay there until I'm gone."

They stopped and stared at me. Backing away, I went to find a horse. I owned one, but I was guessing that he was long gone.

I was right.

The sound of hoofbeats drew my attention to the riders coming into the devastated camp. They were police, and out front was Superintendent Michael O'Hanlon.

"I thought you were still chasing that bastard Kennedy," I said.

"I haven't chased him for a while," O'Hanlon said. "The scoundrel has gone to ground. And it is a big land out there."

"It is."

He looked around. "What in all kinds of shit has happened here?" he asked me.

"There was a riot," I replied. "The Irish and the Chinese."

"A riot? It looks more like a damnable war."

"You could say that," I said. "You wouldn't have a spare horse, would you?"

"Why?"

"I'm going after O'Farrell."

"When you say after, you mean—"

"I'm going to put the bastard in the ground. Right after he tells me what I want to know."

O'Hanlon climbed down from his horse and said, "Jack, you'd better tell me what happened from the start. Before you bloody go anywhere."

REALIZING that I wasn't getting away without giving more details, but not having the time to waste, I rushed through everything I could. Then he gave me a horse, wished me luck, and told me to be in Brewarrina in a week. As I departed, he reminded me of one thing: "You know you can't marry that girl, Jack. Henry Parkes's legislation."

The legislation stated that there could be no intermarriage or social communion between the British and the Chinese. Part of the anti-Chinese sentiment of the time. But I didn't care about it. They hated manhunters, too.

I left the diggings and rode towards Flintville. The town had started out life as a telegraph station before a store followed, and soon after a pub. Then it became a town supporting the surrounding farmers.

There were no police stationed there, however, a constable rode through once a week. If anything was needed, then a rider would be sent to Walgett.

If you needed information, there was one place to go —the pub. It was always the central meeting place of the local people. Tying my horse's reins to the hitching post out front, I pushed through the doors into the dim interior. The number of patrons inside could be counted on one hand.

Behind the bar was a bald middle-aged man. I nodded at him. "Jim."

"Jack," he replied. "Beer?"

"Don't mind if I do."

He poured me one from a barrel and put it on the countertop. I paid for it, and he said, "I hear there was some trouble out at the diggings."

"You could say that. Multiple dead and loads of wounded, most of those will probably die too."

He let out a low whistle. "That's some count. Not since Lambing Flat have we seen anything like that," he said.

"Even Lambing Flat wasn't that bad."

He nodded.

"Has O'Farrell been through?" I asked.

"He was here. Grabbed some supplies and kept going."

"He had a woman with him. Chinese."

"I think he had someone. Left whoever it was outside. Also had his usual crew with him."

"How long were they here?"

"Not long. Why?"

"The woman he had was stolen from the diggings," I said. "I'm trying to get her back."

He looked puzzled. "Why? She's only bloody Chinee."

"What if that was your wife or daughter, Jim?"

"I'd stand at that doorway out there and wave them off," he said in a low voice. "Can't stand the bloody cow, or that daughter of hers."

"*Your* daughter," I pointed out.

"Not my bloody daughter, mate. Belongs to some travelling salesman, she does. The bitch used to hump anyone who would pay her any attention."

Ignoring his complaints, I asked, "Do you know where he was headed?"

"The river."

"Where on the river?"

"Dunigan's."

"What is Dunigan's?" I asked. I'd never heard of it before.

"A place to steer clear of, Jack," he said, his eyes growing wider. "There's nothing but trouble there. Outlaws and no-goods. Run by an American."

Now he had my attention. "What American?"

"Name of Travis. Him and his sister. And that new wife of his."

My heart skipped. "Clara Watson?"

"That's it. She's been running his boats up and down the river. At first, she had her own, now he lets her run all the freight while he does other stuff."

"What other stuff?" I asked.

"Illegal stuff. Selling Chinee women into prostitution. Down at Bourke. Now that the railroad has reached there and the new gold strike, they'll probably want more."

So, the railroad had finally arrived. I knew that it was close, but now that it was here, things were about to change. And Gold—

"What do you mean, a gold strike?" I asked him.

"It's only a whisper, I heard, but apparently a new seam was discovered out past Brewarrina. Word is he's trying to get a rail spur in there. Lobbying the government for it. They refused, but he's got the governor himself coming out to try and change his mind about it."

I shook my head. "If that was true, Jim, it would be all over the damn country by now."

He shrugged. "I only know what I heard."

"All bullshit if you ask me. But tell me about the Chinese."

"He converted the *Murray Flyer*. Now he's called it the *Virginia*. Made it look like some flash boat. But all he does is transport Chinee on it. No one cares, they've had enough of the bastards."

"Who has he got skippering it?"

"Don't know."

The *Murray Flyer* had been a big boat from what I could remember.

"Just Chinese, Jim?"

"No. He's got all kinds. Whites, Chinee, even darkies."

"You a Chinee lover?" a voice asked from behind me.

I turned and looked. The speaker was a big man, Irish if I wasn't mistaken by the accent. Now, I was in too much of a hurry to be dancing with the likes of him, but he had a look about him that told me he was desperate to waltz. It was Jim who spoke first, however.

"Thomas, you don't want to be messing with this man," he said. "He's done nothing to you."

"He's a Chinee lover, that's enough."

"Let me tell you a story about this gentleman here before you try and go a round of fisticuffs with him. Was about fifteen years back when a young man was tricked into going to Greta after a young tearaway by the name of Edward Kelly."

The man named Thomas seemed to be interested now.

Jim continued. "Tricked into it by a trap named O'Hanlon. Yes, the very same Superintendent O'Hanlon who threatened to lock you up last month, and every other month he sees you. Anyway, that young man went on over to Greta, and before he left, was involved in a damn slugfest with young Kelly. That's right, *the* Edward Kelly. You'd know him better as Ned. Up until then, he'd never been beaten in the gentlemanly art of pugilism. But that young man beat him. And then took him to jail. His name was Jack Crowe, and he's standing at this bar right here."

The Irishman looked at me. Even though I wasn't facing him, I could feel his gaze burning into my back. Then I heard him spit on the floor. "What a lot of fucking horse shit."

I sighed and looked at Jim. He shrugged his shoulders and said, "I tried, Jack."

"I don't have time for this, Jim," I replied.

"You can't shoot him."

"I wish I could." I turned slowly and looked at the Irishman. "If you are going to do this, I wish you'd get it over and done with now so I can keep going about my business."

With a roar, the man charged at me. I waited, he got

closer, I waited some more, and at the last possible moment, I hit him with my right fist. Point of the jaw, any normal man's, the blow would have broken bone. This Mick had the hardest jaw I had ever laid fist to.

He rocked back on his heels, shook his head, and stared at me hard. "If that's all you got, Mr. Chinese lover, you'd best start running."

So, being a man who liked to abide by rules and fairness, I hit him again, without him being ready for it. The result was that I wished it was Ned Kelly on the other end, for this damn Irish bastard was still standing.

He moved in close to me, and I held up my left hand. "Wait!"

He stared at me. "Wait for what?"

"This," I said, and with a fluid movement, I took out the Colt from my belt and smashed it up the side of his head.

He fell like a tree, crashing onto the floor, out cold. I breathed a sigh of relief, as one would do when concerned they were about to be hurt badly but escaped by the hair of one's teeth.

I looked at Jim. "That'll do it," he said.

I put some money on the bar. "Will that get him a bottle?"

"Maybe."

"I think he'll need it when he wakes up."

"I'll see he gets it. Are you going after O'Farrell?"

I nodded. "The bastard owes me a life, and I aim to collect."

15

As I rode into Dunigan's, past a towering river gum, a crow, black as midnight, cawed down at me as though he knew something I didn't. Maybe he thought I was death that had come to claim its next victim. And by the look of the new river town, death was what it already had.

For the second time in two days, I saw a tree with ripe human fruit hanging from the branches. This time, they were Aboriginals, and I could feel my anger rising. They looked to be young men, dressed only in rags around their loins. Probably come out of the desert. Nomads wandering the land as they had done for as long as they could remember.

"They're good darkies, they are," a man said as he walked past. He smiled, a toothless grin exposing rotted stumps that had broken away.

"What did they do?" I asked him.

"Stole some meat."

"Maybe they were hungry," I said.

"Maybe. Didn't do them any good. They was tried, then hanged."

I looked at the tree. "Who tried them?"

"Mr. Travis."

"Why not wait for the magistrate?" I asked.

"No need. Like I said, we had a trial, then a hanging."

"Are there police in town?" I asked.

The man shook his head. "No, sir, we have ourselves a vigilance committee."

The more I heard, the more I was thinking that Dunigan's was a river town in America. The Travis influence.

"Cut them down," I said.

"What?"

"Cut them down."

"Bullshit I will."

"I'll give you some money to do it and bury them," I said.

"How much?"

I dug into my pocket and tossed him a coin. "That should do it."

He looked at the coin and nodded. "Fine."

"Do it properly, or I'll come looking for you."

I left him to it and rode on.

There were new buildings going up. One looked like a store, and the second was a pub. The third appeared to be a large house, two storeys at least.

I eased the horse to a stop outside a large barn and climbed down. A tall, thin man came out to greet me. "Hey, bloke, you looking for a place to leave her?"

"Yes."

"How long for?"

"Couple of days, maybe, I'm not sure."

"Sovereign should do it."

Frowning, I said, "Little on the heavy side."

"Not my doing. Mr. Travis sets the price."

"Mr. Travis owns a lot around here?" I asked.

The man nodded.

"He does," said a new voice.

My blood froze. I'd know that voice anywhere. I turned slowly, and my heart missed a beat. She was still as beautiful as I remembered. "Hello, Clara."

"Hello, Jack."

"Been a while."

"Too long."

"Heard you done well for yourself," I said.

"I see you got out of jail," she replied. There was bitterness in her voice.

"Wasn't there for long," I said. "Long enough for you to get married, though."

"Please don't start, Jack," Clara said. "Whatever we had is gone."

"Amazing what money can do for you." It was my turn to be bitter.

"There will be no charge for Mr. Crowe, Jonah," Clara said. "He's an old friend."

"No worries, missus."

She stared at me. I nodded. "Appreciate it."

Jonah took the mare inside, and once he was gone, Clara asked, "Why are you here, Jack?"

"Looking for O'Farrell."

"Why?"

Going to kill him. "He took something I was attached to."

Her expression changed. "Please don't cause any trouble, Jack. Not here."

"Who said anything about causing trouble? I just came to see O'Farrell."

"Is it about the trouble out at the diggings?" Clara asked.

"Word travels fast."

"He said the Chinese went wild and started killing everybody. He said he was lucky to make it out."

"I think Michael O'Hanlon would disagree with that story."

She stared at me. "Would he? Really? From what I've heard, the Chinese are taking over out there. Stealing from the white miners and killing their own. A man named Chen is the one responsible. Maybe he should be hanged, and it might stop."

She was right about Chen, wrong about the rest. "Where's a good place to stay?"

"There're rooms over the pub," she said. "Tell them I sent you and you'll get it free."

"I can pay my way," I replied.

"Suit yourself. If you would like to join us for dinner tonight, the invitation is there."

I stared at her. What was she trying to do? Rub my face in it? "I'll see if I can make it."

"We'll be in the dining room at the pub around seven."

"All right."

"And stay away from O'Farrell, he's a friend of Charles's."

I watched her walk away. Jonah came out and stood beside me, rubbing his head. "Wow, that's the most I ever heard her speak. You two know each other, I guess."

"It's hard to believe."

I went towards the pub, walking along a dusty street lined with wooden buildings and canvas tents. When I reached it, I noticed how close it was to the river and could see a boat tied to the bank. Instead of entering the pub, I kept walking until I stood on the bank looking at what had once been the *Murray Flyer.* Across the front of the wheelhouse on the second deck was a new sign announcing the *Virginia*.

The top deck looked to be all accommodation now. Cabins for those who took voyage on her. I could only imagine what the bottom deck was like.

"She sure looks a beauty," a well-dressed man with an American accent said beside me. He wore a black frock coat and a top hat.

"It is something," I agreed.

"I saw you talking to my wife up near the barn."

I turned and looked at the man proper. So, this is what Charles Travis looked like. "I guess you don't miss much."

"My town," he said. "I don't miss much."

"I kind of figured that."

"Take those darkies, for instance," he said.

"You mean the Aboriginals?"

"Where I come from, we call them niggers."

"I call them Aboriginals."

"I guess you do. Anyway,"—he held out his hand and opened it, exposing the sovereign I'd given the man to cut down and bury—"here's your money back. Those two *Aboriginals* were left there as an example. There are three more behind the pub in chains, lamenting the mistake they made."

I'd already decided I didn't like this man. Now I was wondering how he was still breathing. "You know this is Australia, right?"

"Australia, America, it's all the same. The natives need to learn who their betters are. What do you think, mister—"

"I don't think," I replied. "I just do. I hear that's your boat."

"Yes, it is. We're headed down to Bourke tomorrow to pick up some important passengers for a cruise. Are you looking for some work? I can always use a new man."

"Doing what?" I asked.

"With the important passengers I'll have, I was thinking of putting on some more security. If you're interested?"

"How do you know you can trust me?" I asked him.

"I figure if my wife knows you, then you should be trustworthy enough."

I thought about it. What he was offering was a chance to discover what was going on. I nodded. "All right. I'll do it."

"And your name?"

"Jack Crowe."

I COULD TELL he wasn't happy when I walked away, but he never went back on his word. I stepped up to the pub and entered, my boots clunking loudly on the boards. There were a few customers, but I expected that it would pick up later. I walked over to the counter, and the man behind it said, "Beer?"

"Room."

"Might have one."

"Mrs. Travis said to come here."

The expression on his thin face changed, his eyebrows rising. "If that's the case, then yes, we've got one. Up the stairs and three along on your left. And don't worry about money, it's no good."

"Fine, I'll have a bottle of rum."

"Yes, sir."

He bent low and came back up with one. "No payment necessary."

I took the bottle, nodded, and went upstairs.

The room was small, tidy, and the bed hard. There was a wash dish on a cupboard and a jug of water beside it.

Placing the bottle next to the dish, I walked over to the window and looked out. It faced the rear of the pub, and I had a clear view of a tall river gum. It was solid, the bark on it almost white. But that wasn't what drew my attention. It had five rings driven into it with chains attached. Three of those chains had metal collars fixed to their ends. Each collar was wrapped around the neck of an Aborigine.

I felt my anger rise and turned away from the window. Then I opened the bottle of rum and took a drink.

I WASN'T QUITE drunk when I went to dinner, but in hindsight, maybe I should have been. It might have made the occasion a little more palatable. Apart from Travis and Clara, we were also joined by O'Farrell and Lady Bettina Henry and her husband, Lord Byron Henry. And Travis's sister Alice. Who, by the way, insisted on me sitting beside her.

Why?

I found out five minutes into a meal of steak and fried potatoes when her hand wandered up my leg and started to massage my crotch.

However, before that event, Travis decided to introduce me to everyone. "Mr. Crowe, allow me to introduce you to Lady and Lord Henry. They will be accompanying us on the river when we leave tomorrow."

"Us?" Clara asked, confused.

"Yes, dear, I hired Mr. Crowe as extra security."

"I see. Is that wise?"

He stared at his wife. "I think so."

"I must say, he looks more than capable," Lady Henry said with a glint in her eye. The woman was in her early forties, and I was starting to think had more than an insatiable thirst for excitement. "Where have you come from, Mr. Crowe?"

"Out at the diggings, missus."

"Oh, dear. Were you there when they had that trouble with those heathen Chinese?"

"I was. Though some might say that the Chinese weren't the main perpetrators of the disturbance."

"He's more than capable, all right, Lady Henry," Alice interrupted. She raised a glass of wine to her lips. "Trust me on that one."

"I gather you know Mr. O'Farrell?"

I turned my head slightly to stare at the Irishman. "You could say that."

"Oh dear," said Alice. "Do I detect a slight hint of animosity between the two gentlemen in question?"

"It's nothing I can't beat into the man," O'Farrell growled.

My hand came up from my lap with the Colt in it. I placed it on the table beside me and said in a low voice, "Mr. O'Farrell, I do believe I would like you to try."

"Good Lord," Clara hissed. "Put that bloody thing away, Jack."

Alice clapped her hands. "Oh, goody, some fun at last in this pathetic little town."

"Now, Miss Alice, do not encourage the ruffian," said Lord Henry.

"Shut up, Alice," Travis snapped. "Put the weapon away, Mr. Crowe, or I shall terminate your employment immediately."

I stared at O'Farrell and then took the gun and tucked it into my belt. Travis nodded. "Right, shall we eat?"

Alice Travis leaned close to my ear and said, "Come to my room tonight. I swear that I could ride your cock until the sun comes up."

It almost worked—between the invitation and her forward advances under the table. But I had other things I was going to take care of that night, and an amorous woman wasn't one of them. However, she might just come in useful.

"DAMN, I'VE MISSED THAT," Alice said as she rolled off me and flopped her head down onto the pillow. "You're like a big bull. None of the young men back home used to excite me like you do, Mr. Crowe. Even some of the women."

"What about Lady Henry?" I asked her, feeling the sting of sweat in the furrows opened by her nails in my back. "She seems quite excitable."

"Oh, good lord, yes. That woman will howl the house down if you give her the chance. Her husband is quite impotent. I think he likes other men." Alice rolled on her side to face me. "You stay away from her. I want you for myself."

"Your wish is my command," I replied.

I felt Alice's hand touch my thigh and then move up. I

said, "I saw some Aboriginals chained to a tree out the back."

Alice sighed. "Yes, my brother's way of showing clemency. Leave them chained up until they die of thirst."

It was my turn. My hand touched her silky-smooth thigh and travelled up the inside of it. Her legs parted instinctively. "I sense you don't like what he does."

She sighed. "Not like that."

I reached the coarse hair of her thatch and stopped. She thrust her hips up slightly, trying to get me to add pressure to the small, hard pea that gave her so much pleasure.

"Why don't you let them go?" I asked her.

"Don't tease me," Alice replied hoarsely.

I added the pressure she sought in a circular motion. Her arm wrapped around my neck as she chased my mouth with hers.

I added more pressure, and she bit the flesh of my shoulder. I said, "Where does he keep the key?"

She whimpered in my ear, her movements becoming quicker. "Keep touching me there," she panted breathlessly.

"Where does he keep the key, Alice?" I asked again. This time, my fingers moved lower. I felt her wetness and slipped two of them inside her warmth.

Then, as she tipped over the edge once more, she gasped, "In the office downstairs. Oh, please, ride me again."

ALICE SLEPT SOUNDLY as I slipped out of her room. It was early morning, and the sun would be up in another hour which meant that I had to move now. I crept down the stairs and found a drunk still asleep in the chair he'd passed out in. As I slipped past him, I could smell where he'd pissed himself, a damp mess beneath him in the dim lamplight. He mumbled something incoherent in his sleep, coughed, and then settled again.

I took the lamp from the bar and lit it. The office was at the rear of the building. Opening the door, I went inside. I searched, finding the key in the drawer of the hardwood desk. Then I went out through the rear door to the tree.

"Who are you?" one of the Aborigines asked me in broken English.

"I am here to help. Do not make a sound."

One by one, I unlocked the collars until they were free. "Go. Get away from here. Do not come back to this place."

"You are a good man," the one who spoke some English said. "Not like the tall hat man."

"Tall hat? Yes, right."

"He keep others across the river. They dig for him."

"What do you mean?"

"Four, five suns that way," the man said, pointing to the southwest. "Big hole. Many dig."

"A mine?"

The man shrugged and walked away, the others following him. I still had more questions, but they would have to wait. In a few hours, I would be on a boat headed downriver. And I still had no idea where An Ni was.

16

BY THE TIME anyone realized that the Aboriginals were gone, they were miles away on the other side of the river. I heard the commotion from my room. Walking over to the window, I saw O'Farrell looking up at me. His glare was all-consuming, so I did what anyone else would do —I waved.

When I arrived downstairs, the drunk was gone, but the dampness remained. The Irishman was in a fit of rage, explaining how the Aborigines were gone and that he suspected I was the one responsible. Travis looked at me and said, "Well? What have you got to say for yourself, Crowe?"

"Wasn't me," I lied with a shrug.

"Prove it," O'Farrell snapped.

"What's all the commotion about?" Clara asked as she entered the bar. Gone was the dress from the night before, replaced by britches and a shirt with a coat.

"Crowe let the Aborigines loose," O'Farrell snapped.

"Good," she replied with finality. "The way they were treated was barbaric."

I looked at Travis, who remained silent. There was a smouldering resentment in his eyes at being rebuked by his wife, but he remained focused on me. "You haven't denied it, Crowe."

"It wasn't him," Alice said from across the room, where she sat playing solitaire with a deck of cards. "He was with me."

Travis stared at me, his gaze uncertain. After a moment, he nodded and said, "I want the boat ready to sail in the next hour. I want no further trouble."

"What do you want me to do?" I asked him.

"Find a man called Rivers. Tell him what I just told you. Tell him I want the cargo loaded. He'll be somewhere, just ask around."

I nodded. "Yes, sir."

I left the pub, decidedly relieved that my alibi had held up. I tracked down the man named Rivers at the gunsmith's shop. He was buying a new rifle, which looked like a Snider .557 carbine. "You Rivers?" I asked.

"That's me," he said without turning around.

"Travis says he wants you on the boat within the next hour. He wants the cargo loaded."

The man named Rivers turned and faced me. Looking at him, I recognised him as a scoundrel from down around Hay. His name was Ferris, and he was wanted by the police for robbery and attempted murder.

"Who are you?"

"New man, hired for added security."

"What's your name?"

"Jack Crowe."

His eyes flared and then settled. He knew who I was but tried to remain calm about it. Maybe he hoped I hadn't recognised him. He paid for the rifle and said,

"Come on then, let's get ready. You take your orders from me."

I followed him along the street to a large building. There were two men, both armed, standing outside. They looked at Rivers. The ruffian said, "Get them out, they need to be on the boat."

The building resembled a large barn, but the double doors were barred on the outside. One of the men lifted the metal bar and swung the right-side door open. Then both men disappeared into the dark interior.

At first, all I heard was them barking orders but then came the rattle of chains. Slowly, one at a time, the intended cargo appeared. Chained around the ankles, chained together at the neck by collars.

"What's this?" I asked Rivers.

"The cargo, what the fuck you think it is?"

"But they're people?"

"No. They're fucking Chinee. They don't count."

At first, it was the men. I counted fifteen. Then came the women. Six of them. One was An Ni.

She saw me, and before she could say or do anything, I gave my head a slight shake. "Where are they going?" I asked Rivers.

"The women are going to Bourke. They'll be sold into prostitution for the miners and railroad workers. They go through them like a good dose of the shits down there."

"What about the men?"

"Don't damn worry. Just get them on the frigging boat."

We escorted the bedraggled group along the street towards the river. I walked along at the tail end, where I could keep an eye on An Ni. Dust rose into the hot morning air as they shuffled along. The prisoners looked dejected, accepting of whatever their fate may be. As we passed the pub, Travis was standing on the veranda watching his property parade by. Clara was standing beside him, her face impassive. I couldn't for the life of me work out how she could condone what her husband was doing.

Then I saw something else that gave me concern. As far as I knew, there was no police presence in Dunigan's. Yet here was a trap standing beside Travis. And he was smiling. This was slavery, and it was illegal. But it looked as though money once again spoke volumes.

The river level was up. I guessed there was still water coming down from Queensland.

The Chinese were walked down the bank and onto the gangplank. Then onto the boat. The lower deck had been stripped out and rings installed on the floor where chains could be attached to them.

Once the group was inside, Rivers said, "Chain them down."

"How?"

He tossed me some keys. "They'll help."

I started locking them to the rings, one at a time. When I reached An Ni, I said in a hushed voice, "Are you all right?"

"Are you with them now?" she asked in a harsh whisper.

"No, I came after you?"

"Why would you do that? I'm just a fucking Chinee prostitute."

"Do you want to be sold in Bourke?" I asked her, an edge to my voice. "Do you?"

"What can you do?"

"I don't know, but I'll do something. Just hang in there."

Once they were all secured, I went back outside and found Rivers talking to O'Farrell. The conversation was animated, and they focused their gazes on me once they realised I was there. Rivers went back ashore while O'Farrell walked over to me. "I don't know what your game is, Crowe, but if I get my way, you'll be sitting at the bottom of the river with a blasted rock tied to your feet."

"Maybe I should just kill you now, O'Farrell and get it over and done with." I shook my head. "No, I'll wait. But rest assured, death is coming."

I could see in the black-heart's eyes that my words had gotten to him, and he turned and walked away. I had the sudden feeling that I was being watched, and I turned to see Clara staring.

I walked over to her. "You've changed," I said.

"This bastard country will do that," she replied. "I'm not the only one."

"You shouldn't come on this trip, Clara," I said to her.

"Why? What are you up to?"

"Your husband is a slave trader," I pointed out.

"They're only Chinese, Jack."

"You don't believe that, Clara."

She stared at me for a long moment. "It was you, wasn't it?"

"Was me what?"

"That let the Aborigines go?"

"Didn't you hear Alice? I was with her."

"She wants you to keep humping her, of course she'll say that."

Her words were bitter as though she wanted it to be her. But she'd made her choice, and there was no going back. "What does he do with the Chinese men?"

"I guess you will find out," Travis said from behind me.

I turned and saw him holding a gun on me. Beside him, O'Farrell did the same. "Chain him up with the others."

"What for?" I asked, trying to play for time so I could react. I could go over the side into the water or take my chances going for one of their guns. Neither was good. So, I chose the third option. Stay alive while I can and wait for an opportunity to arise.

MY BODY ACHED, my head hurt, and somewhere in the distance, the dull chug of the river boat could be heard. They had beaten me before chaining me with the Chinese. I guess they thought I'd be less of a threat that way. I moaned and heard An Ni say, "Are you all right?"

I looked at her through my one good eye. The other was already swollen shut. "I feel like shit. How long have we been on the river?"

My voice wasn't much more than a dry croak.

"A few hours. They beat you bad."

I lay there, the throb of the riverboat's motor vibrating through the floor, surprisingly relieving. Around my neck was an iron collar, which I could feel biting into my flesh. My feet and wrists were chained. The sun was still up, and the sound of the steam whistle blowing was long and mournful. I sensed someone standing over me and opened the good eye once more. It was O'Farrell.

"Right where you belong," he gloated. "I must say, you don't look too bad."

"Just goes to show the coward that you are," I grated.

Maybe I should have kept my mouth shut because my words elicited a kick to my ribs, which were already bruised. A cry of pain escaped my split lips, opening them, allowing fresh blood to seep through the cracked scabs.

"Shut your mouth," O'Farrell growled.

I gasped in agony and rolled away from him, the chains rattling. I heard his footsteps retreating and started to tremble as the pain radiated through my entire body.

"Crowe?" An Ni whispered.

"What?" I managed.

"Are you okay?"

"What the hell do you think?"

She never said any more after that, just left me to my pained misery and my steadily building anger.

We kept sailing downstream until dark, when Clara nosed the boat into the eastern bank where it was tied up for the night. I assumed it was to avoid the possibility of snags, but what did I know? I was chained to a ring, anchored to the deck, with an uncertain future.

There was nothing for me to do but lie there listening to the wash of the river as it slopped against the hull of the *Virginia*. Every now and then, a low moan would pierce the false lit gloom. Then I sensed someone standing over me. I opened my good eye and saw that it was a woman. A familiar voice said, "I didn't want this, Jack."

"Well, you got it, in spades, Clara. What I can't work out is why?"

"Charles is charming, funny, wealthy—"

"A rogue."

"I didn't know that until after we were married."

"A bit late then."

"Quite," she replied. "I want to help you."

"Don't bother, I can help myself." Suddenly, I was angry. "You were meant to wait. We were going to be married."

"I know, Jack, I'm sorry. But when news came through that you were in jail for murder, I started to have doubts. Then Charles started saying things and—"

"What things?" I demanded.

"About how you would be hanged. At best, spend the rest of your life in Dubbo gaol."

"And you listened to him."

"How could I not? I was alone. I had no one."

"You had me."

"We could still be together, Jack," Clara whispered.

"No, we can't."

"Why? It's not like there is anyone else."

I remained silent.

When there was no response forthcoming, she asked, "Is there someone else, Jack?"

"Go back to your husband, Clara. He'll be wondering where you are."

Her breath caught in her throat. "I—I'm sorry, Jack."

"Yeah, me too."

She disappeared, and for a while I lay there in the quiet. Then, "Jack?"

"Yes, Annie?"

"Why?"

"Why what?"

"Why didn't you help her?"

"Because I'm busy helping someone else."

The silence came again for just a moment. Then the sound of a body shuffling on the deck, dragging a chain. An Ni said, "I can't reach you, Jack. My hand."

I reached back toward the voice. I felt her hand, and

we grasped at each other. "What do we do now, Jack?" An Ni asked me.

"We stay alive, Annie. Whatever it takes, we stay alive."

THERE HAD BEEN a reason the *Virginia* had pulled into the riverbank the night before. And just as the sun was creeping its way over the eastern horizon, bathing the landscape in an orange hue, we were woken by O'Farrell and Rivers.

All of the men, including myself, and some of the women as well, were unlocked from the deck rings and made to stand up. Myself, I took a little longer than the others, eventually helped by a couple of the Chinese miners. I glanced at An Ni before they led us out and winked my one good eye at her. I said in a low voice, "I'll be back."

"Who the fuck are you talking to?" Rivers snarled.

I turned my head slowly. "You, Ferris."

"Rotten bastard," he growled. "I knew you frigging knew who I was."

"I was going to leave you, Ferris," I said to him. "Now I changed my mind. I'll kill you like the rest."

The killer glanced at O'Farrell. "I told you he knew who I was, O'Farrell. Now he's going to come after me."

"Stop your bleating," the Irishman scowled. "He's going nowhere except out west. No one ever comes back from there. Now, get them on deck."

We shuffled out onto the deck of the *Virginia*. I remember seeing Alice Travis pouting off to the side. She said, "It's a pity. You were such a good hump."

"Most of the devilish ones are," Lady Henry joined in. "A shame I never got to taste the rotten fruit."

"My dear, Lady," Alice said, "the fruit was far from rotten."

These women were touched, I was sure of that. Somewhere etched deep in the memories of my beating, I recalled Lady Henry touching herself as she watched on, excited by the open display of violence. Crazy, the whole bloody lot of them.

The gangway was lowered, and we were paraded up the bank and into the shade of a tall river gum. I looked back at the boat and saw Clara in the wheelhouse. Instead of staring back, she looked away.

A shout from one of the deckhands drew their attention to the plain beyond. Through my one good eye, I could make out the five people approaching. Four riders and a man driving a horse-drawn dray.

At first, I couldn't make out who it was, for the wind was blowing towards us and the dust they were creating acted like a smokescreen. Then once they were close enough, I could see the lead rider. I knew him from a long time back. A scoundrel who should have been hanged without prejudice.

John Kennedy. Wanted man, murderer, bushranger. And the man I had sworn to kill.

The others were with him. Matthew Hill, Mike Gardner, the mad dog kid Billy Wilson, and my old friend George. He was the first to recognise me. "Hello, boss."

"Not your boss anymore, George," I replied.

"You always my boss, Jack."

"Seems like you're with the wrong people this time, George."

"Well, well, well, the manhunter himself."

I looked up at Kennedy. "I always knew we'd cross paths again one day, John. I see you still have my rifle."

He held up the Winchester. It was battered and scratched on the butt from its hard life. "I still have that Colt, too."

A high-pitched giggle reached my ears, and I looked to see Billy Wilson poking at one of the Chinese girls. "I see you haven't put the cur down yet."

"As with all mongrels, you treat them right, give them some food, and you can get them to do almost anything."

Wilson turned his head and looked at Kennedy, an evil grin on his face. "Can I have her, John?"

Kennedy looked at me. "See what I mean?" He turned back to Wilson. "You'll have to wait until we get back."

"I can do that." He giggled.

They began loading us all onto the dray. I guessed there was no way a man could work if he was worn out from walking to wherever he was going. About ten minutes after we were loaded, they set off, headed southwest into the unknown.

As we left the river, I looked back at the boat, knowing that the person I loved, and who infuriated me the most, was still aboard. And I was going to come back and set her free.

THE TERRAIN of the countryside was mostly flat with red dirt and stunted scrub. Larger trees were scattered around, and there were many washed-out gullies. We followed a trail which suggested it had been used many times before. Crows and galahs accompanied us as we moved through the shimmering heat haze. We saw the odd kangaroo, but most seemed to be sheltering out of the heat, unlike us, who were suffering with it.

The Chinese were tough, I had to give them that. They uttered not one word, choosing to suffer in silence. Me, I wasn't so forgiving.

"Must we travel in the heat of the day?" I asked Kennedy.

"The more ground we cover, the sooner we get there," the bushranger said.

"Dead men won't do you much good," I pointed out.

The former trap knew I was right and gave orders to pull off the trail into the shade of a large gum. While we were there, we were given tepid water from a barrel and some dried meat that was like chewing bark off a wattle. I lay on my back looking up through the branches of the tree above when George came over to me.

"Your eye no good, boss."

"It isn't, is it?"

"I fix for you."

He retrieved a knife from his pocket and held it up.

"Whoa. What are you going to do with that?"

"I cut it and then all the blood comes out," he explained.

"You don't want to clean it first?" I asked him.

George nodded. "Okay, boss."

Before I knew what was happening, George had his cock out and was pissing on the knife blade. I was astounded by this and blurted out, "What are you doing?"

"It clean, boss."

"I'm not your boss."

He tucked himself away and shook off the excess piss from the blade. "Keep still."

I'm not sure which shocked me more. The fact that

he was about to cut me or the fact that he was going to use a piss-covered knife to do it, and I was going to let him.

The razor-sharp blade bit into flesh, and I felt the pressure release instantly, then came the warmth of the blood running down my face. George grabbed a mug and washed it with water from the barrel. "There, boss."

I tore a strip of fabric from my shirt and pressed it against the cut. "Thanks, George."

He grinned at me. "Don't worry, the piss not hurt you."

I chuckled. "What happened, George?"

He looked at me, his expression changing. "Them white fellas came after me. The traps. Wanted to lock me up."

"After they got me?" I asked.

"Yes."

"Now you're with Kennedy."

"Yes."

"Hey, what are you doing, you darkie bastard?" Kennedy growled.

"I'm helping my friend."

"You stay the hell away from him."

AFTER THE BRIEF respite in the shade, we travelled for the rest of the day and then bedded down for the night beside a waterhole. The prisoners were chained together so they couldn't run. The sky was cloudless that night, and it got cold quickly. I slept in fits and starts until, at one point, I woke and heard a low whimpering in between an animalistic grunting sound. I opened my eyes and could see by the low glow of the firelight, a pair of buttocks thrusting savagely. It only took me a moment to work out that Billy Wilson couldn't wait and was raping one of the Chinese women.

I moved my hand until I found a rock. As I did, I realised that my eye had gone down considerably. I picked the rock up and threw it at the kid, hitting him.

He stopped what he was doing and looked around. I saw the knife he had in his hand. "Who did that?" he snapped.

"I did, you bastard of a whore."

He came to his feet with a snarl, pulling his pants up. I came to mine. Even though I was chained, I could still stand. The kid stalked towards me, holding his knife out in front like he meant to use it.

"I'm going to kill you, Crowe," he snarled at me.

"You'd better make sure you do, kid, because mongrel dogs like you deserve to die."

He came at me, and I hit him before he could do any damage with the knife. He staggered back and wiped blood from his mouth.

"Enough!" Kennedy snarled from the darkness.

He stepped forward into the orange light of the fire. "Kid, get back to your bedroll."

"I'm not done with the bastard yet, John."

"I say you are. Now, get lost."

The kid stomped off, muttering under his breath. Kennedy looked at me and said, "That boy will kill you, Crowe."

"You've got little faith in me, Kennedy," I replied.

"I just know the type of coward he is."

He left after that, and I managed to go back to sleep.

THE FOLLOWING morning dawned bright and warm, and we were moving before the sun got too high in the sky.

Wilson watched me as we progressed ever westward. The country stayed flat, and the scrub thinned out some. That night we stayed by a waterhole, much like the one we'd camped by last night, and then were up early the following morning to repeat the mile-eating drudgery of the day before.

After the beating that I had sustained, I was now regaining my strength. My eye, with the pressure released, was improving.

At some point after noon, the landscape changed again and became a little hillier. Then I saw the line of trees in the distance, which indicated a water course. Beyond that was the scarified landscape of an open-cut mine.

We crossed the creek and stopped at the edge of the pit. As I looked down, I finally realised what had happened to all the missing Chinese.

17

IN THE TIME that it took us to cover the distance to the mine, An Ni was going through an ordeal of her own. The *Virginia* had kept on down the river to Bourke. In Bourke at that time, the railway had reached its terminus. The new station had opened as well—a grand sight it was.

The railway brought with it an opportunity for the people of Sydney to venture west, and another for freight to be moved directly to the city in previously unheard-of quick times. Eventually, the railway would be the death knell of the river boats.

For An Ni, however, it was just the beginning of her ordeal.

Once the *Virginia* arrived in Bourke, the women were taken ashore and moved to a place across the river, much like a large block-built barn, where they were kept away from the rest of the population.

An Ni, still chained to the others, kept to herself. Then, two hours after they arrived, Travis and O'Farrell appeared with a gentleman in his late forties dressed in a suit and top hat.

"Stand up," Travis snapped at the women.

Their chains rattled as they got to their feet, and he walked around inspecting them as though they were sheep or cattle. He turned to Travis and said, "No darkies this time? The members like the darkies, you know?"

"I'll see what I can do the next time."

The man looked at them thoughtfully. "I suppose they'll do. But I'll not pay top price like last time. This lot—"

He stopped and focussed his gaze on An Ni. "Her. I'll pay top price for her. She's a pretty little thing, I'd wager, under all that dirt. Yes, I'll pay top price for her."

The man's name was Collier, Howard Collier, as An Ni would find out later, and he owned a gentlemen's club in Sydney. One that catered to the needs of upper-class gentlemen desiring a little more out of life. "Get the chains off her. I want to have a better look."

O'Farrell looked at Travis. The American nodded, and the Irishman unlocked the shackles. He grabbed An Ni by the arm and dragged her forward. She struggled against his will, and he was about to strike her when Collier snapped, "Don't you dare."

O'Farrell glared at the man, but Collier ignored the Irishman's hot gaze as he stepped forward.

Collier stood close to An Ni, staring into her defiant eyes. He moved suddenly and ripped open her bodice with a violent jerk, exposing her breasts. He squeezed them, pinching the nipples until they hardened. "A touch small, but a good corset will fix that. Has anyone fucked her?"

"Not since we picked her up from the gold field," O'Farrell said.

"Pity she isn't untouched, but she will do."

"Arsehole," An Ni hissed in a low voice.

Collier's hand streaked out from his side and grabbed her hair. He dragged her head back until it felt as though it could go no further. He leaned in close until she could feel his hot breath on her cheek. "I prefer not to beat respect into you, girl, but I will if I have to. Do as I command of you, and you will be treated better than these other whores. If not, I will put you with them until you are worn out and throw you into the gutter once it is so. Do you understand?"

An Ni felt hot tears come to her eyes. Suddenly, she realised that Collier was a very dangerous man. Worse than any other she had encountered before. She nodded jerkily.

"Good," Collier said, releasing her hair. He turned to Travis. "Now, I want her cleaned up. She will travel with me in my carriage."

"Yes, Mr. Collier," Travis replied.

Collier smiled. "I must say, now that the railway is here in Bourke, it's a lot more convenient than travelling by coach."

He turned back to An Ni. "You will be ready to leave tomorrow. Your life will change forever. Is there anything you want?"

An Ni stared at him. "Yes. Opium."

AN NI WAS TAKEN to a bathhouse to bathe and given new clothes. Then she was put in a locked room in one of the many hotels. It was just after dark when the door opened, and Clara entered. An Ni stared at Clara, her disdain evident. "What do you want?"

"To talk, nothing more."

"What about?"

"Jack."

"You made your decision," she said to Clara.

"Do you love him?"

The question startled her. She'd never really considered it before. "I—I don't know. Maybe."

"I think he loves you," Clara told her. "And that would be a mistake for him."

An Ni just stared at her.

Clara continued. "He could never marry you. It would be best if you forgot about him."

"Careful," An Ni said sarcastically. "The dragon's claws are out."

"Don't be ridiculous," Clara snapped.

"You are jealous, I can see it in your eyes."

"I have a husband."

"But you are not happy. Your husband is nothing more than a criminal and a murderer. Now you are trapped in his world, and the only way out for you is Jack."

"Jack is gone," Clara hissed at her.

"Jack will be back," An Ni scoffed. "You know it, and I know it. And when he returns, people will die. You know what he is like. You hope he will be your saviour."

"Yes," Clara snapped. "Yes, I know what he is like. And yes, I hope he returns. And *yes,* I want him to be my bloody saviour. Which also means that you not being here bodes well for me."

"You are a dreamer," An Ni said. "He is not the man you once knew. He has changed. You changed him. He has become colder, yet he still has the ability to love—*me*. He loves *me*."

"He will forget you, for when he comes, I will remind

him of what we once had, and he will come back to me. We had more than you can ever offer him."

"I can offer him me. It is more than you ever have."

Clara stared at An Ni and then stormed from the room.

An Ni straightened, feeling stronger than she had ever done before in her life.

THE WHISTLE SCREAMED its warning that the train was leaving and that those wishing to travel needed to board, otherwise be left behind. An Ni walked timidly forward, one step behind Collier, one step in front of his man, an ugly brute who was broad across the shoulders and had a scar on his right cheek. Collier had introduced him as Hall. Nothing else.

They climbed aboard the train. Collier's carriage was lavish and spoke of money. An Ni had never seen anything so opulent before and couldn't help but stand agog when she stepped into the coach, not sure where to look first.

"Do you like it?" Collier asked, as though her approval meant everything to him.

She looked at him. The man seemed almost caring, gentlemanly. "I've never seen anything like it before."

"I spent a lot of money on this carriage. My thinking is that if I have to travel, then I might as well travel in style."

The lounge along the wall was hand-carved with velvet coverings. There were landscape paintings on the wall and a large bed pressed tight into the carriage corner. "Where will I sleep?" An Ni asked.

Collier smiled. "With me, of course. I must be sure that my clients will get what they are paying for."

"Of course. Do you have opium?"

The man frowned. "Yes, why?"

"It makes for a much better experience," An Ni said. *For me, especially, you fucking pig.*

Collier looked at Hall. "Where is it?"

"I will get it, sir," Hall replied. His voice sounded like a cross between a seal and a dog's low growl.

An Ni sat down on the lounge and patted it. "Come, sit beside me, Mr. Collier. We might as well start getting to know each other now."

Collier licked his lips nervously. He'd never known a Chinese woman to act like this before. It excited him and made him wary. "You are a little minx, aren't you?"

He stood in front of her, and she reached out for the buttons on his flies. Suddenly, he struck her, hard, with an open hand. Shocked, An Ni sat back, tasting the blood on her lips.

Collier's eyes blazed with fire. "Let's get one thing straight," he growled deeply. "I am the boss, not you. You do what I say."

"Yes, sir," An Ni answered meekly.

He smiled, satisfied she now understood. "So, where were we?"

THANK GOODNESS FOR OPIUM. An Ni breathed a sigh of relief as Collier moaned in his sleep beside her, gently rocking with the motion of the train. The man fucked like a pig, grunting, dribbling saliva onto her back as he ran his tongue through the cleft of her arse.

When he came, he squealed like a pig as well, ejaculating all his seed upon her pale stomach as she pretended to scream in arousal.

Then once he was done, the opium took hold, and Collier fell fast asleep, and she hoped he would remain that way for the next six or seven hours.

He lasted one before waking and taking her again.

Now, as Collier slept, An Ni went through the practice of cleansing herself.

Once completed, she looked out the window as the red landscape flicked by. Trees and washed-out gullies and emus and more trees. The terrain was harsh and cruel and dry. And it took harsh and cruel people to live out here.

She just hoped that I was that type of man.

I WATCHED them hang a man that day. He was taken from a group of men, dragged across to a scaffold where a rope was thrown over. The rope was looped around his neck, and from there, it was wound around the pommel of a saddle, and the horse beneath it walked forward.

If you've ever seen a man hanged, you will never forget such a ghastly sight. Legs kicking, eyes bulging, pissing himself, struggling, fighting for life.

His only crime was disobeying a directive. Kennedy had made an example of him. Just another reason for me to kill the man.

I grabbed the handle of the pick and started to hack at the rock face. I let my frustration flow through the digging tool as I worked on my section. We all had sections. We worked there all day, digging and loading rock into bins where they would be carried away and sorted for gold. We were fed before we started work, and we were stopped three times a day. For water in the morning. For water in the afternoon, and just on dark when we ate and were marched to a set of barracks where we were housed for the night. They didn't chain us, there was no need.

Anyone who tried to escape was flogged with a stockwhip. The women worked alongside the men, and no mercy was given. And of a night, if the guards wanted a little extra, they took it.

"Jack? Jack Crowe?" The voice was whispered through the barracks until I answered.

"What?"

"Where are you?"

"Over here."

I sat up and leaned against the wall. Out of the gloom, my eyes picked up the movement of a man coming towards me. "I was told you were here."

"Who—" Suddenly, I realised the voice—Jim Craig. My business partner I'd left in charge of the freight company we worked together. "Jim Craig?"

"Aye, it's me."

"Goodness, Jim, what are you doing here?"

"The bastards picked me up on the road a month ago." He spat on the floor. "Fucking traps."

"Wait. What do you mean?"

"The bastard has traps on his payroll. They stopped me on the road to Craiglea Station. Went through my freight and accused me of stealing."

"What officer?"

"Sergeant Moore."

"Never heard of him."

"He's a right bastard. Last I heard, he was riding with O'Hanlon."

I froze. "Are you saying O'Hanlon is involved in this?"

"He might be. He's been chasing all around the colony for Kennedy, and strangely enough, the bastard hasn't caught him."

"I can't imagine Michael O'Hanlon being a black heart, Jim."

"I guess that remains to be seen, doesn't it. What are your plans?"

"We're going to get out of here."

"How?"

"I don't know, yet."

"Someone come!" The harsh whisper came from the front of the barracks.

Jim Craig squeezed in beside me, and we pretended we were asleep. The door opened, and a figure filled the void. Footsteps came towards us. I kept one eye opened and saw who the scoundrel was—Billy Wilson, who had come to pay his dues.

He stood above me, looking down, a knife in his hand. I tensed, ready to spring when he made his move. Then, surprisingly, he turned and walked away.

Once he was gone, I said to Jim, "Tomorrow night we will take this camp and free the miners. Do you know anyone who will help?"

"A few."

"Then tomorrow night it is. Bring them here. They think the Chinese are a cowed people. I know different."

CRAIG LEFT ME SHORTLY AFTER, while I went to work making plans in my head. Not that there was much of a plan to be made. We would take out the guards and Kennedy's men and then the bastard himself.

The sun was up and hot, early the following morning. Galahs greeted the prisoners with their chirps while cockatoos just screeched at us. We ate a meal of rice and maggots. Not very appetising, but we did our best to pick the little wrigglers out. Craig sat beside me as we softly discussed what we would try to do that night.

"We have to work in groups," I told him. "Kill the guards and then Kennedy's bastards."

"We will be able to get guns and use them," Craig whispered.

"No," I said, my stare unwavering so he would get the message. "We need to do this quietly for as long as possible."

"Have you thought what we will do once we take the camp?"

"We will worry about that when the time comes."

For the rest of the day, we worked. I was toiling at the bottom of the cut on a section that the mining supervisor wanted a quartz vein followed. It was deep and meant that we would have to tunnel. He brought down dynamite for blasting. It wasn't the first time it had been used since I'd been there.

Using hand drills on the hard rock, the dynamite was then inserted into the bores. The heat was oppressive down in the cut, and sweat rolled off us as though the outback skies had opened and dumped heavy rain upon us without the benefit of being cooled down.

Flies drank persistently at our sweat, and men slumped down exhausted. But we got the rock face ready, and the dynamite was inserted. Fuses were set, and while the supervisor prepared for blasting, he left the dynamite unsupervised. I contemplated taking some and putting them down my pants. Then I remembered how we were searched every day when we left the pit.

"Everyone, get back out of the cut," the supervisor growled at us.

We retreated to the top of the cut while he lit the fuses. Then he followed us to the top, and we waited.

The deep boom of the explosion rolled across the desert, causing birds to take flight from the trees. The ground seemed to vibrate in ever-increasing waves, and as we stood there watching, the rock face bulged, then cracks opened in it before it burst outward like an exploding bubble.

Dust rose into the air like grey smoke from a fire. Rocks eventually settled, and we were ordered back to work.

For the rest of the day, we removed the rubble that resulted from the blast. It was hot, tiresome work, and men died from it.

IT WAS mid-afternoon when things took a surprising turn. A chain gang was formed, and we were using baskets to move the rubble. We'd encountered more falling rocks and debris from the blasting, but it was the heat that killed. Heat and lack of water.

A Chinese miner fell at my feet as he passed me a rock-filled basket, spilling its load. One of the guards came up and kicked the worn-out man in the ribs. "Get up, you lazy Chinee prick."

"Leave him, he's done in," I said. "He needs water."

"Shut your mouth and get back to work." He hovered over the fallen man and drew his foot back.

"Don't—"

His face screwed up, and he took a swipe at me. I moved swiftly, blocked the blow, and knocked him down with one of my own. He scrambled to get his pistol out to shoot me, so I was forced to follow up and kick him in the mouth, shattering teeth.

It felt good, and I was tempted to do it again. But one of the other guards had witnessed the event and shouted a warning, pointing his rifle at me.

Stepping back, I raised my hands. The other guard checked on his fallen comrade and pointed at two other miners. "Help him to his feet and take him up top."

The timid Chinese miners did as they were ordered and helped the stunned guard to his feet. The guard stepped in close to me and snarled like a slavering dog. "You're going to fucking pay for that, bastard. Will be the bite of the stockwhip you'll be feeling before the day is out. Cuts deep it does."

I stared at him, my jaw set firm.

"Get moving," he snapped.

I turned and began making my way out of the pit. Once I was up at the top, Kennedy saw what was happening and headed towards us. "What's going on?"

"The bastard put Tom down. Beat the shit out of him."

Kennedy's eyes narrowed as he stared at me. "Maybe the stockwhip might pull his horns in some."

"That's what I was thinking." The guard gave a sly grin.

Kennedy was about to say more when hoofbeats sounded, and we turned our heads to see horses approaching us. For a moment, I thought it was the heat playing tricks on my eyes, and I shook my head to clear my vision of the confusing sight.

Alas, it was no such thing. It wasn't the heat, and

what I saw was real. Four riders, each in a police uniform. One was black, three were white. One was a sergeant, another was Superintendent Michael O'Hanlon.

"Shit."

18

I STARED AT THE POLICEMAN, not wanting to believe what I was seeing. The horses were eased to a halt, their coats lathered in sweat and dust. The Irishman turned his head, and his gaze locked onto mine.

"I knew you'd wind up here eventually, boyo. All I had to do was let you do your thing."

"You treacherous fuck," I snarled at him.

"Language, son," he cautioned me. "No one likes a foul-mouthed bastard."

"Step down, O'Hanlon, I'll give you fucking foul-mouthed."

The guard who'd marched me up from the pit smashed the butt of the rifle he held, into the lower part of my spine. Pain shot through my body, and I buckled at the knees. I choked off a cry of pain, but my eyes filled with tears as the agony of the blow coursed through me.

My knees landed in the dirt, causing a small puff of dust to rise. I groaned.

"Bastard."

"What are you doing here, O'Hanlon?" Kennedy demanded.

"Travis wants another shipment sent out as soon as possible."

"He's not meant to receive it until the end of the month."

"There have been some issues."

"What issues?"

"Lawful ones."

"That's your problem," Kennedy growled. "That's what he pays you for."

Something wasn't right. I knew O'Hanlon well enough that when he lied, he always picked at the buttons on his uniform with his right hand. He was doing that now.

My gaze diverted to the surrounding landscape when I saw the movement. There were more men in the bush. Was O'Hanlon part of this or something else entirely?

The air was pierced by a warning shout, and chaos ensued. Men went for weapons, and gunfire filled the air.

Me? I dived for the ground, for there is nothing worse than being in the middle of a gunfight without a gun.

Birds took flight as soon as the first shots cracked out. I saw a guard fall, his brains exploding from the back of his head, thanks to a heavy-calibre bullet. Then I saw a trooper fall—the sergeant. I'd never seen him before, and his name was unknown to me, but he died fighting, two bullets in his chest from Matthew Hill.

The trap fell nearby, giving me the opportunity to pick up his pistol. My right hand clawed at the dirt, falling short of the weapon. I lurched forward and grabbed it, pulling it back just as the front hoof of the sergeant's horse stomped down where my hand had been.

I rolled onto my back and brought the Colt revolver up. I fired twice at the nearest killer, and Mike Gardner died with an ugly hole in his throat, blood running like a red curtain down the bastard's chest.

He fell to his knees, eyes wide, as the last thoughts he had turned to *why it was happening to him*. I, on the other hand, had turned my attention to Hill. He had moved his own gun towards me and was squeezing the trigger. The pistol he held bucked, sending the bullet exploding from the barrel to bury itself into the ground beside me.

The Colt I held fired once more, and I saw the bullet strike the killer in the arm. I cursed and fired again. The hammer fell onto a spent cartridge that the sergeant had burned through.

A cold smile spread across Hill's face. "Got you, you son of a prostitute cow," he shouted over the gunfire.

My hand came up and over as I threw the useless Colt at him. The move took him by surprise, but he was nimble enough to dodge out of the way even though wounded. The grin was still on his face, and I knew at that time I was a dead man.

I waited to die.

A shot came.

Hill died.

My head whipped around, and I saw George standing there with a smoking revolver in his hand. He smiled at me, and then his head exploded.

I lurched with surprise as he dropped to the ground, dead. Killed by Billy Wilson, who was living up to his name, grinning like a mad dog. But instead of turning on me, he turned and shot O'Hanlon, who'd already been shot once by the mongrel Kennedy.

The second shot helped the Irishman from the saddle as he toppled sideways, his hand losing its grip on the Colt and the other the saddle as he fell.

Dodging the dead sergeant's prancing horse, I scrambled towards the fallen superintendent. As I grabbed his Colt, he growled, "The bastards got me good, Jack. Blasted good, boyo."

"Just shut up and save your strength," I snapped, and looked through his ammunition pouch. I took out some cartridges and put them into my pocket. Then I turned and looked for the mad dog kid.

I saw him, wild-eyed, firing his gun, knife in his other hand. He'd shot the third of O'Hanlon's traps and was now turning his attention to the fallen man.

The policeman was still alive and held his right hand up in defence of himself. Not that it was much good. I heard Wilson cackle hysterically as he shot the policeman. But not to kill him, he shot him in the stomach, sentencing him to a long, painful death.

But then I watched on in horror as the kid knelt and used his knife, drawing it slowly across the fallen man's throat. Why put one in his stomach?

My anger rose, and I rushed forward, the Colt gripped tightly in my fist. The kid turned and saw me coming, fumbling hastily to bring his gun around to shoot me, but missed. I shot him, though, through the arm, so that he dropped that weapon.

But the bastard still had his knife, and my anger hadn't abated. So the Colt I held spoke again, and this time the bullet bit deep into his other arm, and the blade fell from his grasp. In pain, he sank to his knees, the blood dripping from his hands into the dry dirt as he held them out to his side.

I raised the Colt and pressed it against his forehead,

oblivious to the violence and madness that now surrounded me. The young killer stared at me with crazed eyes and said, "Do it, blast you. Pull the fucking trigger."

And I did, just like that. Blood, brains, and bone exploded from the back of his head, and he died like the dog he was.

I looked around me and saw that the rest of the guards were giving up. More police had emerged from the trees and were surrounding them.

Of Kennedy, there was no sign, and I assumed he'd taken flight.

He would keep, for first, I had a friend to attend to.

I knelt beside O'Hanlon and was joined by another sergeant. The Irishman was coughing up blood and wasn't long for this world. I felt a sadness in my heart that I hadn't felt in a while. Sadness that I was losing a friend who'd helped me over the years, and sadness that I'd doubted his lawfulness.

"You stupid Irish fool, why didn't you tell me?"

"The less who knew the better. I knew Kennedy was out here, and I knew Travis was behind it. But I—" he coughed, "I needed the whole operation."

"What about Travis and Clara?"

"It was Clara who sent word you were here, Jack. Don't—don't blame her, she—she didn't know what she was—was getting into."

I nodded.

With the last vestiges of his strength, O'Hanlon grabbed my arm. "Don't let them get away, Jack. This is what you were born to do. You track them all down."

"I will, Mike, you can be assured of that," I said to him.

His head slowly lowered onto the hard-packed, dusty

earth, and turned to the side, his eyes open, his chest still. I looked at the sergeant. "I'm going to need a horse, food, weapons, and ammunition. Plus, two canteens."

"You'll get all you need," the sergeant said to me.

"What's your name?"

"Ike Webster."

"Take him and bury him back at the river, Ike. He liked it there."

"I'll see to it." He looked around. "What are we going to do with all these Chinese?"

"Jack, are you all right?"

I looked up and saw Craig. "Jim, see that the Chinese get back to the river."

Craig was looking at O'Hanlon. He shook his head. "I always thought that Irish bastard was made of iron."

"Jim, the Chinese," I said, drawing his attention back to the task at hand.

"No worries, Jack. What are you going to do?"

My face hardened. "I'm going after Kennedy."

KENNEDY HAD GOTTEN himself a horse and started back towards the river at a speed that was crazy and unsustainable. Even though he was putting distance between himself and me, I kept the bay horse I rode at an even pace because there would come a time when I would need it, and riding it to death wasn't part of the plan.

That night, I made camp under a large gum. I was still likely a few hours from the river, but it made a huge difference not having a dray in tow. I ate dried meat and drank black coffee.

I was then up as the first ray of red light reached its

fingers across the eastern sky. Pointing my horse east, I found Kennedy's dead mount an hour later. He'd ridden the poor bloody beast to death the day before.

The crows had been picking at it, and the eyes were gone. So too the dingoes, feasting on fresh meat. I scared two off when I came across its remains.

After taking a few minutes to give my horse some water, I kept riding, and a few hours later, I saw the tree line in the distance, which indicated the river.

The boot prints I'd been following led me straight to it and down the bank towards the water. Judging by the marks on the bank, Kennedy had somehow waved down a boat.

How he managed it, I wasn't sure, because the bastard's ugly face was drawn on more pieces of paper than a man wiped his arse on in one of those outhouses. Yet the scallywag had managed to get aboard one, and my guess was he had headed upriver to Dunigan's.

Well, that's the way I was going too.

I stood beside the river and took all my clothes off under the watchful gaze of a couple of kookaburras who seemed to think it funny to see a pale man without clothes on swimming his horse across the river.

Once the horse had clambered out the other side and up the bank, I got dressed, refreshed to have the dust and sweat sluiced away, and we started upriver towards the criminal sanctuary that was my destination.

I let the horse pick its own pace, and once dark came along again, I pushed on, the route shortened considerably due to not following the twists and turns of the riverbank.

Then I saw the lights as they came into view. I drew the horse to a halt and climbed down. I would wait for morning and then go in. Early morning would be best when there weren't too many people around.

The saddle I leaned against a gum along with the Martini-Henry rifle that the sergeant had given me. I dug some more food from the saddlebags and sat to eat beside a small fire I made. Tomorrow I would go into Dunigan's and find the men responsible for the predicament I found myself in. Kennedy, Travis, O'Farrell, and whoever else got in my way.

However, after I had eaten, I leaned against the saddle beside the fire for warmth and stared up at the tiny pinpricks of light, which dotted the night sky. And while I listened to the night animals, I thought of An Ni and what she might be going through.

19

Not that I had any idea, but the train she was on had passed through Dubbo and then Wellington. From there, it went through Orange and Bathurst and Parramatta before reaching Sydney.

It was something like An Ni had never seen before. The buildings, the people dressed in their finery. They had been transported from the station in a highly polished horse-drawn carriage, which made its way to Pitt Street.

It travelled past Her Majesty's Theatre and stopped at a large sandstone-block building on the corner of Pitt and Spring Streets.

What An Ni noticed about it immediately, apart from its grandeur, was the number of horse-drawn buggies parked outside.

Collier placed a calloused hand on her upper thigh. "This is where you will live and work."

"Work, doing what?" An Ni asked him.

"Doing what you're best at, my dear," the man replied with a grin. "Keeping the customers happy. Giving them whatever they require. I do think you will be in high demand."

"Prostituting," An Ni said.

"We prefer to call the ladies who work here *companions*," Collier told her. "And your job is to be companionable."

"Do I get paid?"

"Of course," Collier said with a chuckle. "You'll be provided with a bed and meals along with one sovereign a month."

An Ni knew that a sovereign a month equated to bugger all. "You mean I am to be a slave?"

"Slavery is illegal, my dear."

"So is buying people for their services," An Ni spat back at him.

Suddenly, his hand shot forward and fixed on her throat in a tight grip. An Ni could feel the power in the older man's grasp. She felt her eyes start to bulge and her breathing constrict. Her tongue wanted to protrude from her mouth reflexively. Collier leaned in close and said, "I'll not put up with such impertinence from you or any of the sluts who work for me. If it happens again, I will beat the living shit out of you and give you to the dock workers at Darling Harbour so they can do whatever they want with you. Understand?"

His eyes were like pits of fire, and spittle flew from his lips with almost every word. An Ni nodded as best she could.

Collier released her, and she took a deep breath, taking several minutes for her wildly beating heart to come back to normal. She rubbed at the redness of her throat and tried to steady her breathing.

The older man leaned back against the enclosed carriage seat, revelling in the sense of power he felt surging through him. An Ni's eyes glanced down at his bulging crotch, and she made to climb from the carriage.

Collier reached out and grabbed her by the arm. "Not yet. We are not finished."

An Ni wrenched her arm free and said, "Yes, we are."

THE INSIDE OF THE BUILDING, known as Port Darling, was lined with dark wood. The floors were carpeted, and paintings hung on the walls. Lamps burned dimly, adding to the dark ambience.

It was here that An Ni met Molly Brown, the madam of the establishment. She was a large woman, in breast and belly. Irish she was and tough to go with it. She took one look at An Ni and said, "What's your bloody name, girl?"

"Treat her well, Molly, I've got a feeling she'll go down a treat with the richer clientele."

"Yes, sir," Molly sneered. "Name?"

"I am An Ni."

"Annie it is then. Go upstairs and get one of the girls to show you to a vacant room. In the wardrobe you will find clothes. If they don't fit, make them. You start work tomorrow."

"Doing what?"

"Whatever the gentlemen want you to." She grinned impishly, showing a gap in her front teeth.

With that, An Ni did as she was told and climbed the stairs. The dark-stained wood flowed throughout the building, and the hallway on the second floor was lit by lamps. A young woman was coming from a room and looked at her warily.

"Did Molly send you up here?" she asked, her British accent heavy.

An Ni nodded. "Yes."

"Come on, I'll show you to a room," she said. "My name is Harriet."

"I am An Ni."

"You're Chinese, right?"

"Yes."

"You'll cause a stir around here, a pretty thing like you," Harriet said. "The last one we had did."

"Last one?"

"Chinese girl. All the gentlemen wanted her. I'm surprised her quim didn't get worn out."

"Quim?"

"Good Lord." Harriet chuckled. "Come on, I'll teach you some things as we go."

THE ROOM WAS BIG, much larger than the tent she'd been living in at the diggings. An Ni was actually shocked at the size of it and the steel-framed bed. Harriet said, "This is where you sleep and work, when you're not downstairs."

An Ni turned a full circle, still taking it all in. Again, dark wood panelling, pictures on the walls, wallpaper, a cupboard with a jug of water, and a dish. Then there was a wardrobe.

Harriet continued. "There is a bathroom along the hallway where you can clean up. In the wardrobe are some dresses. We will look at them later. And one more thing. Don't get on the wrong side of Molly. She can be a real bitch."

"Just like Collier."

Fear came to Harriet's eyes. "Don't ever let anyone hear you talking bad about him. The man is dangerous. He's killed girls with his temper."

"Why isn't he in jail?"

"Because he pays the police. Even high-ranking officials. He can't be touched. His money pays for everything."

"Then I will leave," An Ni said defiantly.

"There is no leaving, accept that. Once you are in, there is no out." Harriet turned her back to the new arrival, fidgeted with her dress, and let it drop to expose her back, showing An Ni the crisscross scars that were there. "I thought like you, too. I was wrong."

An Ni stepped forward, and with trembling fingers, touched the knotted scars on Harriet's back. "This is wrong."

Harriet readjusted her dress and turned back to An Ni. "It is what it is. Accept it. Come on, I'll help you get sorted. Tomorrow will be a different day."

That night for An Ni was long and uncomfortable. From different rooms along the hallway, she could hear grunts and moans. Every now and then, there would be a deep growl from the hallway, followed by a slap and a high-pitched giggle. A door would slam and then the noises would start all over again.

THE NEXT MORNING, Molly came to her. "You start work at ten this morning," she told her. "Harriet will bring you down to the lounge. Make sure you are clean and presentable."

An Ni just stared at her.

"Do you understand me, you Chinee bitch?"

"I understand," An Ni said.

Molly had gotten right up into her face after that. "Listen to me. I'm the one in charge around here. You do what I say, or there will be consequences."

Suddenly, the old An Ni flared to the surface. "Get the fuck out of my face, bitch, or I'll cut your heart out."

"You'll what?" Molly couldn't believe that one of the girls was talking to her in that manner. Especially some Chinese prostitute who'd only just arrived. She poked a stiffened finger into An Ni's chest. "Huh? You'll what?"

If the diggings had taught An Ni anything, apart from how to be a prostitute, it was how to be tough. Her father had taught her how to fight. And not just fight, but how to do whatever it took to win. She might have been apprehensive of Collier, but this Irish bitch was a different prospect. An Ni brought her head forward savagely, and her forehead smashed across the bridge of the Irish woman's nose, shattering it.

Molly screeched as she staggered back, blood pouring from her nose. An Ni stepped in close and swung a punch from the hip. She hit the bigger woman flush in the face and knocked her to her knees.

An Ni lashed out with her foot and kicked her in the stomach, causing the Irish woman to vomit onto the floor.

An Ni kicked her again, harder, savagely. The blow rolling Molly onto her back. With a snarl, An Ni dropped to her knees and started punching the madam in the face. Blow after blow after blow. Blood flew, and Molly moaned. An Ni grunted with each blow, letting all her rage out. A short time later, Molly had stopped moving, and the rise and fall of her chest had ceased.

An Ni leaned back and stared at the dead woman

lying on the floor. From behind her, a hoarse voice said, "What have you done?"

The trembling figure turned her head and stared at Harriet. "I—I—" An Ni climbed to her feet. Her hands were bloody, knuckles bruised. "She pushed me."

"Is she dead?"

"Yes."

"Oh, shit, you have to leave."

An Ni started to walk towards the doorway where Harriet stood. "Where? Where will I go? I have no money. I've never been here before."

"I might know of someone who can help. Go to Harris Street, where you'll find the Irish Arms. It's a pub. Inside, you'll find a man called Warren. Tell him Harriet sent you and you need help."

"They will hang me for this," An Ni said.

"No, it won't get that far. Collier will kill you. That is why you have to go."

"Will he be able to get me west?"

"Yes. Maybe. I don't know. Just go, now."

Harriet watched An Ni leave the room and disappear into the hallway. Then she looked down at Molly, counted to ten, and then screamed as loud as she could.

THE STREETS WERE busy with horse-drawn carriages. Ladies in long dresses, carrying small baskets, walked the footpaths while men did the same in small groups, wearing black suits and different types of hats.

Small boys wore hats like their fathers' while knee-length shorts showed long stockings which reached up above their hems. Some stared at An Ni, having never seen a Chinese woman before. Especially one dressed in such a bright dress and covered in blood.

On one of the streets, two horse-drawn drays lumbered along the hard-packed dirt, their loads of wool bales stacked two high.

An Ni stopped a couple and asked, "Can you tell me where Harris Street is, please?"

The woman looked down her nose at the Chinese woman and guided her husband away with a grunt and no more.

She watched them go, confused. Suddenly, she felt alone. She looked down at her hands and noticed the drying blood still on them. An Ni looked around and saw a horse trough at the side of the street. She hurried across to it and started to wash her hands.

The water was cold and clear. She finished washing and shook them dry before she spotted a small market stall near an intersection. An Ni hurried across to the stall.

The man, somewhere in his sixties with a grey beard, removed his hat and said, "Hello there, lass, what is it that old Paul can do for you?"

His voice was heavily accented. British.

"I'm looking for Harris Street."

"Harris Street, lass? Why would you be wanting to find Harris Street?"

"I am looking for the Irish Arms."

He stared at her. "Not a place for one like you, lass, you'd be best to stay away from it."

An Ni looked indecisive. "I was told to go there to get some help."

Paul raised his eyebrows. "In trouble, are you? You'll only find more there."

"There is a man there called Warren. I was told he could get me west."

"What are you running from, girl?" Paul asked her. "I can see the fear in your eyes."

"A man named Collier."

"Howard Collier?"

"Yes."

"Good Lord, lass, you are in trouble." His gaze went over her shoulder. "And here it comes. Get under the stall."

"What?"

"Get around here and get under the stall, blast your eyes, girl."

An Ni cast a glance over her shoulder and saw the two men in suits looking around. It didn't take much to work out they were searching for her. Before she could do as instructed, she locked gazes with the men. They began moving quickly towards her.

An Ni turned to run but tripped on a hole in the street. She fell to her hands and knees, and when she tried to rise, fell again.

Then they were on her.

"Hey!" protested the old man. "Let her go."

One of the men, a big fellow with a moustache, shoved him forcefully to the ground. "Piss off, old man."

Then, they started to drag An Ni, kicking and screaming, back to where she'd come from.

WHACK!

"So, you like to bloody well fight, do you, you damn Chinee bitch?" Collier snarled. The blow had been hard but not as vicious as An Ni had expected. "Come on then, you bloody cow. Let's see you do it."

WHACK! He hit her again, and she staggered back. "Come on, damn your eyes. Hit me!"

An Ni could feel her anger rising again with her fear. Was he going to kill her? If he were would he have done it by now?

WHACK! A third slap and that was enough to tip An Ni over the edge.

Collier was starting to think she was too scared to be doing anything about it, and her sudden fury took the older man by surprise.

The punch was filled with power from hard work, her bunched fist like a hammer. It crashed into Collier's jaw and made him stagger. But he had been only expecting one and when she hit him again, he went down, blood flowing from his mouth.

Collier's two bodyguards lurched in to help their boss out but not before An Ni had hit him for a third time. Her blows came like streaks of lightning.

"I'll kill you, you bastard!" she screeched, as they pulled her away from him, thrashing around like a wild animal.

Collier shook his head and climbed to his feet. "Don't hurt her. Not at all."

An Ni stopped struggling when she realised that there was no way to break free of their grasp. She spat vehemently on the floor and said, "Go on, you bastard. Kill me and get it over with."

"Kill you?" Collier chuckled and shook his head. "I'm not going to kill you, girl. You're a fighter. Grace Patterson better watch out for you. By God, but you're a fighter."

"Grace Patterson?"

Collier spat blood. "She's a bare-knuckle fighter, so she is. Said to be the best in Sydney. By my reckoning, not anymore. You will beat her, I know it."

"You mean fight?"

"Not fight, girl, win." Collier looked at one of his men and said, "Get a message to Lester Parker. Tell the bastard I have a woman who will belt the shit out of that prostitute of his."

The bodyguard nodded. "Now, sir?"

Collier looked at him as though he was stupid. "Now? Of course, bloody now. Tell him I have a hundred sovereigns' bet that my girl will pound his wench into the ground."

"Yes, sir."

Collier looked back at An Ni. "Oh yes, she will."

That was what was in store for An Ni. She had been chosen for the art of fisticuffs, while as the sun came up out west the following day, I was preparing to ride into Dunigan's to exact bloody vengeance on the men responsible for all that had happened.

And I meant to have it.

20

WATCHING ME FROM A THICK BRANCH, a crow was the only witness as I checked my weapons. I made sure both the Martini-Henry and the Colt were loaded before I climbed upon the mare. As I did so, the bird cawed at me, most likely saying goodbye, and good luck, and I'll peck out your eyes once you're dead.

I kneed the horse forward and rode toward the township. Woodsmoke hung over the small riverside port like a morning mist. The Martini-Henry rested across my lap, ready to use.

Circling around, I came in on the blindside and eased the horse to a stop. I climbed down and let the horse stand.

A steam whistle's high-pitched blast sounded from the river, indicating a boat was getting an early start. I walked between two buildings: a saddler and an ironmonger. Pausing at the corner of the building, I checked both directions along the street. Information was what I needed, and I thought of the man at the stable.

Making my way along via the rear of the buildings, I

reached the stable, heading around to the front and went inside. He was in there mucking out a stall. Looking up at me, he said, "You're back. You owe me money, mister."

I drew the Colt and pointed it at him. His hands shot up, and he said, "I don't want it that bloody much."

"I'm going to say some names, and I want you to tell me if they're in town or not. Understood?"

"Sure."

"Travis."

"Yes."

"O'Farrell."

"Yes."

"Kennedy."

"Who?"

"John Kennedy."

"The bushranger?" He seemed genuinely surprised.

I nodded. "Yes."

"No."

"What about Travis's trap friend?" I asked.

"Sergeant Moore? Yes, he's here."

I hesitated. "Clara Travis?"

His hesitation was longer than mine. Then it turned to anxiety. "He—he shouldn't have done it."

My blood ran cold.

"Shouldn't have done what?"

He stared at me. "He chained her to the tree."

Suddenly, my apprehension was gone and then came the anger. My jaw clenched and through gritted teeth, I asked, "Why?"

"I don't know. He chained her up last night."

"If you know what's good for you, you'll stay here," I said to him.

"What are you going to do?"

"Bring justice to Dunigan's."

I worked my way to the prison tree where I found Clara huddled in a ball, battered, bruised, but still alive. She looked up when she sensed me there. "Jack?"

I crouched beside her. "What's happening, Clara?"

"Kennedy came here and said about the police and the mine. Somehow, Charles figured out I sent Michael O'Hanlon a message."

"I don't understand."

"I knew what Michael was up to. You see, it was me who originally told him. He pretended to be bad to get Charles on his side. Charles didn't suspect because some of the traps were already working for him."

I looked at her face. There were bruises and scrapes, and it made me angry. "Are the keys inside?"

"Charles has them."

"Where is he?"

"Inside, I think."

"What about Kennedy and O'Farrell?"

"I don't know about Kennedy. O'Farrell will be with one of the girls."

I stood and nodded. "I'll be back."

Carrying the Martini-Henry in my left hand, I took out the Colt with my right and went in through the back door. The bar area smelled like stale grog and vomit. I saw why as I almost trod in a pile of spew. I made my way towards the office where the key was usually kept.

The key wasn't there.

I went back out into the main bar just as a man was walking downstairs.

Ferris.

Taking cover behind the bar, I waited, hoping he would go away. Instead, he approached it and leaned across for a jug. Only to find the barrel of my Colt poking up under his unshaven chin.

"I—ah—I—ah—"

"Just shut up or you'll have another hole in your head," I said in a low voice, as I came to my feet.

Ferris's eyes widened as he realised who it was. "Jack —don't—don't—d—d—do anything crazy."

"Where is Travis?" I asked him.

"Upstairs in one of the rooms with Hettie."

"Who is Hettie?" I asked.

"One of the prostitutes."

"What about Kennedy and O'Farrell?"

"I'm not sure."

"What about that crooked bastard Moore?"

"I'm here, you murderous bastard." His voice boomed across the room.

I whirled and saw the bearded trap standing on the stairs, gun in hand. He looked like one of the gums on the riverbank. Tall, straight.

He fired at me as I threw myself sideways. I disappeared back behind the bar as a lead bullet punched into the timber.

Normally, one would think twice about shooting back at a trap, but this bloke was bad to the core and would kill me in a heartbeat. So I didn't think about it, I just did it. Crawling to get a line of sight, I stayed low behind the bar for cover.

My first bullet flew wide as I fired without aiming. The second missed as well, although not quite as wide. Moore fired a shot back and the round chewed splinters from the rough bar top, not far from my head.

I ducked instinctively, allowing the trap to fire another two times. Then I came back up and fired. This time, the bullet flew true, and the trap grunted, buckled at the knees, and fell down the stairs, his forehead smacking into the floor when he finally reached it.

Then I turned, looking for Ferris. The damn fool had had a chance to run and never took it, true to the coward he was. There were several choices of what I could do with the scoundrel. I took the first one that came to mind and shot him.

He fell to the floor, landing on his knees. He cried out, "You've killed me, you bastard!"

"Not yet," I replied, and shot him dead.

I heard footsteps overhead beating a distinct path across the floor. I hurriedly reloaded the Colt.

But the threat didn't come from upstairs, it came from behind me. I sensed the movement and then came the crash of gunfire. I felt the bullet bite deep and staggered.

Turning, I saw O'Farrell standing with a wolfish grin on his hate-filled face. He should have shot me somewhere vital, for I wasn't dead, and I shot him.

His hate turned to surprise as my bullet punched into his chest. He slumped to the floor, and I shot him again.

Pain radiated out from the wound in my side. I staggered towards the doorway at the rear, and as I passed through it, bullets hammered at the wood surrounds as Travis joined the fight.

But Kennedy was still out there somewhere, and I was wounded, hit hard, and bleeding badly.

I lurched out the back and crashed into a ramshackle shed near the prison tree. "Jack!" Clara exclaimed as she saw my plight.

I ignored her and staggered along the rear wall of the pub, my back turned to the doorway I'd just passed through.

Travis appeared, gun in hand. He snarled with rage when he saw me. Then he saw that I was wounded, and exultation replaced his anger.

"Jack, look out," Clara called out.

I turned, my reflexes slow from the wound. I fell, tripping over a tree root. It saved my life for at that moment, Travis fired, and the bullet passed harmlessly over my head.

I fired back at him and saw Travis stiffen. He cried out in pain and lurched back, fighting to bring his gun into line. He fired, and the bullet ploughed into the dirt near my leg.

My thumb curled the hammer on the Colt back, and I fired once more. This time, the bullet hit Travis in the chest. He fell back dead under the tree that he'd chained his wife to.

I managed to claw my way to my feet, my strength ebbing even as I did so. I staggered over to where Clara was under the tree and fell again, losing my grip on the Colt.

Ferris was dead, O'Farrell was dead, and Travis was dead, too. Still, there was one person who wasn't, and he emerged into the sunlight, casting a giant shadow over me.

"I should have killed you those few years back when I had the chance," Kennedy sneered.

"Leave him," I heard Clara say. "Can't you see he's wounded?"

"He'll be dead in a moment, missy. Then I might take you for myself."

I rolled onto my back and was blinded by the sun because the movement had taken me out of Kennedy's shadow. He sneered at me. His gun centred on my face, and I can honestly say, at that moment, I had never seen the opening of a gun barrel look bigger, even through blurred vision.

Then, everything went black.

21

Lester Parker stared at An Ni with disdain. He was sizing up the Chinese girl that Collier boasted would slay Grace Patterson in the pugilistic art of bare-knuckle fighting. He shook his head. "If you think I'm going to match Grace against her, you're mistaken, Collier. Grace would kick her arse halfway across Sydney."

They were standing in Collier's private office. With dark wood panels, a polished hardwood desk, and other expensive furnishings, it matched the rest of the club.

The waterside worker's boss shook his head once more. "She'll have to prove herself first."

Collier pointed at the bruise on his cheek. "What does that tell you?" Collier said.

"That you walked into a fucking door."

"She killed Molly Brown with her bare hands, she did."

An Ni's eyes widened at the revelation. She'd never stopped hoping that I would come for her but now, even more so.

"Molly Brown was a mole, and if what you say is true,

got what she deserved. No, the Chinee tart proves herself first."

Collier nodded. "When and where?"

"Tomorrow. Down at the Quay. I'll have a girl there waiting. And bring some money, so I'm not wasting my time." Parker gave An Ni another once-over. "If she wins, we'll talk."

Parker left, escorted by a big dock worker who doubled as his bodyguard. Collier stared at the closed door for a moment before saying, "You'd better win tomorrow, girl, because if you don't, I'll leave you down at the Quay for the dock workers to play with. Be damned if I won't."

"What am I supposed to do?" An Ni asked.

Collier gave her a perplexed look. "Haven't you been listening to anything? You have to fight. Bare knuckles against another woman."

"What do I get if I win?"

The man chuckled. "You get to fight again. Against the best that Sydney has to offer. Grace Patterson. Unbeaten, she is. Put the women she's fought in hospital. Knocked one stupid cow so silly that her head hasn't been right since. Lives in some institution for people who aren't right."

"What do I get if I beat her?" An Ni asked him.

Collier leaned forward in his chair. "If you beat Grace Patterson, girl, you can have anything you want."

"I want to go back out west," she replied.

Eyes narrowed, the crook thought for a moment before giving a slow nod. "All right," he lied. "If you beat Grace Patterson, I'll put you on a train out west."

Satisfied, An Ni said, "Then I will win."

"You'd better, girl. You'd bloody better."

THE FOLLOWING DAY BROUGHT RAIN, and An Ni thought for a moment that it might have been a sign of things to come. Curtains of water swept in from across the mountains, through Parramatta, and into the city itself, turning gutters into raging torrents.

Drivers sat hunched atop their carriages as they waited for their masters to emerge from whichever establishment they were in. There were no ladies on the streets—heaven forbid they get wet or drowned, even by the savage weather.

Between heavy showers, the sky was leaden, ominous-looking and every so often, the rumble of thunder could be heard.

Inside her room, An Ni stared out at the morning storm, dressed in only pantaloons, no corsets, or petticoats. Her top half was exposed, her nipples hard against the chill draught coming in from the hallway under the door. Goose pimples erupted all over her skin.

Harriet opened the door and walked in without knocking. She looked at An Ni as if her nakedness was normal and said, "It is a bugger of a day out. Early morning storms this time of year are not normal."

"Maybe it's saying something to me," An Ni suggested.

"What are you going to wear?" she asked.

An Ni pointed at the bed where a plain grey dress lay. "Collier sent that thing."

"Okay. Let's get you into it, but first, a corset."

"No, no corset. If I'm to fight I need to be able to move."

"I don't know how you can be so calm."

"One thing my useless Father taught me was how to

fight in the way of the ancient Chinese. A martial art called Shaolin Kung Fu. I will use it when I fight."

"Aren't you scared though?" Harriett asked her.

"I am. But the fight is in the mind. Besides, what can I do? If I win the next fight, he said he will put me on a train that will take me to Bourke. Once there, I can try to find Jack."

"Who is Jack?"

An Ni hesitated, thoughts tumbling over in her mind. Then she nodded as though her answer was definite. "He is the man that I love."

Harriett sniggered.

"What?" An Ni demanded.

The prostitute looked at An Ni. "You're serious?"

"Yes."

"You know you wouldn't be the first prostitute to fall in love with a screw."

"It is different."

"It won't matter anyway."

An Ni was confused. "Why?"

"Because if you win, there is not a hope in hell that Collier will let you go. You'll be too valuable to him."

"But he said—"

"He's a liar, Annie. Just like the rest of them. If you win, he'll make you stay. Most likely lock you up to keep you. The man is a crook and has influence."

An Ni's heart fell, then she shook her head—no. She would fight and then she would be free. "Help me with the dress."

No sooner had it slid on when a knock came at the door. Collier entered and nodded appreciatively. "Not the best of weather, but still, you'll be fighting with a roof over your head."

"Is it time to go?" An Ni asked.

"Aye." Collier saw the corset on the bed. "You're not wearing a corset?"

"Have you ever tried to hump a woman with a rope tied around your cock, Mr. Collier?"

"I can't say that I have."

"Then don't tell me how to fight."

Anger flared in Collier's eyes, then just as quickly disappeared. A cold smile came to his lips, and he said, "Shall we go now?"

"Yes."

THE STORM EASED SOMEWHAT the closer they got to the Quay. The driver pulled the horse and carriage to a halt outside a large warehouse, and Collier and An Ni alighted in what was now nothing more than fine drizzle. The sky was still a grey overcast, but that was all, not the angry dark ones which had dropped at least two inches of water on the sprawling city.

An Ni followed Collier inside the large warehouse. The interior was cool and dark thanks to the overcast. But someone had lit kerosene lamps and placed them to cast light.

The fight was to be witnessed by a dozen or so men who were gathered, talking. As soon as they saw Collier enter with An Ni, the small groups they were gathered in broke up, and they all stared at the Chinese girl. She heard someone say, "She's not much to look at. Pretty, aye, but she's not got much meat on her bones."

Another man spoke, his accent British, thick, "I've seen some of the Chinese fight. Special way they have. Quick with their hands and feet. Mark my words."

"The only thing she could do quick is pull her underdrawers off," another man sneered. "It would make my c—"

"That's enough," Parker said as he came into view. Beside him was a woman. Solidly built, her dark hair tied up, she had a crooked nose where it had been broken before. And a dress with a corset. "Is your girl ready, Collier?"

"As ready as she can be, I guess. Shall we have a small wager?"

Parker nodded thoughtfully. "Twenty sovereigns?"

"I was thinking a hundred," Collier shot back at him.

"How about we start out small. If your wench gets through, then maybe we can up the ante a bit."

"All right then." Collier turned to An Ni and whispered, "It's a bit like boxing, girl. You'll have a break after three minutes and then go at it again. The fight keeps on until one of you can't fight anymore. Understand?"

"I understand."

An Ni was guided to the fighting area, where she looked around briefly before coming to stand facing the woman she was to fight. The woman spat on the hard floor, flexing her jaw maliciously and said, "You'll not walk away, Chinee bitch."

An Ni said nothing, but moved to her right as the woman began to circle her. The watchers stepped forward, enclosing the fighters in a human ring.

Lizzy threw a punch at An Ni's face, which was evaded easily. Then came another two, both avoided.

"Come on, you bitches, fight!" a dock worker snarled.

Lizzy's face contorted with rage, mostly at her failure to land a blow, but also at the taunt, and she threw a wild right. A haymaker designed to put the smaller Chinese woman down.

An Ni was nimble and went under it, coming up

smoothly and swiftly. Then she hit Lizzy with a two-punch combination a professional would have been proud of. Lizzy's head rocked back, and blood appeared from her cut lip. She took two backward steps, surprised by the Chinese woman's speed and power.

Off to the side, Collier grinned at what he was witnessing, while Parker suddenly looked worried.

An Ni moved to her left and struck again. Her hands moved blindingly fast. Two more blows and Lizzy had a broken nose to go with her cut lip.

Lizzy swung wildly, trying to stop the Chinese woman's onslaught.

An Ni once more ducked to avoid the blow, this time, however, when she came up, she hit Lizzy just under her heart with the heel of her hand, stopping the woman in her tracks. Lizzy's eyes bulged, and she fought for breath as a great whoosh escaped her lungs. Before she knew it, she was hit twice more and sank to her knees.

An additional brutal blow, and Lizzy toppled onto her side and never moved, out like a lamp.

The crowd stood in stunned silence at what they had just witnessed. An Ni stared down at Lizzy as though making sure her opponent was still alive. The woman groaned.

It was Collier who broke the silence. "I do believe we have another fight to arrange."

Parker looked up from his fighter and stared at Collier. "I guess we do. How about three weeks from today?"

"No," An Ni snapped. "Tomorrow."

Collier nodded. "Three weeks will be fine. Where?"

"Beaumont House," Parker said. "The gardens there are quite substantial. There will be room for many spectators. We'll make a show of it."

Beaumont House was a large estate on the Parramatta River. The owner, Oliver Beaumont, owned a shipping fleet of six vessels. At one time, that number had been nine, but the fickle weather of Bass Strait had claimed one, the Horn another, and the heads off Sydney the third. People had died, but the shipping line carried on.

"All right," Collier said, "I'll see you there."

"One other thing, Collier," Parker said with a sly grin.

"What's that?"

"Bare knuckle brawl."

"You changing things to suit yourself?" Collier asked incredulously.

"Take it or leave it."

"Oh, I'll take it. Bet your life on that one."

Uncomprehending what had just transpired, An Ni stared at Collier. Reading the confusion on her face, he spread his hands and said, "It just means you can hit, kick, bite, scratch, headbutt, shit like that."

With that explanation, An Ni began to worry.

22

IT TOOK me four days to wake up after being shot, and another week passed before I was able to get up and around. During that time, Clara was by my side, making sure I wouldn't die. And I spent it thinking of An Ni.

A well-known Chinese flower was the Lotus. It was said to grow in murky water, but was the most beautiful flower. Well, An Ni had grown in murky water. Years of being dragged around the various gold diggings as a child and then as a young woman working as a prostitute to put food in her mouth. But beneath the dirt and tough exterior, I was sure there was that beautiful flower they called a Lotus. And I meant to find her to prove it.

Swinging my legs over the side of the bed, I put my feet on the wooden floorboards. Sitting up made my head spin, and I was still weak but had spent far too long lying around. I needed to be up and about.

I fumbled into my clothes and then crossed to the door. Placing my hand on the knob, I was surprised when it opened by itself to reveal a policeman standing in the hallway. I recognised him right away. Ike Webster, the sergeant from the mine who'd been with O'Hanlon.

"Going somewhere?"

"Downstairs," I said. "To the bar."

"What for?"

"I figure if I can make it that far, I can make it to Sydney."

He looked puzzled. "Sydney? What for?"

"I have to find someone."

"No, you have to stay here. There are questions that need to be answered about what went on. The magistrate will be here next week."

"You know what happened," I said to him.

"You shot a policeman," Webster said.

"He was a criminal," I said defensively. "He tried to kill me."

"And I'm sure that will all come out, but until then, you need to stay put."

"The hell I do."

He looked grim. "You either stay of your own accord, or I'll make use of that tree out the back."

"Fuck you," I hissed.

"If you try to run, I'll come after you, Jack, me, and the others."

By others, he meant the three other traps that were attempting to bring law and order to the portside town. I nodded. "Am I under arrest?"

"No."

Then I sprang. I didn't want to, but I wasn't about to let him stop me from doing what needed to be done. I had almost reached him when my weakness overcame me, and I passed out on the floor in front of him.

Webster looked down at my prostrate form at his feet

and shook his head. "Shit. Now I have to get you back in bed."

"THE FACT REMAINS that you shot a police officer," Magistrate Jonas Wyler said, glaring at me from behind a desk. Considered a tough man of dubious morality.

I could already feel the noose tightening around my throat and swallowed hard.

The dusty courtroom was packed with people waiting to hear my fate. Sitting behind a desk, Wyler's grey hair looked like he'd walked through a *willi-willi* on the way to court, and his eyes were set deep in his head. The man was looking to hang me for something I did in self-defence. This was a hearing, not a bloody trial.

"Your Honour," Webster said, "Greg Moore was a hellion and a scallywag. He was paid to look the other way when Charles Travis and his henchmen were kidnapping Chinese immigrants and enslaving them to work in his mine."

"My brother did no such thing, Your Honour," Alice Travis blurted out as she stood to be seen. Attired totally in black, she was portraying a grieving sister. But I knew better—the woman was a she-wolf in a dress. Dangerous and conniving.

Wyler glared at her for the outburst, causing her to adjust her dress to reveal a little more pale cleavage for the magistrate's hawkish eyes. "Please be quiet, madam. I can handle this."

"Yes, Your Honour," she acquiesced, nodding coquettishly but remaining on her feet for a few seconds more.

His eyes lingered on her breasts until she sat down,

and I felt the sinking feeling in the pit of my stomach expanding.

Webster continued. "Not only that, Your Honour, but Travis had the scoundrel Kennedy and his murderous cutthroats in his employ as well. He—"

"Who is on trial here, Sergeant Webster?"

"Sir?" Webster looked confused.

"I asked who was on trial here?"

"No one, Your Honour. It is an inquest to find out what happened regarding the death of Superintendent O'Hanlon. Mr. Crowe's friend, I might add."

"Which sent the defendant on a murderous rampage."

"He's not a defendant, sir," Webster pointed out.

"He's whatever I bloody well say he is," the magistrate snarled.

"Sir, he was acting under the instruction of Superintendent Michael O'Hanlon," Webster persisted. "His last words were for Mr. Crowe to track them all down."

"And you witnessed this?"

"Yes, Your Honour."

Wyler looked displeased. "But I bet he didn't say to go and murder them, did he?"

"No, sir."

"There, the truth at last."

"Right after he swore Mr. Crowe in, he said, "Hunt those bastards down and kill them, Jack. They don't deserve to live."

I couldn't believe what I had just heard. Webster had just lied under oath in the name of saving me from a man who seemed to want me to hang.

"He did no such thing, sir," Wyler blustered.

"Were you there, sir?"

"I was not, sir."

"Then you could not know what was said. And I have just said under oath that what I say is true."

The magistrate stared hard at Webster. "Damn your eyes, sir. Take the scoundrel away and lock him up. The charge is murder of a police officer. And by golly, he will hang for it."

The room burst out into uproar at the magistrate's words. Stunned, I glanced at Alice Travis, who smiled smugly at me. And then at Wyler, who caught sight of her. He gave her his own grim smile and licked his lips, giving certainty to the collusion they were guilty of.

Webster leaned close to me and said, "This is not over."

I could not keep the helplessness from my voice when I muttered, "From where I'm standing, it pretty much looks like it is."

"Your Honour," Webster called out.

"What?" The magistrate's voice was impatient.

"Is that your last word, sir?"

His eyes narrowed. "Damn right it is."

Webster nodded, and I could tell by his expression that it indeed was not over. He said, "Holland and Forrest, arrest the magistrate for accepting a bribe."

"What do you think you're doing, Sergeant?" Wyler blustered furiously.

"Reynolds, Allister, arrest Miss Travis for bribery."

Suddenly, her smugness was gone, and she looked terrified. "Jonas, do something."

"Shut up, blast your eyes." He turned his attention back to Webster. "What do you think you're doing?"

"Your Honour, I have a witness who saw Miss Travis coming from your room this morning in a certain state of undress."

There was a gasp from the female element of the courtroom crowd.

"So?"

"That same witness said you kept them awake half the night playing...ah...*horsey*. I think that's what they called it." A loud guffaw came from somewhere at the back of the room. "I may not be able to prove that bribery was taking place, but I can lock you up for it until the replacement magistrate arrives and he can sort it out."

"That is blackmail, sir, of the lowest order," Wyler said indignantly.

"And humping a suspected criminal is not, sir?" Webster asked. "I still intend to arrest her, but as for you, Your Honour, your next decision will tell the tale."

The magistrate glared at me and said, "The defendant is free to go without charge."

I turned to Webster, who was grinning. He said, "I told you it wasn't over."

Behind us, Alice Travis was protesting her innocence as she was led away. Then I saw Clara. She was smiling at me, yet her eyes showed concern. I slapped Webster on the shoulder. "Thanks, Ike."

"Not a problem. At least you're free to go to Sydney now and find that girl."

I nodded. "But first, there is something I have to take care of."

He looked at Clara. "Yeah, I guess you do."

Everyone filed from the makeshift courthouse, leaving myself and Clara alone. She took several tentative steps toward me and said, "That was almost disastrous."

I shrugged. "Thankfully, Webster had that ace up his sleeve."

"Are you staying?"

I could sense a hint of hopefulness in Clara's voice, and I almost hated to shatter her illusions. I shook my head. "No."

"You're going after *her*, aren't you?" She looked at the floor to hide her feelings.

The way she said *her* was almost bitter. I didn't want to part on bad terms with Clara, but what we had was gone, replaced by what I felt for An Ni. "I gave her my word that I would find her."

"She is a prostitute." The words were designed to slap my face.

"She is a victim of circumstance, a lot like you," I pointed out, refusing to take the bait.

"Do you love her?"

"I do."

"You don't even know who has her?" Clara asked.

"I intend to find out."

She stared into my eyes, searching for some lifeline, before relenting and said, "His name is Howard Collier. He owns a gentlemen's club in Sydney on the corner of Pitt and Spring Street. Be careful, Jack, he's a bad man. A killer who has connections."

"I'm a killer too," I reminded her.

"Sydney isn't like out here. Let me come with you."

"Why would I do that?"

"I can help."

I wasn't sure. She could see my troubled mind.

She placed a reassuring hand on my arm and once more stared into my eyes. "It's all right, Jack, I can help, I promise. I've been to Sydney before."

With a nod, I acceded to her wishes. "All right, Clara. That would be good. Thank you."

23

WHILE I HAD BEEN DEALING with my issues, An Ni had been waiting for the fight that would set her free. And the day Clara and I were to climb aboard the train at Bourke for our journey to Sydney, An Ni was in a carriage on her way to Beaumont House with Collier by her side.

"Today is the day, my dear," he said to her wolfishly. "The day that you win me a lot of money."

"The day that I win my freedom, you mean," An Ni reminded him.

His head snapped around. "What? Oh, yes, yes, that's right. We can't forget that, can we?"

The carriage lurched as it hit a hole in the road and then righted itself. The day outside was sunny with a slight breeze coming off the ocean. As they rounded a corner, An Ni sighted the river to their left. They travelled further past green fields before turning through a gateway outlined by stone pillars on either side.

Crossing the boundary onto the property transported them into another world, the grounds large with well-tended gardens dotted throughout. The carriage's iron rims ground on the gravel driveway, and the driver pulled the horses up at the base of a grand staircase leading up into the large, sandstone-built house.

Collier climbed out and helped An Ni down. A man attired in a formal suit emerged from inside and stood at the top of the steps. "Everyone is around the back in the garden, sir."

"Thank you," Collier said, and began walking around the back with An Ni following.

She had never seen anything like it before. The grounds were massive. Trees and gardens as far as the eye could see. Not sure whether she was impressed with it all, she considered that the outback had much of the same, and that maybe it was prettier.

Stopping abruptly as she rounded the house, An Ni took in the gathered crowd and breathed in deeply. Men in suits. Women in sundresses, holding parasols and fans. Children running around playing. Collier looked back at her. "Is there a problem?"

"Who are all these people?" An Ni asked uncertainly.

"They have come to see you fight," Collier told her. "Jim Lyons, owner of Lyons Furniture. General Ron Fitzgibbons, formerly of Queen Victoria's Royal Dragoons. Now he is an advisor to Lord Farragut. Lloyd Gilmore from Bathurst. He owns Gilmore Mines. Those are but a few."

"Surely a fight is not that important."

"Don't you believe it. You see, Grace Patterson hasn't been beaten for two years. But don't you worry, today is the day."

They approached the crowd of people who slowly turned to look at the newcomers, a clear pathway opening through the throng. Almost immediately, the whispers began from behind hands.

"She doesn't look like much," one young woman said.

"She is so thin," said another.

"Grace will kill her..."

"Is this your Chinee girl, Collier?" an older man called out.

"It is, Oliver."

The man walked over to them, escorted by a dour-faced woman in a blue dress. She looked to be in her sixties, with a generous coating of powder and rouge on her wrinkled skin. The man, while the same age, had lines like dry creek beds across his clean-shaven face. His eyes narrowed, and he said, "What do you think, Priscilla? Will she beat Parker's whore?"

The woman named Priscilla looked down her nose at An Ni and sniffed, saying, "I doubt the poor girl would have enough stamina to clean our floors, Oliver, dear."

Beaumont grunted. "You're probably right, but what the blazes. I'll have a hundred sovereigns on her anyway. What say you, girl, are you a good bet?"

"I'm a good fuck."

Priscilla Beaumont recoiled in horror. However, the coarseness of An Ni's language brought forth a loud guffaw from the old man. "My goodness, Collier, you've got a winner there, I should think. I'll have two hundred on the wench, and if she wins, we'll talk business."

They walked away, and An Ni turned to Collier. "What business?"

He stared at her. "Nothing for you to worry about."

A young man in a soldier's uniform approached them. He held out a glass for An Ni. "A tot of rum before you start, miss?"

"No, thank you."

"It might help to dull the pain."

"So does opium."

He smiled at her. "Sorry, I don't have any of that." He suddenly looked confused. "What is it, anyway?"

"Never mind. I doubt you could handle it." An Ni took the rum and threw it back. Pulled a face and said, "Tastes foul."

The young man nodded. "Yes, it's an acquired taste."

"Here is the competition," Collier said.

An Ni looked in the direction he was staring and saw the solidly built woman walking towards them, accompanied by Parker. Her head was shaved close to her scalp, and her nose appeared to have been broken at least once in her life. A scar on her right cheek gave her a mean look, while her eyes were as black as the night and seemed to pierce An Ni's soul.

"What do you think?" Collier asked her.

"She is big."

Grace stopped short of An Ni and looked down into her eyes. She screwed up her face and sneered. "Are you the Chinee slut I'm fighting?"

An Ni just stared at her, showing no emotion.

At the lack of response, Grace began to get angry. "Dog got your tongue. I hear you eat them. That's why there are no dogs on the gold fields."

An Ni smiled. "You'd best stay away, then."

Grace stepped closer, and Parker grabbed her arm. "Let it go, it's almost time."

The larger woman spat at An Ni's feet. "I'm going to kill you, bitch."

They walked away, and Collier said, "She's mean, isn't she?"

"Yes."

He looked at An Ni's face. "Getting nervous?"

"No."

The truth was, she was doing a stellar job of hiding it. She was scared. The woman was a monster in human clothing. An Ni didn't doubt the veracity of Grace's statement that she'd kill her. She looked more than capable. An Ni had to rely on her skill as a Shaolin fighter.

"Don't go getting cold feet on me now, girl," Collier snarled. "I have a lot of money riding on this outcome."

"Then why don't you fight her?"

The man grabbed her wrist, squeezing tightly. "Don't you answer me back, girl. I own you."

It was the moment that realization dawned on An Ni that Collier wasn't going to keep his word. Harriet had been right. Somehow, she had to try to get away again. It was all she could do. But first she had to get through the fight.

"Come on," Collier said. "It's time."

THE YOUNG MAN who'd offered An Ni the rum stood between both women and said, "I'm only here to make sure that no one dies. That's all. You fight until one of you can fight no more."

He stepped back, and the crowd shuffled around. It surprised An Ni that the women seemed to enjoy the anticipation, too. She stood off to one side while Parker talked to his fighter for the final time. Then it began.

Grace walked straight in and threw a punch at An Ni, who ducked away to the side, circling to the left. Grace followed her and threw another, which An Ni dodged as well.

"Keep still and fight, bitch," Grace growled. The

words were followed by a grunt as she swung and missed again.

This time, however, An Ni reacted. Two swift blows smashed into the face of Grace Patterson, stinging her like an insect. The woman had a hard head.

She grinned wickedly. "That's better, little Chinee girl. Come and get some more."

The noise from the surrounding spectators began to rise at the sight of An Ni fighting back.

Grace moved in, and her opponent caught her with a straight left jab to the chin. Grace shook it off and closed in further, so An Ni hit her again.

Grace was expecting it and moved her head slightly so that the blow glanced off. However, before An Ni could retreat, Grace hit her with a solid blow of her own, and the Chinese girl went down bleeding from the mouth.

The response the blow evoked from the crowd was a raucous cheer. An Ni climbed to her feet and dabbed at her cut lip.

While she did that, Grace moved in again to try and take up the advantage. An Ni lurched back out of reach.

She circled to the right this time and moved in close to hit her opponent. A solid blow just under the right breast hurt the larger woman but did little to stop her. Instead, Grace seemed to feed off the pain and lashed out with a right hook, which connected.

An Ni staggered back, tripped over the hem of her dress, and fell. Taking advantage, Grace kicked her in the ribs, eliciting a cry of pain. But the bigger girl wasn't done. She kicked her again, harder this time.

An Ni moaned and rolled over, arching her back to try and rid herself of the pain. Grace leaned down and snarled, "How'd you like that, you prostitute bitch?"

An Ni started to climb to her feet, and Grace hit her again, knocking her flat. She could taste the blood in her mouth, and her head spun. She tried to climb again, and Grace kicked her.

This time, An Ni rolled away, crying out with pain and anger. She forced herself to her feet and tore at her dress. The fabric came away and left her in her undergarments. Nostrils flaring, she bunched her fists and spat blood on the green grass at her feet.

"By God, Collier," Beaumont called out. "But she looks bloody angry."

Collier ignored the comment, concentrating on his fighter, worried that he might be about to lose a small fortune. He glanced at Parker, whose face wore a smug expression.

Meanwhile, all that was going to change because the prostitute known as An Ni was about to turn into an angry storm lashing Sydney late on a summer's afternoon.

Wanting to keep her advantage, Grace closed in like a large predator about to take down its prey. She swung wildly, wanting to end it all with one blow. Her senses heightened by her anger, An Ni went under the blow, came up, and shaped to throw a right hook, but instead brought her elbow around, driving it into the other fighter's jaw.

Grace staggered back, the blow stunning her. Her hands dropped, and An Ni pirouetted like a ballet dancer. As she came around, she lifted her right foot, the momentum sweeping it around in an arc until it hit the bigger fighter in the side of the head.

Grace staggered once more, hurt by the blow.

Grinding her teeth, An Ni used all the skills taught to her by her father and rushed in while the bigger girl was incapacitated. The Chinese girl hit her twice in the face, hard enough to rock her head back. Then a third blow, this time to the stomach, doubled Grace over. Then An Ni brought her elbow down on the back of Grace's neck and dropped her to the grassed area.

"Whoa, what the blazes is that?" Parker snarled, stepping forward.

"You never said a word when your girl was kicking the shit out of mine, Parker, get the buggery out of it."

Grace climbed to her feet and screwed her face up in anger. "Is that all you've got, you Chinee bitch?"

An Ni went to hit her again, but Grace grabbed the fabric of her bodice and pulled her forward. As momentum took over, Grace brought her forehead down in a vicious headbutt, which luckily caught An Ni on the forehead instead of the bridge of her nose.

It still opened a cut, however, and An Ni reeled away, shaking her head.

"That's it, show the bitch what it's all about," Parker growled.

Blood ran down An Ni's face in a long stream. She wiped it away with her hand and straightened up.

"Is that all you've got, bitch?" she snarled, returning the favour.

"That's it, girl, you've got her measure," Beaumont called out. "Just see if you don't."

The headbutt was designed to end it all, but it hadn't, and Grace was feeling the aftereffects of it. With arms outstretched, she lurched forward. Her hands formed claws as she reached for An Ni's throat.

The fight was brutal, both girls bleeding, but neither willing to back down. For Grace, it was pride, for An Ni, it was all about survival.

Just as Grace's hands were about to wrap around the

Chinese girl's throat, An Ni dropped, doing the splits on the grass. Just as she landed on the ground, she hit Grace in the stomach, then twisted herself, sweeping the larger girl's legs with her own.

With a cry of alarm, Grace fell onto her back, leaving herself exposed. An Ni rolled over and brought her elbow down into the middle of her opponent's face, breaking her nose and knocking out her two front teeth.

Just to be sure, An Ni hit her again.

Panting, she climbed to her feet and looked around at the stunned crowd. Grace Patterson hadn't moved. She was checked out by the young officer, who looked up and said, "She's still alive."

"My goodness, Collier, that's some fighter you've got there," Beaumont said, clapping him on the back.

"You could say that, sir."

"I did, I did. Now we need to talk business. I'll give you a thousand sovereigns for her."

An Ni turned to stare at the shipping owner. "No, I'm going back west. I was told if I won, I could go."

"Were you now?" Beaumont said, amusedly. "What do you say, Collier?"

"Sorry, Mr. Beaumont, I'll not sell her. She's mine."

"Two thousand."

"No."

Beaumont nodded. "Can't say as I blame you. But I wouldn't let her go. She's too valuable for that."

Collier stared at An Ni. "Oh, I'm not letting her go anywhere. She's all mine."

An Ni spat blood on the ground and decided then and there that she was going to have to kill him if she ever wanted to be free again.

24

I'D NEVER BEEN to Sydney before and decided right then that I didn't like it. The smell, the sights, the people. It was nothing like things were in the outback.

"Are you all right?" Clara asked me. "You look... uncomfortable."

"Not as uncomfortable as some of these people we keep walking past," I replied.

"Maybe it's because of the rifle you're carrying."

I glanced down. "Well, I wasn't leaving it behind. I may have use for it."

We checked into a hotel on a busy street not far from the place we needed to go, so Clara told me. In separate rooms, we cleaned up, and I had just finished dressing when Clara knocked on my door. When I opened it, she stood before me wearing a cream-coloured dress and matching bonnet. As she entered the room, she said, "I was thinking that maybe I should go and see Collier by myself, first, Jack. He knows me, and he might respond better if I'm on my own."

Her words made sense, even if I didn't want to let her go alone. "All right."

Against my better judgement, I waited in the room that cost more than I made in a week. But I wasn't paying for it. That was Clara's money.

I crossed impatiently to the window and looked down onto the street through the lace curtains. Horses and carriages, people, hustle and bustle. A bloke could swing a possum by the tail and kill at least ten people by the time he'd done a full circle.

There was a knock at my door. I frowned and opened it. Standing in the hallway were two thickset men holding handguns pointed at my belly—policemen. But what did policemen want with me? Perhaps something had happened to Clara. My heart quickened. Then I realized that they wouldn't be pointing guns at me if Clara had been hurt in any way.

"Are you Jack Crowe, sir?"

I nodded. "I am."

"Then you'd best come with us."

"What if I don't want to?" I asked them.

The taller of the two, a man with a bushy beard, said, "If you don't, we'll just shoot you here with the law on our side."

"I guess I don't have a choice then, do I?"

"No, sir."

So, they escorted me downstairs and out onto the street. They loaded me into the back of a horse-drawn wagon that had ***POLICE PATROL*** painted in bold letters on the side.

Both men sat up front after chaining me to a large ring in the back. We travelled through the streets, and they took me to a large building. I assumed that it was the gentlemen's club that Collier owned.

I assumed correctly.

I WAS SHOWN into an office where two people waited for me. The man called Collier and Clara. Upon seeing her, I soon realised that she had orchestrated the whole thing, but to what purpose I had no idea.

It was Collier who spoke first. "It would seem that you are to be a pain in my side, Mr. Crowe. However, I have a proposition for you."

My eyes went to Clara. "I don't know why, but it seems that you have a habit of betraying me."

"I'm not betraying you, Jack. I'm about to offer you something wonderful, a new start for you and for me," she said, her voice full of enthusiasm.

"I'm listening," I replied. I couldn't really do anything else.

"There is a ship leaving for Africa in an hour," Collier said. "Passage is to Durban. Two tickets. One for you and the other is for Miss Watson."

"Why?" I asked.

"Why what?"

"Why are you doing this? Why not just kill me?"

"I'm doing it for Clara. She asked—"

"Jack, don't you see? We can leave here and start a new life. It will be marvellous."

"Marvellous for who?"

Collier said, "You will also be given one thousand sovereigns to start a new life. You hunted men here in Australia. Over there, you could hunt something else."

I looked at the pair as though they were mad. "What if I decide not to?"

"The harbour is deep," Collier said matter-of-factly.

Clara stepped forward, grabbing my arm. "Please be sensible, Jack. She's not worth it. She's Chinese. Why would you want her when you can have me? She's a prostitute."

"She's a bloody good fighter," Collier said. "Besides, I own her, and she will stay here with me."

"Can I see her?" I asked.

Collier thought about his response and nodded. "I guess so. Wait here."

Wait here? It wasn't like I was going anywhere. There were still two armed traps in the room, and I was chained at the wrist with manacles. I had no doubt I would end up in the harbour should I refuse, but I wanted to see An Ni to make sure she was all right.

I'd not heard about the fight, so when she appeared, dressed in a drab grey dress, battered and bruised, I was shocked by the sight. My jaw set firm, my anger rose. "Are you all right?"

An Ni looked up at me, for the first time, seeing that it was me in the room. She smiled and went to step forward, but Collier held her back "No, there will be fine."

I swallowed my rage, pushing it below the surface, but wanting to kill the man who had done this to her. "Are you all right?" I asked again.

"I prayed you would come," she said to me. "Knew you would keep your word. I am fine."

"What happened to her?" I asked Collier.

"She had a fight with another woman," he said to me. "She also killed a woman who worked for me. With her bare hands. Can you believe it? I could have had her hung for that, but I chose another path."

"Is it true?" I asked An Ni.

She nodded sombrely. "Yes. She was a mean woman. Harsh."

I nodded. I knew how she felt.

"Have you come to take me away?"

I shook my head. "Not today," I told her. "It's complicated."

"But you promised me, Jack. You love me, and I love you, and you said you would come for me. Well, here you are."

"I have to go away," I told her. "It's not my choice. I'm sorry."

"You must take me with you," she said. "Please, Jack."

I could see the tears in her eyes. "I'm sorry."

"Then get word to my father. He will come."

"Your father is dead," Clara said, her words cutting deep.

My head snapped up as I looked at the woman I was starting to despise. I tried to read her face to see if she was lying, but I couldn't tell. An Ni shook her head. "No, you lie, bitch," she hissed.

Collier slapped her, hard. I lurched forward but was met with two Colt handguns, halting my progress. My eyes narrowed. "You're lucky I don't kill you, Collier."

"I'm starting to lose patience with you, Crowe." The *mister* was gone. "Don't make me change my goodwill."

I reined my temper in. While I was alive, I still had hope of freeing An Ni. Dead, I was no good to anyone. I forced the tension from my body.

"Good choice, Crowe, good choice. Unchain him."

One of the traps stepped forward and unlocked the manacles. I rubbed my wrists, pleased to be free of the irons.

Collier went over to his desk and picked up two tickets from the polished top. "Here." He proffered them to me. I took them with my right hand, my eyes holding his stare. While we did so, my left took his letter opener from beside the inkwell.

I turned away and walked towards the door.

"One more thing, Mr. Crowe."

Mister, again. His confidence returned. I waited.

"Do not return to Australia. If you do, I will have you hung."

I took another two steps, and as soon as I reached the two policemen, I exploded, and people died.

The letter opener came up as I drove it up under the bearded policeman's chin. I didn't try to extract it. I just left it there, and he died with it buried deep. As he fell, I managed to get his Colt free from the flapped holster on his hip. It was slow, cumbersome, and his friend began to draw his weapon.

He would have shot me—in the back—but An Ni's reflexes were lightning fast, and she kicked him behind the left knee. The trap cried out as his joint gave out, and he fell.

I turned and clubbed him unconscious with the Colt before he could get up. Then I turned on Collier. His hands shot up in a defensive posture. "Whoa, Crowe, just take the Chinee slut and go."

"Jack, what have you done?" Clara gasped.

I ignored her and remained focused on Collier. I knew what was going to happen. He was one of those people who would come after me. Of course, he would. I would always be looking back, wondering where he was. And more importantly, An Ni would never be safe while he still drew breath.

Collier must have realised what I was thinking and took a step back, his mouth open in protest, just as I shot him. He fell to the carpeted floor and convulsed once before he died.

I turned and looked at Clara, who thought that maybe I would shoot her, too. She gasped, "You're a rotten murderer."

I walked around the desk and opened every drawer I could find. What I was looking for was in the last one—money. I needed money, so I took it. Most probably, the sovereigns Collier would have given me anyway.

"Jack, take me with you," Clara tried desperately once more.

I just glared at her. I walked over to An Ni. "Are you coming with me?"

"Where?"

"Well, we can't stay here anymore. As Collier said, there is a ship waiting."

"Yes, I will come with you."

I looked at Clara and said, "Have a good life, Clara."

As we left the room and walked along the hallway, her voice could be heard reverberating behind us, screaming at me.

EPILOGUE

ABOARD THE FALCON, TWO WEEKS OUT OF SYDNEY

I STOOD at the rail with my arm around An Ni's waist. We both rocked with the motion of the ship as it beat its way up the South African coast towards Durban. A gull came in and landed on the rail before squawking at us and then taking off.

"How do you feel now that you can see it?" I asked An Ni.

She rested her head on my shoulder and said, "I'm excited."

I kissed her forehead, and she wrapped her arms around my waist. We'd heard on the way over that Africa was a land of opportunity just waiting for someone to come along and take it.

"Have you thought about my offer, Mr. Crowe?" a voice said from behind me.

We turned and saw the Englishman, Thomas Graves. A former general from India, the man was grey-haired, with a lined face, and a mouth that constantly chewed cigars. He was also now headed to Africa to make his fortune hunting. The market was ivory, and it was said to be available by the thousands of pounds.

And I needed money and a place to start.

"You'll be working with natives, mind," Graves continued. "It'll be dangerous work, but I will supply you with all you need."

I nodded. "I'll do it, Mr. Graves."

His expression turned doubtful. "I'm not sure that it will be all that suitable for your wife to travel with you."

Oh, I think I forgot to mention that An Ni and I were married, the ship's captain performing the honours. I said to Graves, "Annie goes where I do. Besides, she is more than capable of looking after herself."

"Suit yourself, Crowe. Suit yourself."

I nodded.

"Come and see me after the ship docks. I'll have money for you to buy supplies and wagons, and guns."

"Thank you, General."

Although he was no longer one, he never corrected me. I used it as a term of respect, and he liked it because it linked back with his days in command of the 56th Foot Infantry Regiment.

He left us there, and An Ni and I went back to watching the coast as it slid past. "Are you sure you want to take me along with you, Jack?" she asked.

"Of course, I do," I reassured her.

"But if it is as dangerous as they say, then—"

I placed a finger on her lips. "Quiet. It'll be fine."

Two hours later, the ship dropped anchor in Durban harbour, and we went ashore.

I LEFT An Ni at what passed for a cheap hotel. It was clean, but that was about all. Not that I had plans on being in Durban long. I needed weapons, wagons, supplies, and most of all, men—good men that I could trust. I asked around, and the one name that kept coming up was an Irishman named Seamus Finnegan.

I'd learned that Finnegan was a hunter who had his own bearers and knew the interior like the back of his hand. If there was one issue the Irishman had, it was that he liked to drink. However, it was that vice that made him easy to locate.

I walked into the tavern and found him seated at a corner table with a half-empty bottle beside an empty mug. I took my own bottle over and stood in front of him, waiting for an invitation to sit. Not that it was forthcoming. The unshaven ruffian who sat hunched before me, was short on manners and long on insults.

"What do you want, you son of a motherless whore?"

"Are you Seamus Finnegan?" I asked him.

He nodded. "I am. Who are you?"

He was drunk, that was for sure, but maybe his inebriation would prove a moment of weakness I could use to my advantage. I sat down and filled his mug with rum from my bottle. "My name is Jack Crowe. I'm looking for a hunter and a guide for an expedition into the interior. I was told you were that man."

He stared at me through bloodshot, grey eyes. "Oh? What makes you think I would work for you?"

"Two hundred pounds and a cut of all the ivory we bring in."

"How much?"

"One percent," I said to him.

His eyes narrowed. "Ten."

I was prepared to pay that much, but I had a feeling I could get him for less. "Two."

"Fuck off. Eight."

"Five, and that includes all your bearers."

He nodded abruptly. "Fine."

Depending on what we got, five percent was a lot of money. "We will need wagons, oxen, guns, and ammunition."

"Meet me here in the morning, and I will take you to get what you need," Finnegan said.

"First thing in the morning, and be sober. Or I will cut your percentage."

"I don't drink when I'm working," he said to me. "In spite of what the rumours say."

I nodded. "All right, I'll see you tomorrow."

I left the tavern and returned to the hotel, finding An Ni asleep on the bed. She stirred when I sat beside her, and she opened her dark eyes. She smiled at me. It made her face light up, and my love for her came to the surface. My hand reached out, and a finger stroked her cheek. "Did you find him?" she asked sleepily.

"Yes. I have to meet him tomorrow morning."

"That is good."

"I have to go and see the general, now," I told her.

"Not yet," An Ni said to me, grabbing my hand. "First, you must give me a child."

"Really?" I was shocked at first but that quickly vanished.

"Yes. I want a child. You will give it to me."

I leaned down and kissed her. "I like that idea."

"I thought you might."

THE FOLLOWING MORNING, I met Finnegan where I'd left him the day before. He was sitting at a table drinking coffee, clean-shaven, and ready to work. He stared at me for a moment. "You are Crowe?"

"Yes. Do you remember me?" I asked him.

"I do. Vaguely."

"Then you will remember our deal," I reminded him.

"I do," he said again.

"Shall we get started?" I asked him.

"Do you have any idea what you'll need?" Finnegan asked me.

I didn't, and I said as much. "This is my first time."

"Then I'll have to teach you as well," he said doubtfully. "What did you do in Australia?"

"I ran a freight business," I replied.

"What else?"

"I hunted."

"That's something. Hunted what?"

I hesitated before answering. "Men. Bad ones."

He thought I wasn't serious for a moment and then realised that I was. He nodded. "Nothing more dangerous."

"Yes."

"All right, you're going to need wagons. Maybe five or six. Twelve oxen to pull each of them, which comes to seventy-two, might be better if we get a hundred, as they tend to get eaten sometimes. We'll also need enough provisions for six to twelve months."

"That long?"

Finnegan nodded. "It'll take us two months to get where we're going. Two months to get back. No sense in going all that way just for a small load. I expect to be able to load fifteen tons of ivory. Hopefully, twenty thousand sovereigns depending on the market. At worst, fifteen."

"Fine."

"I'll supply the bearers. Sixty of them. They'll carry what won't fit in the wagons. Also, some will be able to detusk the elephants. We can live off meat from the game we kill."

"It sounds like you've got it all sorted," I said to Finnegan. "There is one thing. My wife will be coming."

"The hell you say. No women. Nothing but bloody problems."

"She can take care of herself."

He was angry about it, but let it go. "Fine, but if she gets eaten by a lion or trampled by a damn elephant, it's not my problem."

"Let's go get what we need then," I said.

When we went outside, we were joined by a Black man. He was solidly built, with defined muscles, and an air of authority about him. Finnegan said, "This is Mthunzi. He is a Zulu warrior. He takes care of the bearers, the scouts, and whatever else needs doing with the natives."

I held out my hand. "My name is Jack Crowe. Pleased to meet you."

The Zulu looked at Finnegan and then back at me. Finnegan said, "He's not used to being treated as an equal. I'm about the only other one who does it."

Mthunzi took my hand. "Thank you, Nkosi."

I looked questioningly at the Irishman. "It means Lord," he said to me.

Nodding, I said to Mthunzi, "It's just Crowe. No need for Nkosi."

"Yes, Nkosi."

"You won't win, Crowe. Let it go."

The wagons were first on our list, and the ones we found were solid and sturdy. Just what we needed for the rugged interior we were heading to. They cost us one hundred sovereigns each. Then came the oxen and the supplies. With those covered, we bought weapons and ammunition.

This, I left up to Finnegan, who bought three Holland and Holland .557 Black Powder Express double-barrelled big game rifles. We also invested in four revolvers for personal protection.

By the end of the day, everything we needed had been purchased, and the expedition was all but ready to move out.

IT WAS two days later that we left Durban, heading north towards Matabeleland. The general came with us, riding the wagon alongside An Ni. Finnegan and I both rode horses while Mthunzi walked along with the rest of the bearers.

For the first two weeks, we travelled north at a slow pace. Through rolling lands, across deep gullies, laying eyes on wildlife like I'd never seen before. Lions, hyenas, zebras, and vast herds of cow-like things called wildebeest. Even giraffes. Plus other native animals I'd never even dreamt of.

Finnegan hunted antelope to keep us in fresh meat. We took sufficient for our needs from the carcass, leaving the rest for the carrion eaters.

I was awestruck and fell in love with the landscape and all the majesty it held. It would be some time before I tired of what surrounded us.

A LOOK AT: RETRIBUTION: A TEAM REAPER THRILLER

BY BRENT TOWNS

EVERYTHING COMES AT A COST...

Author Brent Towns keeps the action coming thick and fast, let's you up for a breath and then drags you back in for more.

After he is betrayed and shoots the two most powerful men in the Irish Mob, John "Reaper" Kane is forced into hiding. He thinks Retribution, Arizona, is the perfect hiding place, but he is wrong. Underneath the old, crusty surface of the dying town, hides the Montoya Cartel, for they use it as a funnel to ship their drugs across the border.

Trying to lay low in a town gripped with lawlessness is impossible for the ex-recon marine, especially after the local sheriff is brutally murdered by the Montoya Cartel's sicario, leaving an old friend, Deputy Sheriff Cara Billings, the only person standing between them and the town.

Things go from bad to worse when Kane is arrested by Cleaver, the deputy in the cartel's pocket, for shooting a local gang member.

Enter DEA Agent Luis Ferrero who has expressed to his bosses for a long time the need for a task force to fight the cartels on their own ground. He's about to get his wish, and to head up his team, he wants the Reaper.

AVAILABLE NOW

THANK YOU

Thank you for taking the time to read *The Lotus and the Dragon*. If you enjoyed it, please consider telling your friends or posting a short review. Word of mouth is an author's best friend and much appreciated.

Thank you,
Brent Towns

ABOUT THE AUTHOR

A relative newcomer to the world of writing, Brent Towns self-published his first book in 2015. *Last Stand in Sanctuary* took him two years to write. His first hard-cover book, a Black Horse Western, was published the following year.

Since then, he has written twenty-six western stories, including some in collaboration with British western author, Ben Bridges; several action adventure novels, such as his bestselling *Team Reaper* series; the novelization to the 2019 movie, *Bill Tilghman and the Outlaws*; as well as scripted a handful of Commando Comics. Not bad for an Australian author, he thinks.

Often up until the small hours of the night, bashing away at his tortured keyboard in Queensland, Australia, Brent loves to lose himself in the world of fiction. If you're interested in sharing your thoughts in more detail, scan the QR code below! Your feedback is invaluable to him—and often helps shape his future writing endeavors.

www.ingramcontent.com/pod-product-compliance
Lightning Source LLC
LaVergne TN
LVHW040216110826
845146LV00005B/1301

* 9 7 9 8 8 9 5 6 7 5 2 7 4 *